Never Marry
A Scandalous Duke

Never Marry
A Scandalous Duke

RENEE ANN MILLER

The Infamous Lords Series

ZEBRA BOOKS
KENSINGTON PUBLISHING CORP.
www.kensingtonbooks.com

ZEBRA BOOKS are published by

Kensington Publishing Corp.
119 West 40th Street
New York, NY 10018

All Kensington titles, imprints, and distributed lines are available at special quantity discounts for bulk purchases for sales promotion, premiums, fund-raising, educational, or institutional use.

Special book excerpts or customized printings can also be created to fit specific needs. For details, write or phone the office of the Kensington Sales Manager: Attn.: Sales Department. Kensington Publishing Corp., 119 West 40th Street, New York, NY 10018. Phone: 1-800-221-2647.

Zebra and the Z logo Reg. U.S. Pat. & TM Off.

First Printing: July 2022
ISBN-13: 978-1-4201-5007-0
ISBN-13: 978-1-4201-5008-7 (eBook)

10 9 8 7 6 5 4 3 2 1

Printed in the United States of America

*To Christina Hovland for her support and friendship
and for reading my stories
even when she was busy writing her own.*

Acknowledgments

This story would not be possible without so many wonderful people. First, a shout-out to my editor, Esi Sogah, and the staff at Kensington. Thanks to John for his never-ending encouragement. Last but not least, my gratitude to romance readers who share their enthusiasm for the genre.

Chapter One

Dorchester Hall
Richmond, England

Lady Sara Elsmere released a taut breath and tried not to fidget. Any attempt at blending into the background while standing in the Duke of Dorchester's ballroom was a challenge when wearing a pink gown adorned with enormous silk peony flowers the size of a serving dish.

Father's words replayed in her head. *The gown gives you a youthful glow.*

That statement was utterly absurd. Plain old poppycock.

In truth, the ball gown made her look foolish. Yet, no amount of arguing had changed Father's mind. So here she was, trying to disappear into the gold-flocked wallpaper and failing miserably.

She desperately wished Father would stop forcing her to attend such gatherings in hopes someone would make her an offer. The gentlemen at these social events had little interest in a twenty-seven-year-old entomologist who collected butterflies and laughed nervously whenever a man asked her to dance.

As she glanced at the women dressed in their finest

gowns and the men in their evening attire, the memory of her first Season replayed in her mind. She'd been older than the other girls, having attended Bedford College. Father had thought educating a woman a waste of time and money, but it had been one of her mother's dying wishes. During most of the evening, no one asked her to dance, and she'd come to realize that her age and the fact she was a bluestocking who studied insects made her less appealing to most marriage-minded gentlemen of the *ton*.

Then Sir Harry approached, and her dance instructor's words replayed in her head. *No. No. No. Your right foot first. Not your left. You are the most blundering dancer I have ever had the misfortune to teach.*

By the time Sir Harry asked her to dance, her fear that she might fall, or cause him to fall, had gotten the better of her, and she'd begun to laugh. Not a girlish giggle that a man might find cute or endearing, but a high-pitched, nervous laugh. Heads had turned toward her, and the more everyone gawked, the more she'd laughed. Her second ball during that same Season had been another utter disaster. The same thing had happened when Lord Gilbert asked to partner with her.

Being a bluestocking had made her less appealing. Laughing uncontrollably when asked to dance had sealed her fate as a wallflower.

Shoving her memories aside, Sara scanned those waltzing and caught sight of her sister being twirled around the dance floor by some young buck. A bright smile wreathed Louisa's face, and her partner had the look of a man who thought everyone envied him. Sara was sure many did envy the fellow. At eighteen, Louisa had made her debut in society this year and instantly become the Season's incomparable. Every man wished to dance with her, and Sara could not blame them. Her sister was not only beautiful, she also sparkled and thrived under the spotlight.

While Sara collected butterflies, Louisa acted the social butterfly, flittering around with her grace and beauty, drawing everyone's regard. How two sisters could be such opposites befuddled Sara's mind. Yet, she was relieved that her sister did not suffer from the same quirk that rattled Sara when asked to dance.

She searched the crush for her brother. Ned was probably in the cardroom with their host. She didn't care for Ian McAllister, the Duke of Dorchester. He was one of the last remaining members of a set referred to in the scandal sheets as the Infamous Lords—a group of rakish noblemen. Though most had married and given up their wicked ways, Dorchester, who looked to be in his early thirties, appeared quite determined not to change. And the *ton* seemed more than willing to forgive the coldhearted womanizer, especially when he was serving them an abundance of champagne and French cuisine.

She wondered what women saw in him. Yes, he was handsome. Yes, he was lean with broad shoulders. But surely there had to be more to a gentleman for a woman to fall at his feet. Yet, only last year, it was said that a young debutante swooned and collapsed to the floor when he'd done nothing more than say hello.

Turning her mind away from the scandalous duke, Sara peered at her father who stood across the ballroom engaged in conversation with another gentleman. Perhaps it was not as much a conversation as it was an argument, since Father's face had turned the same shade of red when she'd balked at wearing the atrocious pink gown.

Sara bit her lower lip and eyed the wide doorway several feet from where she stood. With Father, Ned, and Louisa preoccupied, a better opportunity to slip out of the ballroom might not present itself. She edged toward the opening. She'd heard that the Duke of Dorchester's Richmond estate possessed an exemplary library, and she was on a mission to hide away in it for the remainder of the evening. Surely, afterward, she would garner Father's wrath when they returned home, but she would rather absorb one of his verbal tirades than remain in the ballroom a minute longer.

As fast as she could move, while dragging twenty pounds of silk, tulle, and oversized faux peonies, she slipped through the archway. A sense of elation drifted through her as she made her way down the wide corridor with its red Turkish runner.

A male servant, dressed in a tailored black suit, stepped out of a room and nearly collided with her.

"Forgive me, madam. Are you looking for the retiring room?"

She shifted from one foot to the other, while deciding how much of the truth to reveal. "Actually, I'm looking for the library."

The man's eyes widened, and he averted his gaze. "Of course, madam. It is the next door to your left."

"Thank you." As Sara moved down the wide corridor, she glanced over her shoulder. There was something unsettling about the way the footman had looked at her—as if she'd startled him—as if she was not what he'd expected.

Well, she had gotten that look enough times in her life. She shoved her thoughts away. Perhaps the guilt of sneaking off was causing her to overanalyze the man's expression. Most likely, he thought her brazen for leaving the other guests to indulge in a book.

She opened the door he'd indicated and softly closed it behind her. Gas wall sconces set low illuminated the library, which was one of the largest she'd seen, and she'd seen more than her fair share since they were her solace during these gatherings.

The scent of the leather bindings filled her nose as she scanned the tall mahogany bookcases that lined three of the walls. Each of them had a sliding ladder so the uppermost books could be reached, and in the corner of the room a metal spiraling staircase soared to a second-story balcony with even more bookshelves.

With such an extensive collection, she felt almost positive she would find something to read that would be more stimulating than the ballroom, possibly something on entomology.

As she made her way to the bookcases to her right, she peered up at the ceiling's lovely mural. Puffy white clouds dotted a blue sky, while winged cherubs, wearing crowns of flowers, fluttered about. The angels held flutes and harps. Such a whimsical scene almost tempted her to lie on her back and stare at it. She tamped down such a foolish inclination and continued toward the bookcases.

She squinted at the small writing on the bindings and removed her spectacles from the side pocket sewn into the skirt of her gown. As she scanned the books, she saw titles by George Eliot, Daniel Defoe, and even spotted a book of poetry by Robert Burns. She could not envision the present duke reading the latter. From what she'd heard, he was more likely to engage in reading something more scandalous than poetry, such as *Memoirs of a Woman of Pleasure*.

Footsteps sounded in the corridor, along with a man's voice.

She spun around to see the door handle being turned.

Had Father or her brother tracked her down? She didn't wish to return to the ballroom, not when there were so many books to be explored. Shoving her glasses into her pocket, she made a mad dash for a narrow alcove between two of the bookcases and flattened her body into the space.

The young, widowed Lady Cleary, wearing a bright yellow gown, stepped into the library with the Duke of Dorchester. He closed the door behind them.

Sara swallowed. Why wasn't the scandalous man with his guests?

That answer came to her as soon as the widow skimmed her palms up the duke's chest and leaned into him.

In response, Dorchester curled his large hand around the back of the woman's neck and brought his mouth down on hers.

Goodness! She had thought Lady Cleary wiser than this. Didn't the woman realize she was the affair of the year? Hopefully, the woman wouldn't fall too deeply in love with Dorchester before the scoundrel moved on to his next conquest.

Sara thought of the servant she'd almost bumped into in the corridor and how he'd looked at her. Had he believed she'd been heading to the library for an assignation with His Grace? That would explain his odd expression, since Sara didn't resemble the seductive Lady Cleary, especially in this outlandish gown.

She opened her mouth to say something, but the sight of Dorchester lowering the shoulder of Lady Cleary's ball gown and kissing the pale skin caused her to clamp her mouth tight.

Now what should I do?

She could close her eyes.

Yes, that would work. She pinched them shut.

Lady Cleary started panting and making mewling sounds. "Mmm. Oh yes, Ian. That feels so . . . Yes, there."

Though Sara fought the urge to open her eyes, curiosity got the better of her and one eyelid slowly lifted.

Dorchester was pressing his thigh between the woman's gowned legs, while kissing her.

Sara opened her other eye and tilted her head to the side. Why was Lady Cleary arching and purring like a cat? What Dorchester was doing to the woman looked rather uncomfortable.

Suddenly the gentleman stilled.

Feeling a shiver of apprehension, Sara clapped a hand over her mouth. Had she made a noise? The possibility caused her heart to pound wildly. So loud, she feared they would hear the intense *thump, thump, thump* in her chest.

The duke glanced over his shoulder. Though handsome and in possession of striking features, including dark hair, a firm mouth, and a square jaw, she'd always thought the man possessed an aura of danger. Perhaps it was his piercing blue eyes that looked as if they could scour one's soul to find their weakness.

Trying to make herself invisible to his gaze, she pressed her back more firmly against the wall. As she did, one of the blasted round peonies fell off her gown and rolled out of the alcove.

Dorchester's menacing glare settled on the faux flower before narrowing in on her like a periscope. He peered at her with the same contemptuous arrogance most of the men at the London Society of Entomologists offered her when she handed in one of her articles for publication.

"Ian, you tease, don't stop. I'm almost there," Lady Cleary snapped, clearly agitated.

He turned back to the woman. "I think it best you return to the ballroom, darling."

"Ian, what is the matter?"

"I believe I heard a rat."

The widow let out a *squeak* and inched up the skirt of her gown.

He opened the door.

"It's not fair of you to leave me in such a state. Why don't we go into another room?" she suggested, sounding hopeful.

"Sorry, darling. I need to deal with this."

"Yourself? Don't you have legions of servants to tend to such a detestable task?"

"I prefer to catch this one myself."

That statement made Sara's heart pound even harder. She normally only laughed when a man asked her to dance, but she tightened the hand over her mouth, suddenly fearful a nervous giggle would bubble up her throat.

Lady Cleary blinked and appeared ready to question him further, but something in the duke's expression must have halted the action. The widow's skirts swished as she exited the room.

With a heavy hand, Dorchester closed the door, leaned back against the surface, and folded his arms over his ample chest. "I'm not particularly fond of Peeping Toms who get their jollies from watching others."

Peeping Tom? How ridiculous. She'd not set out to watch his sexual escapade. She'd stepped into the library to escape the ball.

Infuriating, arrogant man! Sara's nervousness turned to agitation. She ran her hands down her gown and stepped

NEVER MARRY A SCANDALOUS DUKE   9

out from her hiding spot. "It was not my intention to spy on you, and I'm deeply offended that you would suggest such a thing. Your unfavorable comment leaves me demanding an apology."

Ian drew in a deep breath. "You think I owe you an apology, Miss . . . ?"

"Miss Elsmere. Lady Sara Elsmere."

Yes, that was her name. He'd seen her before. The Earl of Hampton's daughter. The bluestocking who laughed uncontrollably whenever a man asked her to dance, causing men to avoid her at these gatherings as if she were a leper.

"I only stepped into the room so I might read."

"Really?" He cocked a brow at her.

"Yes, really. If you think I wanted to watch you . . ." She waved her hand toward him as she appeared to struggle with what to call what she'd witnessed. Her already-rosy cheeks deepened in color, settling on a shade nearly as pink as her full sensual mouth. A mouth incongruous with everything else about the woman who styled her brown hair in a taut bun, and wore a frilly, overly embellished gown, which hid all her curves and made her look rather silly.

As if he'd said the comment out loud or she'd gleaned what he'd been thinking, she stuck out her chin. "My father chose this abomination. So don't judge me."

"Aren't you rather old to be having your father dictate your clothing?"

"I am. But if I want my father's benevolence, I must wear such an atrocity. Now if you will excuse me, I fear this conversation has grown tiresome." And with that said, she marched toward the door. Her gaze seemed to settle on the large faux flower on the rug. For a minute, Ian thought she intended to retrieve it.

"You may keep the peony, Your Grace. Perhaps your haberdasher could add it to one of your hats, or you could gift it to Lady Cleary for not finishing what you set out to do."

Few people talked to him without deference. The prickly Lady Sara was an anomaly. Oddly, he found her intriguing, especially her tart, sensual mouth. For a split second, he thought about asking her if she wished to be tutored in what she'd seen.

Where the deuce had that foolish thought come from? Ian gave a slight, imperceivable shake of his head to scatter such a renegade idea. He had no interest in a prim, hoity-toity wallflower.

She'd nearly reached the door when a man's panicked voice calling out her name echoed in the hallway. "Sara, where are you? Damnation."

Bloody hell. It wouldn't be wise to be found alone with the woman. Ian stepped into the shadows.

Lady Sara opened the door and her brother rushed over the threshold. The man was breathing heavily. His face was ghostly pale.

"Ned, what is the matter?" Lady Sara gripped his sleeve.

Her brother's Adam's apple moved but nothing came out.

"Ned, you're frightening me." She grabbed his shoulders and shook him. "Tell me."

"It is Father. He collapsed."

"Collapsed?" Her voice trembled.

"Yes," her brother replied. "Dr. Trimble said he suffered apoplexy. H-he's dead."

Chapter Two

A year later . . .
Dorchester Hall, Richmond

Normally, anyone bursting into the Duke of Dorchester's office without knocking would have received a withering scowl, along with a severe dressing-down. In fact, at the age of thirty-two, Ian could not recall a servant ever having the temerity to do so until a moment ago.

Yet, the sight of Gertrude Winterbottom, his wards' nanny, halted his rebuke. The middle-aged woman looked as if she'd fallen into a puddle of muck and, knowing the two mischievous boys he was guardian to, she probably had.

The woman swiped at the dirt splatters on her face, smearing them across her cheeks, making her look like a rugby player on a wet and foot-trampled field. "Those boys are demons. The devil's spawns!"

Sadly, he was sure the two lads had been called worse.

"Look what they have done to me. They pushed me into a puddle of muddy water." Winterbottom fisted her hands into her dirty gray skirt and shook the garment as if to add more potency to her declaration.

Ian knew nothing about children. He'd been shocked

after his cousin's death, three months ago, to learn he was the boys' guardian. If he'd agreed to that, Finley must have plowed him with too much drink beforehand.

"I resign my position, effective immediately," the nanny proclaimed, drawing him from his thoughts. She exhaled a gusty breath as if blessedly free from an anchor tethered to her waist.

Resign? That wouldn't do. Instead of railing at the woman for barging into his office, Ian decided to haggle with her. Something he excelled at since learning that money was the supreme bargaining weapon in any negotiation. That, and the threat of ruining a person. But he was sure the pious Gertrude Winterbottom had no skeletons in her closet that he could use against her.

So the money it was. "I'll increase your pay."

"No. I have had it, Your Grace. Yesterday I found worms in my bed and today this." The nanny's voice grew an octave higher with every word she spoke. "My sanity is worth more than the very generous salary you pay me. Though such an exorbitant amount should have forewarned of what would besiege me in this house. Might I suggest you hire a zookeeper to tend to those boys?" With rivulets of filthy water running off her straggling hair, the woman stormed out of the room, leaving a trail of dirty shoe prints in her wake.

"Bugger it," Ian grumbled. Not another one. That made three nannies since the boys had come to live with him. And Gertrude Winterbottom had been the only one to apply for the position from the Governess and Nanny Association in London—a place that housed women of those occupations, while they awaited positions. Word of the two hellions and their recent pranks appeared to have scared away everyone with even a modicum of sense.

He stood, strode from the room, and retraced Winterbottom's muddy shoe prints down the corridor, then through the morning room, and to the terrace outside into the bright May sun.

Not seeing the hellions, he made his way down the steps and into the gardens. "Edward! Jacob! Where are you?"

The leaves on one of the oaks shook ever so slightly.

Ian glanced up to see his eight- and seven-year-old wards sitting on one of the branches, peering down at him. With their round faces and rosy cheeks, they looked like Raphael's two cherubic angels in the *Madonna di San Sisto*, but they were anything but. They were more like the bow-and-arrow-carrying cherubim in the master's *Triumph of Galatea*.

Brushing his coat back, Ian set his hands firmly on his hips. "What did you do?"

"Nothing, Cousin Ian," Edward, the elder of the two, said.

"Nothing," Jacob echoed.

The two little terrors stared down at him with no sign of contrition on their faces. In fact, their expressions remained as deceptively innocent as that of two newborn babes.

Ian thought of Edward and Jacob's father who'd acted a hellion when younger. Yet, Finley had always possessed the ability to deflect attention from himself with the same guiltless expression, leaving Ian to be solely blamed for whatever prank they'd conjured up. But even so, he had cared for Finley, until Ian's father had commanded that they refrain from seeing each other. For a lad already lonely in his father's dictatorial house, it had felt like a severed appendage.

Shoving his thoughts aside, Ian released a slow breath. "So Miss Winterbottom falling into a muddy puddle was an accident?"

The two boys looked at each other as if silently communicating an answer. Their regard returned to him. "She tripped on her skirt," they said in unison.

Ian presumed with a fair amount of help. "Well, you have sent another one packing."

Both of their mouths turned up into broad smiles.

"Pleased with yourselves, are you?" He infused a hard edge of steel into his voice. The same tone he used when he wished to place a modicum of fear into others.

Neither child seemed to notice, for their smiles didn't waver in the least.

How was it nearly everyone who dealt with him appeared either in awe or terrified, yet he couldn't handle two tiny boys? "Before leaving, Miss Winterbottom suggested I might hire a zookeeper instead of a nanny."

"Does that mean we can get a lion or an elephant?" Exuberance sparkled in Jacob's eyes and an even broader smile stretched across his full cheeks.

"No, it does not," Ian replied.

Edward shoved an elbow into his younger brother's ribs. "No, silly. He means to take care of us."

The excitement disappeared from Jacob's countenance. He blinked. "Are you going to hire one, Cousin?"

Ian hesitated before responding, letting them ponder that possibility. "Of course not. Now get down from there and go into your room to contemplate the gravity of what you have done."

Looking less guilty than they should, both boys climbed down from the tree and marched toward the house.

Ian watched them playfully pushing and shoving each other as they made their way up the terrace steps, then into the house. He rubbed at the back of his neck. He might be a force to be reckoned with in the House of Lords, and a savvy businessman, but he freely admitted he didn't know how to raise these two boys. His own father had only taught him how *not* to raise a child, believing that a leather strap or birch rod was the answer to everything. Ian would cut off his own arm before he struck them.

Perhaps he should hire two nannies. One for each boy. No, he would not separate them. They'd already had to contend with the deaths of their parents, and he clearly remembered what it was like to be isolated and kept away from others.

Footsteps tapped against the flagstone.

Ian glanced over his shoulder to see his closest friend and business partner, Julien Caruthers, the Earl of Dartmore, strolling toward him. He and Julien had attended university together.

"Lost another nanny, did you, old boy?"

"Yes. How did you know?"

"Just saw old Freezerbottom mumbling to herself as she carried her suitcases down the stairs."

"Winterbottom," Ian corrected. "Yes, they did everything they could think of to traumatize the woman and send her packing. I'm at a loss what to do. For a moment, I contemplated doing as she suggested."

"And what was that?"

"Hire a zookeeper instead of another nanny."

Julien laughed. "Maybe you need to get married, old chum. Perhaps if the boys knew they could not get rid of a maternal figure in their lives they would not try so hard to do so."

His friend had married his childhood sweetheart and now talked ad nauseam about the blissful state of matrimony. Ian, on the other hand, had only considered marriage once, but Isabelle had turned out to be a manipulative, devious, and money-grabbing liar. After professing her love to him, she'd married his father, a man she knew he despised. It appeared Isabelle had cared more about becoming a duchess than about him. Father and Isabelle's ultimate betrayal had taught him a painful lesson—one he would never forget. Never allow yourself to be ravaged by sentimental emotions.

His current arrangement with the widow Lady Randall suited him fine. Neither asked anything from the other except sensual gratification. No emotional entanglements.

"Whomever I married would not think it their responsibility to tend to my wards. She would just hire a nanny. Then I'd not only have an unhappy nanny, but a wife I do not want."

"Well, you do have a point there, but perhaps you could find a wife who is a helpmate. Someone who wouldn't completely fob off the job of helping to raise the lads. A woman who is maternal in nature."

A foolish idea by a man totally besotted with his wife. Wishing to change the subject, Ian set a hand on his friend's shoulder. "What brings you here?"

Julien removed a letter from the inside pocket of his coat. "This arrived at our Magnus Shipping Offices. It appears our newest steamer is on schedule and will be ready to enter service shortly."

"Excellent. Then we'll retire the *Calypso* from our fleet. I can tell by your grin you have more news."

"I do. I think I've convinced Bertram Floyd to sell us his ironworks company."

Ian smiled. With the move to build iron-hulled ships, Floyd's business would see substantial profits in the coming years. It would also cut Magnus Shipping's cost in producing their fleet, since they could supply the iron to Carver's Ship Building, another business they hoped to purchase.

"I will not attend!" Lady Sara Elsmere bounced up from where she sat and squared her shoulders.

Her brother, the Earl of Hampton, sitting behind the massive desk that used to be their father's, narrowed his eyes. "Yes, you will. It is high time you stop spending your days examining dead bugs."

"Ned, butterflies are not bugs. They are Rhopalocera. A division of *Lepidoptera* family of insects."

"I do not care what they are called. Since Father's death, I have not forced you to go about in society, but now that our period of mourning is over, you must find a husband."

Her brother sounded just like their dear departed father. Adamant and unwilling to understand how she felt when she attended balls. The men who took part in the marriage mart were not interested in a bluestocking who favored spending her time studying the habitat of butterflies. Especially a woman who possessed a reputation of giggling like a schoolgirl when asked to dance.

After Father's passing, she'd been stricken with grief, but the last year had allowed her to remain home and not be subjected to the whispers that other members of the *ton* made behind her back.

"I insist you find a husband this Season." Ned pounded his fist against his blotter, rattling the inkpot on his desk tray.

"You know I don't wish to marry. I wish to dedicate my life to the study of butterflies. I am an entomologist."

"Father should never have let you attend college."

"It was one of Mother's dying wishes that I further my education."

With a scathing look, Ned stood and raked his fingers through his brown hair before he marched to the round marquetry table in the corner of the room. He picked up a large white box with a pink ribbon, returned to where she stood, and thrust it at her.

"What is this?" she asked, taking the package.

"Your costume for Lord and Lady Farnsworth's masquerade ball next week."

"I told you I'm not attending."

"You are, or I'll cut off your allowance."

Her mouth went dry, then slack. She used her allowance to fund her studies. Ned knew as a woman she would have a difficult time getting a benefactor. She glared at him. "You wouldn't."

"You know I don't make threats lightly."

She did know that. Her brother could act contemptible when he set his mind to it. Once, after they'd argued, he'd removed several of her preserved butterflies from their glass-and-wood cases and destroyed them.

"You need to find a husband, and that won't happen hiding away in your study."

It wasn't fair that her brother who was two years younger than she controlled her future because he was a man, or that her father had stipulated that she didn't get her own inheritance until she married. And even then, her husband would try to control it.

"You are handsome enough," Ned added.

Handsome enough. Father had always used the same words to describe her. Somehow they'd never sounded like a compliment when Father spoke them, and they didn't sound like one when Ned said them either.

"Maybe if you wore your hair differently. Not pulled into such a severe bun. Why don't you style it the way Louisa does her hair?"

She was waiting for that comparison. Why didn't her family understand that she was different from Louisa? Most likely, her sister would once again be this Season's incomparable. She wanted that for her. It would send Louisa over the moon. Make her smile again. Something she hadn't done much of since Father's death. Sadly, it wasn't as much because Father was gone as it was because Louisa missed the limelight—missed being the center of attention.

"Allowing a few tendrils to soften your face would help," Ned said, interrupting her thoughts.

Ignoring his comment, she set the large garment-sized box Ned had thrust into her hands onto the corner of the massive desk and unfastened the large pink ribbon tied about it. If she wanted to continue her studies, it appeared she'd have to attend Lord and Lady Farnsworth's masquerade ball next week. She lifted the lid, exposing a frilly gown that looked plucked from a different decade, along with a wide-brimmed straw hat and a gold Venetian mask.

She removed the dress from the box. The skirt of the blue gown was embellished with layers of fabric and a plethora of bows at the hem. Though not as outlandish as the gown Father had insisted she wear to the Duke of Dorchester's ball last year, it definitely wasn't meant to escape attention.

Her gaze narrowed on the neckline, which seemed to be missing several inches of fabric. "Where is the rest of the bodice?" she asked.

Ned's brows drew together. "What do you mean? It looks fine to me."

What did she mean? "Exactly what I asked. The décolletage is cut exceedingly low. I will not wear this ridiculous costume."

"You most certainly will."

"So I am to attend as a lady of the night?"

Her brother's nostrils flared, and he pointed toward the sidewall. "Don't be silly. This is a shepherdess's costume."

Sara's gaze settled on the shepherd's crook leaning against a bookcase. It was embellished with a blue satin ribbon that wound up the staff. She thought of what she wanted to do with that staff, and it had nothing to do with sheep herding. But if she cracked it over her brother's head, he would definitely cut off her money.

"I am too old to wear such a costume."

"You are twenty-eight and sitting firmly on the shelf. It is time you did something about it."

"Why is it that a man of twenty-eight is in his prime, while a woman of the same age is considered a spinster?"

As if the question confused him, Ned blinked. "It just is."

"That isn't an answer."

His jaw tensed. "Next week you will attend Lord and Lady Farnsworth's masquerade ball, or I will not give you a penny more to study your insects."

Heat scorched her cheeks.

"Wallace will help you dress and style your hair," Ned added.

"I can do my hair and dress myself. I don't need the lady's maid's help. As always, she can tend to Louisa."

"I'm not asking you, Sara."

"What difference does it make?" She plucked the hat with its enormous brim out of the box. "This atrocity will hide my hair."

"Not the back of it, if you leave it loose."

"Loose? You're taking this a bit too far."

He flashed a smug look. "Your days of hiding away with your collection of dead bugs is coming to an end."

"Insects! And you cannot force me to bend to your will."

"I can if you don't want me to toss that *insect* collection of yours into the Thames."

The beats of her heart escalated. She could not believe that her brother had not only threatened to withhold her allowance but was threatening to destroy years of work. Specimens that she'd collected over the last decade. She narrowed her eyes and opened her mouth to tell Ned exactly what she thought of him.

Her brother held up a hand. "I mean it. There will be no negotiating."

Knowing she had little choice, she stormed out of the room, with the hideous costume in her hands.

Chapter Three

In the carriage on the way to Lord and Lady Farnsworth's masquerade ball, Sara twisted her hands together as a dreaded sense of apprehension grew within her. Hopefully, once there, she could hide in the library. That thought brought her back to last year. To the Duke of Dorchester's ball and what had happened there, and how the odious man had accused her of spying on him minutes before Ned had told her about Father.

After Father's apoplexy, several men had carried him into a drawing room. She could still remember the stillness of his body stretched out on a sofa, the bluish color of his lips, and the look of sympathy on Dr. Trimble's face when their eyes met. That look had revealed all. Ned had not been trying to frighten her. Father *was* dead.

Sara sniffled and blinked at the tears prickling her eyes.

"If you think tears will make me feel guilty that I'm forcing you to attend this ball, they will not," Ned snapped.

In the dim compartment, she could see her brother's scolding gaze centered on her. Father had never brought her to tears, and if Ned thought he could, he was disillusioned. "Have you ever known me to cry over being forced to do anything?"

Ned's mouth twisted as if that realization agitated him. "I cannot say I have. Then what has you upset?"

"I was remembering the last time we attended a ball. I was thinking of Father." He might not have been the most demonstrative father. He might have sometimes been cruel with his comments, but he had been her father.

"A sad time, indeed, but I suggest you do not cry, or you'll end up looking like Louisa did before we left the house."

She brushed at the dampness at the corners of her eyes and thought of their sister. Since Father's death, Louisa had been anxiously counting down the days until she could, once again, attend social events, but she was sick with a devil of a cold.

"I wish you were the one sick," Louisa had wailed, sitting in her bed with tear-filled eyes and a red nose. *"You don't even want to go."*

Louisa's rather thoughtless and petulant comment hadn't upset Sara, since she also wished her sister was going instead. Louisa, unlike her, would not be twisting her hands nervously into knots while contemplating how to sneak into the library.

The carriage pulled up to the Farnsworths' town house where a line of carriages stood, and liveried footmen helped guests out of their vehicles.

Ned picked up his Venetian mask and slipped it on. He wore a white wig and long cape of red velvet.

Sara slipped her half mask on and alighted the vehicle, assisted by a footman whose gaze settled on her low décolletage.

"I'll never forgive you for making me wear this ridiculous costume," she whispered to Ned as they made their way inside.

They stepped into the ballroom, and she noticed several

men turn and stare at her. Men rarely stared at her. They avoided her. Obviously they had no inkling who lay behind the mask. Otherwise they wouldn't have given her a second glance, even in this silly costume with her breasts tightly corseted and all but spilling forth. They probably thought she was Louisa.

"Ah, I believe I've spotted Sir Charles," her brother said, holding out his arm for her to join him.

"I need to find the retiring room and freshen up."

Ned's mouth twisted. "We just arrived."

"I'll be back in a few minutes," Sara replied, having no intention of joining her brother and his friend. She intended to find Lord and Lady Farnsworth's library.

As she wove through the crowd, she spotted another Bo Peep. Same dress, same silly hat, same mask, and the same blue ribbon adorning her shepherd's crook.

How original of her brother.

She moved to the perimeter of the room where the crowd wasn't as thick. A fellow wearing pantaloons, a frilly white shirt and cravat, along with a half mask, stepped in front of her, forcing her to stop.

Was he about to ask her to dance? Sara waited for her nervous giggle to start. It didn't. If she searched for an answer as to why, it could only be attributed to the mask she wore. She felt less exposed. People weren't staring at her, waiting for her to make a complete cake of herself. That anonymity caused a sense of calmness she rarely experienced at a ball.

The gentleman grinned and his gaze briefly dipped to her breasts. "I've always had a fascination with nursery rhymes."

That made sense since his peachy skin with nary a

bristle of growth implied he'd recently stepped out of the nursery.

Maybe if she didn't say anything he would go away.

"Might I get you a refreshment, Lady of Mystery?"

Blast it. Not talking to him had only piqued his interest. She shook her head.

He glanced around before returning his gaze to her breasts.

She fought the urge to try to tug up her bodice.

"Are you looking for someone specific?" he asked.

Not someone, but someplace. The library. However, if she came across her brother, she might strangle him.

"I've changed my mind," she said, forcing her voice to be deeper than it usually sounded. "I am thirsty." She left out the part for her brother's blood. Making her wear this outfit was beyond the pale. "Would you be so kind as to get me a libation?"

The fellow smiled and scurried off toward the refreshment room.

As soon as the young buck dashed away, another man dressed as a gladiator moved toward her. Before he could reach her, Sara headed through the closest archway.

As she moved down the corridor, she heard the squeak of hinges. A masculine hand reached out and clasped her fingers.

Startled, she dropped the shepherdess's crook she held in her other hand, as the man pulled her into a dark room, closing the door behind them.

"What took you so long?" a deep voice asked.

Before she could respond, the man's mouth settled on hers in a soft, yet demanding, kiss.

For a moment, she was stunned. Confused. She'd never

been kissed before. Well, not like this. She attempted to open her mouth to tell him there was some case of mistaken identity. But she realized, rather quickly, the mistake was hers when the man's tongue entered her mouth to stroke hers.

The beating of her heart kicked up into a canter. Not from fear. No. Something foreign. Something primal unfurled within her. Surely there was a scientific explanation, but presently her mind could not grapple with a hypothesis since she was growing too warm to think.

Gathering some semblance of sanity, she lifted her hand to the man's chest, intent on pushing him away. Her palms settled against a linen shirt. Under the thin fabric, she felt the hard planes of his muscled chest. As if her hands possessed a mind of their own, her palms skimmed over the surface while her nose drew in the spicy scent of his skin.

He made a noise that seemed to signal he approved of her touch. One of his large hands slid from her waist to the small of her back, pulling her closer to him, while his tongue continued to tangle with hers.

This was ridiculous. She needed to push him away. She was about to do so when the door opened. The gas wall sconces in the corridor sent shafts of light into the dark room.

The man holding her growled as if angered by the intrusion. He pulled his lips away from hers. The light shining into the room illuminated whom she'd been kissing.

Goodness. The Duke of Dorchester. She almost choked on the air she drew into her lungs, while her legs grew weak as her gaze drifted over him. He was dressed like a pirate with a white billowing shirt, tight fawn-colored breeches with a thick black leather belt, and knee-high boots. Instead of a Venetian mask, he wore an eye patch and looked as if he'd purposely not shaved his normally clean jaw, leaving it shadowed by a day's worth of beard. He looked every bit the marauding pirate.

Her gaze shifted to the person standing in the open doorway. Ned stood there, holding the shepherdess's crook she'd dropped.

"Hampton, this room is occupied. Go away," Dorchester growled, clearly agitated by the intrusion.

"Your Grace," Ned said. "What are you doing with my sister?"

"Your sister? I have no interest in your sister."

Sara's gaze veered to the other Bo Peep in the corridor, standing behind her brother.

Dorchester must have seen her as well, for he mumbled an oath and tugged off his eye patch. His dark, almost menacing, gaze pivoted to Sara. It seemed to settle on her mouth before he lifted off her mask.

"Why didn't you say something?"

"Say something?" She could feel her face heating. "How could I speak with your tongue in my mouth?"

"Would you remove your hands from my sister, Dorchester?" Ned actually sounded irate.

A collective gasp rose outside the room, and Sara realized more guests were gathering in the corridor. The buzz of conversation grew so loud, it sounded as if they stood near a sizable hornet's nest.

As if a log tumbled off a grate to roll too close to his feet, His Grace stepped back, removing the pleasant warmth and scent that radiated off his hard body.

"Dorchester, I believe we need to have a conversation in private. Tomorrow afternoon at my town house," Ned said, looking stone-faced.

Sara's stomach felt as if it was heaving upward. Did her

brother want the scoundrel to offer for her? The idea was preposterous, and by the look on the Duke of Dorchester's face, he thought the implication distasteful, as well.

As their carriage rumbled through the streets of Mayfair on their way home after an early departure from Lord and Lady Farnsworth's masquerade ball, Sara watched as Ned nibbled on the nail of his index finger.

"Now you've surely sealed your fate," he said.

Yes, now she would be branded a woman of loose morals. It was something she actually wouldn't mind. She could stay home and continue her studies.

Ned scrubbed a hand over his face. "Perhaps His Grace will do the honorable thing and offer for you."

She doubted the Duke of Dorchester knew the meaning of the word *honorable*. Anyway, even if he felt socially pressured to marry her, she would not accept. "He won't offer, and even if he does, I will not marry the scandalous man."

Ned's eyes widened, making the white part more visible in the interior of the dusky carriage. "Yes, you will. He would be the best offer you've had."

"Ned, if he does propose, he will be the only offer I've ever had."

As if that wasn't quite true, her brother averted his gaze.

"Did someone else ask for my hand?"

Her brother's gaze returned to hers. "Yes."

Though she didn't wish to marry, a spark of excitement shot through her. Someone had wished to marry her. Someone not forced to wed her. "When did this transpire?"

"Earlier today."

The only person who'd called on them at the town house today had been Lord Montgomery. He was a septuagenarian who was nearly in his eighties. He was like a benevolent grandfather.

She swallowed the thickness collecting in her throat. "Lord Montgomery?"

Ned nodded.

Well, he might be a better alternative than the Duke of Dorchester. Yet, as that thought worked its way through her mind, she could not stop herself from comparing the two men's physiques and how solid His Grace's chest had felt under her palms. Feeling her face grow warm, she shoved that wicked thought away.

"I'm almost positive Lord Montgomery will withdraw his offer once he hears about your sordid liaison."

"I've already explained what happened. It wasn't a liaison. It was a case of mistaken identity. And if you hadn't made me wear that godawful costume, it would never have happened."

"That very well might be true, but who would believe such a tale? I was not the only witness, and you didn't look as if you were protesting. Not in the least."

She wanted to argue that she hadn't done anything untoward, but she recalled the way her mouth moved against the duke's and remembered her tongue tangling with his. Worse, she remembered how her initial shock had dissipated, leaving her feeling lustful.

Scientists weren't lustful. They were pragmatic. Sensible. It must have been due to her shock. Yes. Surely that was the reason.

"Did you notice something about your interaction with

Dorchester?" Ned leaned forward and braced his forearms on his thighs.

Yes, she'd noticed quite a lot about the man's body in those breeches. "I'm not sure what you are referring to."

"You didn't laugh. Not once."

She hadn't, had she? But it was difficult to laugh while kissing, especially the way Dorchester kissed. "I normally only laugh when asked to dance. I hate the idea of everyone watching me, waiting for me to start laughing. I fear it so much, it happens."

"So kissing is fine, but dancing isn't?" Her brother huffed as if frustrated beyond words. "That makes no sense."

She agreed that it seemed irrational, but many fears were.

"Most women fall over themselves to be with him." He leaned back against the squabs.

True, women flocked to the Duke of Dorchester like butterflies to nectar. There was something about the cold-hearted scoundrel that appealed to women.

"I don't find him handsome in the least," she said, shoving thoughts of the man's body from her mind.

"Everyone thinks him handsome."

"There are different types of handsome. He might be visually appealing to some, but I don't care for him, which makes him not handsome to me in the least."

Her brother made a sound that clearly conveyed his disbelief.

"You've gotten yourself into a fine mess this time," Julien said, stepping into Ian's library after Lord and Lady Farnsworth's masquerade ball.

Ian leaned back in his chair, tipped his tumbler of

whiskey to his mouth, and downed the last drop. Titillating news traveled through the *ton* with the speed of a peregrine falcon. "So the gossip is already spreading?"

"Indeed. My wife and I stepped into Lord and Lady Farnsworth's ballroom to be inundated with the scandalous news of your indiscretion. I don't understand. You and Lady Sara Elsmere?" Julien's brows drew together on his forehead. "What were you thinking?"

"It was a misunderstanding."

"Really? You just happened to be in a dark room with her. You just happened to be holding her close? You just happened to have your tongue in her mouth?"

"Yes." Ian stood and refilled his glass.

"Well, that makes no bloody sense."

"I thought she was someone else."

"Couldn't you tell it was Lady Sara? Her nervous giggle should have been enough to give her identity away."

The woman hadn't laughed at all. Not a peep. In fact, she'd kissed him with an astonishing amount of passion. "If you must know, she didn't giggle once. And she damn well knows how to kiss."

His friend's lips twitched. "They say it is always the shy ones who are the most surprising at bedsport."

He wouldn't know. He didn't usually associate with women who were shy. Surely the widow Lady Randall who was supposed to meet him in that dark room at the Farnsworths' ball would not have fallen into that category.

As if banshees were invading the house, screaming rang through the corridor outside the library. Ian's ward Edward, wearing a pillowcase like it was a cape, darted past the open door, followed by Jacob, brandishing a play sword, followed by Ian's elderly butler, Jeffers.

Ian glanced at the clock on his desk. Nearly midnight. What were those two hellions doing up?

"Still haven't found a new nanny?" Julien asked.

"No, the Governess and Nanny Association hasn't sent any new candidates. If they don't soon, I'll need to place an advertisement in a newspaper."

Julien tapped a finger against his chin. "Have you thought any more about what I said the other day?"

"About getting married?"

"Yes."

"No. Of course not."

A ridiculous smile lit up Julien's face. "Besides her nervous laugh, Lady Sara seems a sensible woman."

"Good God, Julien, have you been drinking?"

"Think about it. I believe she collects bugs or insects, or something or other. From what I've heard, she wishes for her inheritance to continue her studies, but she won't get it until she marries. Why not offer her a marriage of convenience?"

"Because I have no desire to marry."

"Like so many other gentlemen, are you bothered by the fact she is a bluestocking?"

Intelligence, whether a man's or woman's, was something to be admired. "No."

"I think you should know that Bertram Floyd approached me only minutes after I heard what happened."

The look on Julien's face reflected that Ian would not like what his friend was about to tell him.

"He was quite upset about what transpired between you and Lady Sara. You know he was a friend of her father."

He did know that. He also knew the pious man had walked with Gladstone trying to save the souls of the prostitutes in the East End.

"I fear he is questioning his decision to sell us his ironworks company."

Damnation.

"After the gossips spread word about this indiscretion," Julien continued, "I have a feeling if you do not marry Lady Sara, several of our business ventures will not come to fruition."

Yes. Some of the moral sticklers they did business with would not want to deal with him. Duke or not. It was fine if they thought him a rogue when it came to widows, but despoiling an unmarried virgin was a whole different kettle of fish.

"If you make her an offer—a sensible one—and concoct a tale that you have been secretly betrothed, it might soothe some of our more pious capitalist companions."

Edward and Jacob darted by the room again. Somehow they'd lost Jeffers. Hopefully, the gray-haired retainer wasn't lying on the floor clutching his chest and gasping at his last breaths.

Ian marched into the corridor. "Edward, Jacob!"

Both children halted and turned to look at him, their mouths gaping.

"I thought you were gone out, Cousin," Edward said.

"I was out. But as you see, I have returned. Is this how you behave when you think I'm not home?"

Neither child answered.

Hearing a noise, Ian turned to see a winded Jeffers making his way toward them. The butler looked close to expiring.

"To bed. Now," Ian said. "I shall be up in ten minutes to check on you. If you are not tucked in with your hands and faces washed and your teeth brushed, you will not be allowed to leave the schoolroom tomorrow." He'd sworn he would never make that threat to the boys. It stunk with the echo of his father's voice.

Heads cast downward, the children shuffled off toward the stairs.

Ian turned to see Julien peering at him. "I know what's going through your mind, Ian. You are not your father."

He didn't like being so transparent. He hardened his features—drew up the façade that left one wondering what thoughts traversed his mind.

Julien clapped him on the back. "Think about what I've said."

After Julien left, and Ian made sure the boys were in bed, he lounged in the chair near the hearth in his library with a newly topped-off glass of whiskey.

The faces of his two young wards drifted in front of his mind's eye. Over the last few months, he'd come to feel a strong emotion toward his wards. But he clearly had no inkling how to raise the lads. They were better off being raised by someone else. Someone who could lavish love on them.

Since they'd come to live with him, he'd sworn he would not confine them to the schoolroom from dusk to dawn, learning Latin, geography, and mathematics. That they would not be struck with a leather strap if they did not earn a perfect score on an assignment, and they would never be sent to bed hungry for not living up to anyone's expectations.

He wanted them to have a childhood. Not to be raised with absolutes, where rules were chiseled in stone.

He was scared he might ruin them emotionally, as his father had him, if he became too involved in raising them. The lessons he'd learned from his father would do that. Though he didn't wish to marry, Julien was correct. A marriage of convenience would be different. His wife would not expect flowery sentiment. He feared that emotion had died a quick death after Isabelle and Father's betrayal.

He thought of Lady Sara. He'd noticed her once at a garden party last year before her father's death—before she'd gone into mourning. She'd not spent her time with the other ladies as her vivacious sister had, but had stood with several children near the lake, helping them sail their boats. Her expression had been open, loving, as she'd engaged with them. So unlike the nervous shy woman she was when he'd seen her at balls, mostly trying to blend into the background so no one would approach her. But that time he'd seen her with the children. . . . Perhaps she could give Edward and Jacob the love he felt incapable of giving them.

Good Lord. Was he seriously considering offering for the woman?

He tipped his glass of whiskey to his lips and drained it dry.

Chapter Four

The afternoon following the Farnsworths' ball, Sara sat on the cushioned window seat in her bedroom and flipped through the pages of her favorite book, *The Caterpillar, Marvelous Transformation, and Strange Floral Food*, written by a woman pioneer in entomology.

Usually she became engrossed in the pages, but today her gaze kept veering outside the mullioned glass panes. She doubted the Duke of Dorchester would call on her. But as that thought drifted through her mind for the umpteenth time, a shiny black carriage pulled in front of her family's town house.

The vehicle's door opened and the man in question stepped out with the grace of a big cat.

Behind her spectacles, she blinked. Sara would have bet her inheritance Dorchester wouldn't have shown up. Perhaps he was here to tell her brother he'd not marry her.

The wind caught his long coat, swirling it behind his legs as he moved toward the door at a speed that relayed he was in a hurry to get whatever he'd come here to convey over and done with. As if sensing someone watched him, he glanced up.

Sara quickly ducked her head. She didn't want him to think she'd been pining away for his arrival.

A few minutes later, a heavy knock sounded on her bedchamber door. "Sara, Dorchester is here!" Ned sounded shocked, as if he couldn't believe it as well.

She set her book down and opened the door. "He probably only wishes to inform you he will not ask for my hand."

"Good God, woman. He would have sent a note if that were the case, or done nothing at all."

Sara bit her lower lip. Did her brother truly believe the duke was here to offer for her hand? Do what society expected of him? That was as unlikely as her flying on the delicate wings of a butterfly.

"Very well. I shall see him."

Her brother's gaze drifted over her simple brown dress. "I suggest you change into something more stylish. Something not so bland."

She glanced down at herself. "No. This is fine."

"Why must you be so stubborn?"

Ignoring her brother's glower, Sara tipped her chin up and strode out of her bedroom.

She descended the stairs, Ned trailing behind her. Once at the drawing room's closed double doors, Ned set a hand on her arm, halting her from opening them.

"Sara," Ned whispered in an agitated voice. "At least remove your spectacles."

Perhaps she was more nervous than she realized since she'd forgotten she wore them. She removed her reading glasses and slipped them into the side pocket of her dress.

Ned opened the doors, and they stepped into the room.

The Duke of Dorchester, who'd been staring out the window, turned around. The hard angles of his face didn't shift into a smile. His piercing blue eyes drifted over her before moving to regard her brother. "Hampton, might I speak with your sister alone?"

An expression of hopefulness lit up Ned's face as his gaze volleyed back and forth between her and the duke. "Yes, of course." Ned pulled the doors closed behind him, leaving her alone with Dorchester who stayed near the window as if frightened she might start laughing if he moved nearer.

Wanting to prove he did not intimidate her, that she didn't feel at all nervous in his company, she strode closer to where he stood. "If you have come here to inform me you will not marry me, you could have sent a note."

"Perhaps I've come here to ask for your hand."

That possibility *did* make her nervous. "M-my hand. Surely you are not serious."

"I was thinking that we might make a deal."

She wasn't in the habit of making deals with the devil. She narrowed her eyes. The man was a cutthroat business-man. He stomped on others to get what he wanted. Any deal he made would only be to his advantage. "Oh, I cannot wait to hear what you propose."

A couple of feet separated them, but with one step he closed the gap.

This close in the brightly lit room, she realized his eyes were the brilliant color of the male species of the Adonis blue butterfly. Striking. For a moment, she felt almost mes-merized by the rich color.

Mesmerized? Foolish woman, she reprimanded herself and drew in a deep breath. The same spicy scent that she recalled from when he kissed her drifted to her nose. She found it very male and very pleasant. She had found the kiss very pleasant as well, but those things weren't reason enough to marry the man.

"What is your proposition, Your Grace?"

He braced his feet apart and placed his hands behind his back, causing his broad shoulders to look even wider. "If we marry, I won't touch your dowry or your inheritance. You may do whatever you wish with the funds."

Her mouth went slack. She snapped it closed. His proposition sounded too good to be true. There had to be more to it than that. "I think you are leaving out several details, Your Grace."

This earned her a smile, though there was something cunning in it. She presumed it was the way a fox grinned seconds before he leaped on an unsuspecting rabbit. "How astute. I'm not in the habit of making deals without getting something in return. This incident—"

"You mean when you pulled me into that dark room and kissed me?"

"Have you forgotten that you kissed me back, darling?" He drew his finger down the side of her cheek.

The light touch felt like a breath against her skin. A tingling sensation moved slowly through her body. Wishing for a barrier between them, Sara stepped back and folded her arms across her chest. "I was confused."

"Were you? That's not how I would describe it."

"You're insufferable."

"Let us not squabble over semantics. This incident has put me in a bit of a bind. If I don't marry you, several of my business associates might not wish to continue doing business with me. They are men of connection. Men that I need to deal with. I don't wish for my companies to suffer. So if we marry, in public you will play the devoted wife."

"That might be difficult. I don't like you."

"You liked me well enough in that dark room."

Heat crept up her cheeks. Beyond the pale for him to mention that. "I didn't realize who I was kissing."

"So you are in the habit of kissing men in dark rooms?"

The blackguard was twisting her words around. She ignored that comment. "Is there more to this deal?"

"Yes. You will help raise my two wards as if they are your own children."

"Wards?" She couldn't have been more startled if he'd pinched her bottom. She wasn't aware he'd become the guardian of any children. "When did this happen?"

"Three months ago."

"How old are they?" She heard the almost wistful tone in her voice.

"Seven and eight. Two boys."

When younger, she'd dreamed of having children. Mothering two young boys would not be a hardship. "Is there more to this deal?"

"We would need to come to an understanding about the marriage bed."

"The marriage bed?" Heat flooded her body. "What do you propose?"

"That would be up to you."

"Up to me?"

"I'm not a monk, darling. If you refuse me your bed after we consummate the marriage, I will discreetly take a lover."

"I've seen how discreet you are, Your Grace."

"Would you then prefer we live like husband and wife in every sense of the word?"

"No!"

"You cannot have it both ways."

She presumed she couldn't. "I need to think about this."

"Yes, do that." He pulled out his gold pocket watch and flipped it open. "You have exactly five minutes to respond to my marriage proposal."

"F-five minutes." Though she usually only giggled nervously in a crowded ballroom when asked to dance, the absurdity of having to make such a life-changing decision in such a short time nearly caused her to laugh hysterically. "You're not serious?"

"Absolutely. I am helping you as much as you're helping me. Something I'm not accustomed to doing. So yes, you have"—he peered at his watch again—"four minutes."

As Ian waited for Lady Sara to give him an answer, he thought he might have gone mad. He could not see himself married to the woman who stood before him. They didn't know each other. And though most women fawned over him—he was a duke, after all—Lady Sara clearly stated she didn't like him. And yet he was here. He thought of Edward and Jacob, along with Julien's comment about their business connections—men like Bertram Floyd turning their backs on them. He'd worked too hard to surpass the wealth his father had attained to let it slip away.

He glanced at his watch again. "Three minutes."

Sara looked as if she stared into the face of a lion. Yet, she didn't giggle.

"Why must I answer you now?" she asked.

He wasn't quite sure why the ultimatum of now or never. Most likely because he wished to get this over and done with. His gaze moved to her mouth. He remembered the kiss they'd shared. Good Lord, she'd kissed him with such want with that pouty mouth of hers. But as she'd said, she hadn't known whom she was kissing, but a fire burned within the woman and, in truth, he wouldn't mind setting it loose in his bed if that was the type of marriage she wanted.

"Two minutes."

She snagged her lower lip between her teeth. "If I have a contract written up, stating that my dowry and inheritance will be mine to do whatever I wish with, will you sign it?"

The minx was clever. Every business arrangement should be put down in writing. "I am a duke. Isn't my word enough?"

She tilted her chin up and held his gaze. "No."

Though he would have kept his word, he admired that she was keen enough to know one should get everything in writing. "I will."

"Then I accept your marriage proposal. How could I not when it was offered with such flowery sentiment?"

He heard the sarcasm in her tone. He leaned forward and drew in the pleasant floral scent drifting off her body. "You want more sentiment? Then we should seal our deal with a kiss."

Her eyes grew wide, yet she stood her ground.

He realized that her large hazel eyes were quite lovely with their golden specks around her irises.

She tapped her cheek. "You may kiss me here."

"A man should give his betrothed a suitable kiss." He drew the pad of his thumb over her bottom lip.

Her lips parted, and he experienced the warmth of her breath on his skin. She briefly closed her eyes, then as if regaining her composure, she tipped her head back and held his gaze like a general in the Grenadier Guards. "Very well, if you insist."

He set a hand on her forearm and skimmed his palm

over her sleeve, while his other hand cupped her cheek, angling her face to his.

Sara's eyes drifted closed, again, while her mint-scented breath brushed against his lips.

Ian's mouth was only an inch from hers when the double doors burst open, and Sara's brother rushed into the room holding three glass flutes in one hand and a bottle of champagne in the other.

Eyes wide, Lady Sara stepped back.

Ian tried not to growl at the man. For some strange reason, he'd desperately wanted to kiss Sara. Perhaps to disavow his memory that the kiss between them had been so incendiary.

Yes, of course, that was the reason. Nothing else made sense.

Chapter Five

Ian stood with his feet braced slightly apart, hands clasped behind his back, and stared down at his wards' round and deceptively innocent-looking faces. His future wife had sent a letter yesterday, requesting she meet Edward and Jacob.

Bathed, with their hair combed, and not a stitch of dirt on them, they looked the picture of obedient children.

"I want you both to be on your best behavior," Ian said.

As was their way, Edward and Jacob peered at each other as if silently communicating before returning their gazes to him.

"Well?" Ian used his stern voice. The one that made grown men look ready to weep but seemed to have little effect on the two scamps sitting before him in his library.

They nodded their heads.

"Good." He removed his watch from the fob pocket of his waistcoat and flipped the timepiece open. "Lady Sara and her brother, Lord Hampton, should be here shortly."

While waiting for their guests, Ian had directed the boys' tutor to sit in the library with them and make sure they didn't get into any mischief. Mr. Marks, a lanky fellow in his mid-twenties, had grown up the youngest child in a family of twelve and seemed immune to any pranks they played on him. Both Edward and Jacob seemed to have decided the man a hopeless cause when it came to attempting to get the tutor to quit, and had all but given up trying.

"Can't we go out and play, Cousin?" Edward asked.

If he allowed that, they'd come back full of mud, looking like the rascals they truly were. "No. Definitely not." Ian turned to the tutor. "Thank you, Marks. I'll take it from here."

"Yes, Your Grace." The tutor gave the boys a cursory glance before he stepped from the room.

"Is this Lady Sara going to be our new nanny?" The devilish gleam in Edward's eyes revealed the child was already concocting ways of frightening off the woman.

"No, she's not a nanny. I've asked her to marry me."

Edward's eyes grew exceedingly round before he crunched his face.

"Will she be our new mama?" Jacob asked.

For a brief second, Ian saw a glimmer of hope in Jacob's eyes, conveying how the boy missed his mother. "No. But she will help care for you, and she is quite nice."

"I don't want a new mother." Edward stubbornly set his hands on his narrow hips. "I want my mama to come back."

What does one say to that? Ian squatted down in front of both boys. "As I've explained, your mother and father did not wish to leave you."

"Excuse me, Your Grace," his butler said from the doorway. "Lord Hampton and Lady Sara have arrived. They are in the gold drawing room."

"Thank you, Jeffers."

Ian stood. "Now, men, let us be on our best behavior."

A few minutes later, Ian stepped into the drawing room

with the boys begrudgingly trailing him. Lady Sara stood beside her brother, dressed in a plain brown day dress, similar to the one she'd worn when he'd called on her and asked for her hand. Once again she wore her hair in a severe bun at the nape of her neck. Her gaze was not on him but on the children.

A tentative smile turned up her lips. She looked almost infatuated by the boys.

Her gaze shifted to him, and her smile fell away. He recalled what she'd said about not caring a great deal about him. That suited him fine. He didn't give a tinker's curse what she thought about him as long as she tended to the boys, and hopefully loved them as a mother would. And acted the devoted wife in front of the men he did business with.

"Lady Sara, Hampton, how nice of you to call on us. May I introduce you to Edward and Jacob?"

"Master Edward, how wonderful to meet you." Smiling, Lady Sara bent and extended her gloved hand to Edward.

Edward limply grasped her fingers.

She shook his hand, then reached out to shake Jacob's. "Master Jacob." Smiling, she glanced from one child to the other. "You are both so handsome."

Neither said a word.

"Boys, what do you say?" Ian prompted.

"Thank you." Jacob gave a weak smile.

Edward dug the toe of his shoe into the carpet and mumbled a thank-you.

Lady Sara smiled as if she hadn't noticed the boys' less-than-enthusiastic response. "Edward, Jacob, I hear you have a lovely garden. Would you like to give me a tour?"

Ian saw a devilish spark light up Edward's eyes, and the

image of their last nanny, Miss Winterbottom, covered in mud, flashed in Ian's mind. "Why don't we all go?"

"Your Grace," Lady Sara said, "I think it would be best if just the boys and I go. It will allow us to get to know one another."

That was what he was worried about, but what could he say? "Very well." He gave his wards a stern look. "I expect you both to be on your most gentlemanly behavior."

As Sara and the boys made their way out of the room, she bit the inside of her mouth. The children's less-than-enthusiastic response clearly indicated they were not pleased about the upcoming marriage between her and Dorchester.

Perhaps they believed she would try to replace their mother. She could understand them not looking favorably on that. It could not be easy for them to go through such loss and upheaval in their lives. She comprehended their sorrow. She'd lost her own mother when twelve. Mother had possessed a great fascination for botany and exotic plants. Sara and Mother had visited gardens and exhibits presented by the Royal Horticultural Society. It was from these outings that Sara had come to be fascinated by the life cycle of butterflies. Like herself, Mother had been a bluestocking, though Sara believed her father only saw Mother's beauty, not her intellect. Losing her mother had caused Sara such melancholy. Especially since Mother had never made her feel as if she were a square peg that didn't fit into a round hole.

Pulling herself from her thoughts, Sara peered at the two small boys before her as the three of them moved down the corridor. She could love them like her own if they would allow her the opportunity.

"This way." Edward stepped into a morning room with two sets of open French doors.

As soon as they walked onto the flagstone terrace, Sara's gaze moved to the lush garden that lay beyond. Excitement shot through her. It boasted a plethora of plants that would attract butterflies. There were milkweeds, cornflowers, yarrows, and other plants rich in nectar. "What a lovely garden."

"It's got spiders. Big, hairy-legged ones," Edward, the eldest of the two boys, said as if trying to frighten her.

"Really? How wonderful."

The child's brows pinched together, and he frowned.

"Will you give me a tour?" she asked, trying to contain her excitement.

"There really are bugs." Jacob peered up at her.

"Yes, I'm sure there are." She anxiously walked down the granite steps that led from the terrace to the gardens.

The boys trailed her.

She bent down to examine the underside of a leaf, which showed that an adult caterpillar had already laid eggs on it. When she straightened, she noticed Edward whispering into his younger brother's ear.

Jacob grinned and nodded.

She suddenly suspected that the two boys were not as angelic in nature as their sweet faces would have one think. "I bet you play all sorts of games in this garden, don't you?"

Edward lifted one shoulder in a shrug.

Jacob's smile broadened. "We do. We play pirates and Robin Hood."

"I used to love playing pirates with my brother when we were younger." That had been before Ned learned that being Father's heir would give him absolute power over her life.

"Girls cannot be pirates." Edward kicked a pebble and sent it skittering in front of them across the path.

"But they can," Sara said. "Have you not heard of Anne Bonny and Mary Read? They were two female pirates, but they were not the only ones. I might have a book about them."

"Will you read it to us?" Jacob asked, eyes bright with anticipation.

"I will." Sara gazed at the older brother. "Would you like that, Edward?"

This time he shrugged both of his shoulders.

They reached a fountain with a mermaid who held a large shell that water overflowed from to settle into the fountain's base. Sara sat on the raised edge, removed her gloves, and dipped a hand into the cool water.

"We'll be back." Edward grabbed his younger brother's hand. "We need to show you something."

Perhaps she was making headway. Sara smiled and nodded.

A few minutes later, the boys ran back up to her.

Edward sported a mischievous grin on his face. Flecks of dirt circled the right cuff of his once-pristine white shirt, while his other hand was hidden behind his back.

He stepped in front of her. "We have a surprise for you. Close your eyes and hold out your hand."

Her gaze shifted to Jacob, who was gnawing on his lower lip as if a bit concerned about what his brother was about to do. Obviously, whatever Edward intended to give her was meant to cause her some discomfort. What they didn't know was that nothing found in this garden could make her uncomfortable. Everything about it was glorious.

"Very well." Setting her gloves down next to her, Sara closed her eyes and held out her hand. Something both gritty and slimy was placed in her palm.

"You can look now." Almost uncontained anticipation laced Edward's voice.

Sara opened her eyes to see a long pink worm with bits of dark soil clinging to its body wiggling in her hand. "Ah, an earthworm. And a fine specimen indeed, if I may say so."

Both boys' mouths went slack-jawed.

"Did you know that worms are called invertebrates because they, unlike humans, have no backbones?"

Just then, the Duke of Dorchester and Ned rounded the bend in the garden path.

His Grace's eyes settled on the worm in her hand and his jaw tightened. "What is going on here?" he asked, peering at the boys.

"Nothing." Sara stood and set the worm onto a cool spot under a bush. "I was explaining about invertebrates to the boys."

Now it was the duke's turn to look startled. His gaze volleyed from her to the children, then back to her.

On the other hand, Ned looked like he wanted to rail at her. "Forgive my sister. She favors herself some type of entomologist."

"That's not true. I don't favor myself as one. I am one." She kept her gaze on the duke, wanting to see his reaction. His expression gave nothing away. At least it did not reflect the disdain on her brother's face. Sara dipped her hand into the fountain's water to remove the bits of soil from her palm, then picked up her gloves from where she had placed them.

Dorchester stepped up to her and offered Sara his arm.

For a brief moment, her body tingled over the thought of touching him. Why? She didn't even like the man. Then why was she going to marry him? She reminded herself he'd offered her freedom. Freedom she might not have if she married another gentleman. She might not even have sovereignty over her own body. At least he had given her a choice.

She wrapped her hand around his arm. Almost immediately her mind shot back to that dark room at the masquerade ball and the feel of his hard chest under her palms.

Would he kiss her the same way he had at the Farnsworths' ball? A wave of anxiousness, or perhaps desire, flittered through her body. Her steps slowed.

"Is something the matter?" Dorchester asked, matching his gait to hers.

Yes, the thought of making love to you is a bit disconcerting. "No, I was thinking of your two wards."

He stiffened slightly—an almost imperceivable movement. Sara suspected he was waiting for her to make some derogatory comment. She was more than aware that the two boys had tried to scare her off. If they thought a prank with a worm would accomplish that, they were mistaken.

"They are charming boys," she said.

As if she'd said something outlandish, he blinked, then laughed.

Though she had witnessed the occasional quirk of his lips, along with a rare smile, Sara couldn't recall hearing him laugh. He always looked so formidable. So serious. There was something appealing about the sound of his laugh. She shoved that thought away.

Her brother who walked several paces ahead of them

briefly turned around with a clearly startled expression on his face.

"You're being too kind, Lady Sara. They are devilish children, but you are wise enough to have figured that out. As I am astute enough to know that you did not dig up that worm, yet I have a feeling you can still care for them, perhaps even come to love them."

She peered sideways at him. He might not like to show his softer side, but he had one. Otherwise he would not care whether she loved the boys or not. She'd thought his proposal was motivated by his desire to save his business connections, the mention of the wards an afterthought. But it was not. That knowledge made it easier to accept the bargain they'd made.

"Do they have a nanny and a tutor?" she asked.

"They have a tutor, Mr. Marks, but at present they are in need of a nanny."

She would bet they had scared the last one away with their antics. "Might I ask how many they have had over the last few months?"

His deep blue eyes held her regard. "Several. Does that knowledge make you want to default on our deal?"

"Not in the least, Your Grace." She glanced at her brother. "You're offering me freedom from being under my brother's thumb. I now realize that I would do almost anything to precipitate that."

"Even marrying a gentleman you don't particularly care for?"

She looked ahead. "Even that."

Chapter Six

The two weeks preceding Sara's wedding seemed to come and go as quickly as a spring thunderstorm, leaving her anxious on her wedding day.

It didn't help that while Sara sat at the dressing table in her bedchamber as Wallace, the lady's maid she shared with Louisa, tried to wrangle her hair into some intricate coiffure, her sister prattled on endlessly about the Duke of Dorchester.

"Though he looks rather intimidating, he's devilishly handsome," Louisa said. "And he is in possession of an athletic build. I bet his tailor doesn't need to add a stitch of padding to the shoulders of his coats." Her sister flopped onto Sara's bed, arms akimbo, and released a dreamy sigh.

As Wallace wrapped a thick strand of Sara's hair about the curling tongs, Sara noticed the lady's maid smile. At least someone was enjoying Louisa's prattling.

"I can't believe he asked you to marry him." Louisa rolled onto her stomach, propped up her chin in her hands, and scrutinized Sara. There was a plethora of unspoken insults in her sister's words, along with the critical look she bestowed on her.

Yet, Sara couldn't believe it either. And not just for the reasons her sister had listed ad nauseam over the last couple of weeks—such as the duke being strikingly hand-some, wealthy, and sought after, while implying Sara was plain and sat firmly on the shelf. The main point of this odd union could not be overlooked, which was the unmit-igated fact that neither the duke nor she felt any meaning-ful affection toward each other.

Ha! An understatement. They simply didn't like each other. He'd not even bothered to call on her since she'd met Edward and Jacob. But they had corresponded, mostly to iron out the details of their wedding and for Dorchester to let Sara know that he had procured a special marriage license from the archbishop, bypassing the need to have the banns read for three consecutive weeks.

Over that point, Ned had railed on endlessly that mar-rying a duke should be done in grand style, with everyone who was anyone invited, but Sara had asked Dorchester if they might be married in a simple ceremony at her family's town house. She wanted a short list of guests—those who would not make her more nervous than she was about her decision to marry the duke.

Thankfully, he'd agreed.

As far as him courting her, why would he? She needed to remember that to Dorchester this was like any of his other business transactions. Cut-and-dried.

"Last year, I heard he had an affair with Lady Cleary before his latest liaison with Lady Randall." Louisa's voice pulled Sara out of her thoughts.

Sara knew all about Lady Cleary. She remembered Dor-chester and the widow's assignation in his library.

"Do you think he'll have affairs while married to you?"

"Of course not," she replied, even though that was one

of the worries that had kept her awake during the night. He'd said he'd be faithful if she decided that they would share the marriage bed. He'd implied it, hadn't he? He'd not pressed her on the subject in their missives. He probably hoped they would consummate the marriage and live separate lives. She still hadn't decided. She shoved thoughts of that away. Right now, her main worry was what would happen if Dorchester didn't show up, and she was left standing before the clergyman, utterly humiliated.

She examined her reflection in the mirror above her dressing table and tried to ignore the dark smudges under her eyes.

"You know they say he's as rich as the queen." Her sister's gaze met Sara's in the mirror. "It's a shame you don't care about how you look. You could go to Paris and buy every gown at the House of Worth, yet you're content to wear such unflattering clothing. But as a duchess, you'll have to do better. Dorchester can't have you looking no different than a maid working at one of his estates."

Sara's stomach was nervous enough. She wished her sister would take her uncharitable comments and leave the room. "I bought several new gowns at Madame Renault's."

"You did? When?" Louisa shifted upright into a sitting position.

"I went the day after Dorchester called on me. They were completed this week and are already packed away in my trunk."

"Why didn't you ask me to accompany you? You don't have a great deal of fashion sense, and I could have helped you."

She wasn't sure how much more she could take of her sister's cutting comments without saying something she might regret. And she knew doing so would only cause

Louisa to pout and cry, and Ned would blame Sara. "I went early in the morning, both times. You were still in bed."

Louisa glanced at the simple cream-colored gown draped over a chair and crinkled her nose. "Is that what you intend to wear?"

"Yes. It is one of the gowns I purchased from Madame Renault's."

"You definitely should have had me accompany you to the modiste. A wedding gown should have more embellishments."

A throbbing started in Sara's head. "Darling, shouldn't you be getting ready?"

"I need Wallace to help me, and she's been trying to make you look presentable."

The lady's maid set the curling tongs down. "There, miss. All done."

Sara's gaze shifted from her sister's reflection in the mirror to her own. The maid had styled her hair with the front sections swept upward and the back left loose to trail down in a mass of flowing curls. She bit her lip.

"You don't like it, miss?" Wallace asked.

"No, it's lovely, but do you think it looks too young?"

"Don't be silly," Louisa said, slipping off the bed. "Many women, even ones your age, are wearing it this way. If you would spend more time reading fashion magazines and less time with your insects, you would know what's in vogue."

"Thank you, Wallace." Sara stood. "It does look lovely. Now you can go and coif Louisa's hair."

The maid smiled. "Yes, miss. Then I'll return to help you get dressed."

"I want pearls wrapped in my hair," Louisa said as she

strolled toward the door. "And I'm going to wear my newest gown. The lavender one."

A worried expression settled on Wallace's face. The lady's maid realized, as Sara did, that Louisa was trying to outshine Sara.

"Perhaps you should save that one for Lord and Lady Pendleton's upcoming ball," Wallace suggested.

"But I want to wear it. I'll be . . ." Her sister's voice trailed off.

She knew what Louisa had begun to say. That she'd be the center of attention.

"The guest list will be quite small, Louisa." Sara forced a smile. "You probably should save it for the ball."

"Yes. I guess that would make more sense." Louisa was almost through the doorway when she pivoted back. "Are you nervous?"

"A bit."

"I hope you won't giggle and embarrass Ned and me."

"You know I usually only giggle when asked to dance."

Her sister's lips twisted the same way Ned's did when he judged her. "I would think marrying someone as formidable as the Duke of Dorchester would make you even more nervous."

Sara realized it could happen. Her stomach fluttered.

"My friend Annabelle told me she sometimes gets nervous when she must play the piano at her mother's musicales. Do you know what she does?"

No, but Sara was anxious for any tidbit that might help. "What does she do?"

"She pretends that everyone in the room is naked."

Naked? Sara felt heat move up her neck to settle on her cheeks. "I don't think that would help me, Louisa."

"Well, they aren't completely naked. Annabelle says her

imagination isn't that creative. The men are still dressed in their smalls. If you get nervous, you should try it." Louisa smiled as if she thought herself a kind benefactor, then both she and Wallace stepped out of the bedroom, closing the door behind them.

What poppycock. Envisioning men naked surely would not help her nervousness, it would make it worse. Especially if she was imagining the duke naked. She glanced at the clock. In less than two hours, she would become the Duchess of Dorchester.

If her betrothed showed up.

As the reverend read the vows, Sara's nose twitched from the abundance of flowers placed around the drawing room. She presumed Ned had ordered them to impress Dorchester. However, His Grace's face looked as serious as a mourner's during a funeral procession.

Most likely, he was questioning his decision to marry her as much as she was doubting her decision to marry him.

Maybe they were both mad for going through with this.

Standing next to him, his height, the breadth of his shoulders, everything about him made her feel so small even though she was five feet and six inches. Her stomach gave a nervous roll. A strong desire to flee washed over her. Hoping to calm herself, she drew in several deep breaths.

They must have sounded like gulps because both Dorchester and the clergyman peered at her.

Her future husband cocked a brow.

Sara had a feeling he was silently hoping she would run so he would be free of this entanglement. Perhaps running would be for the best. She glanced over her shoulder at the double doors before her gaze settled on her brother. Ned must have realized what thoughts were playing through her mind since he shot her a warning scowl. This morning he'd made a point of telling her that Lord Montgomery had not withdrawn his marriage proposal, and that if she didn't go through with this wedding, she would find herself marrying the elderly gentleman in the future.

Attempting to calm her fraying nerves, Sara reminded herself that she would control not only her inheritance but her dowry, as well. Yet, her heart began a steady increase in her chest.

Louisa's words about how her friend Annabelle imagined people naked to ease her apprehension flashed in Sara's mind. She peered at the clergyman. It seemed a sacrilege to envision him that way, so she glanced at Dorchester. She could easily imagine him naked. All she had to do was think of the print she'd seen of the statue of the *Farnese Hercules*—an impressive, brawny depiction of the god. Starting at Dorchester's shoulders, she visually began stripping off every stitch of his clothing as her gaze traveled over his muscled body. At his hips, she swallowed and decided to toss a loincloth on him before moving farther down to his bare legs.

Though she had managed to distract herself from her nervousness, Sara almost giggled over the silliness of it all. She pinched her lips tight.

Her expression must have looked rather odd because the clergyman gave her a strange look, which caused Dorchester to glance at her and arch his brow again in that arrogant way of his.

She ignored him, mentally repeating *I will oversee my own funds. I will oversee my own funds.*

For that reason alone, it was worth marrying the man.

She started to repeat the words again in her head only to hear the vicar pronounce them man and wife.

Realization that it was too late for either of them to back out hit her like a bucket of cold water. She looked at Dorchester's solemn expression and gulped down the fear rising within her. She had made her bed and would have to lie in it, and perhaps, at least for tonight, she would not lie in it alone.

Chapter Seven

The wedding breakfast had concluded over an hour ago, and the few guests invited chatted in the drawing room.

"You look absolutely lovely," Nina, Sara's dearest friend, said. "And your wedding ring is breathtaking."

Sara pulled her gaze away from where Dorchester stood talking to her brother and Baron Ralston, Nina's husband, and studied the three-stoned diamond-and-gold ring on her finger. It *was* stunning. "Thank you, Nina, and thank you for coming."

"I would not have missed it for the world."

Nina was the only one Sara had told about this marriage being a farce. The only person whom she'd divulged the full extent of the conversation she'd had with Dorchester— that this was nothing more than a marriage of convenience. That the tale bandied about as fodder for the *ton*—the lie that they were already secretly betrothed when found kissing at the masquerade ball was sheer claptrap. Though she realized Nina would have realized that since she'd not spoken favorably about Dorchester on more than one occasion to her closest friend and confidante.

"You did wonderfully." Nina clasped Sara's hand.

"Except that one time when I imagined Dorchester naked."

"You . . . you what?" Nina's eyes widened.

"Louisa said it might help my nervousness if I imagined those around me naked."

Nina laughed.

The men turned and looked at them.

Louisa, who stood near the mantel eyeing Julien Dartmore like the man was a French pastry, gave them a curious look. The man's wife had not attended since she and her daughter were in the country visiting Julien's family. Her sister sauntered toward them. "What's so witty?"

"I was telling Nina about the advice you gave me this morning."

"About imagining people naked? Well, if I felt nervous, I would try it, but I don't feel the least bit anxious, especially when a man wants my attention. In fact, I think I'll go engage Lord Dartmore in conversation. It's a shame he's married." Louisa took one step away from them, then pivoted around. "Did you try it? Imagine someone naked?"

"Just once," Sara replied.

"Who? I bet it was Dorchester."

"How do you know I've not already seen my husband naked?" Sara replied, shocking not only Louisa but herself with such a scandalous comment. But she had to admit it felt good to stun her sister and momentarily leave her speechless.

"I'm sure you haven't," Louisa replied.

"How do you know?" Sara arched her brow in the same arrogant way the duke did.

"Because I know you. You would never—"

"You thought I would never marry. Yet, here I am married

to one of the most sought-after men in all of England. Perhaps you don't know me as well as you thought."

Louisa gaped.

"Dear, didn't you say you wished to go speak with Lord Dartmore?" Sara asked.

Her sister blinked, then without a word she walked away.

Sara watched her stroll toward the men. Her sister had nearly reached them when Ned walked up to Louisa.

Next to her, Nina chucked. "Well done, Sara. It was long overdue that you turned the tables on your younger sister."

"I shouldn't have said what I did. It was a blatant lie, and though I love my sister, she has been rather trying today."

Nina squeezed her hand. "I think everything between you and Dorchester will work out."

"I dearly hope you are right. Though I'm not sure how it can be when we feel the way we do about each other. But I keep reminding myself that he will allow me the use of my own funds to continue my studies. Surely that has to account for something."

Nina nodded, then glanced at Edward and Jacob. "Are you getting along with his wards?"

Edward and Jacob sat on the sofa. Both boys looked fidgety, as if the ability to sit still took a great deal of effort. She'd noticed Dorchester talking to them a few minutes ago. She had a feeling he'd instructed them to behave.

"This is the first time I've seen them since I visited Dorchester Hall. But as I told you after my visit there, they are not overly pleased to have me joining their family."

"Well, if the best they can do is try to scare you away with a worm, they will not succeed. I have no doubt you will win them over."

"I have a feeling it might not be such an easy task. I should go and talk to them." She pressed a kiss to her dear friend's cheek. "Thank you. You always make me feel better."

As Sara headed toward the boys, she heard a loud grumbling from her sister.

Louisa was glaring at Ned with narrowed eyes. Her angry regard shifted from their brother to Sara before Louisa marched out of the room.

Wondering what in the blazes was going on, Sara walked up to a red-faced Ned. "What is the matter with Louisa?"

Her brother released an agitated huff. "I informed her that Wallace will be going to Dorchester Hall to serve as your lady's maid."

"Why?"

"I will not have my sister, married to the Duke of Dorchester, arriving at his residence without a maid to attend to her. Especially since Louisa has fashion sense, and you possess none. And it was Louisa who mentioned how you might embarrass us when you attend social events with the duke dressed no better than a servant. So I'm not sure why she stormed off in such a hissy way."

Dorchester had said he was helping her as much as she was helping him. Listening to the way her brother and sister talked about her, she realized how correct he was. "Very well, but Lord and Lady Pendleton's ball is in two days. Let Wallace stay until then so she might help Louisa get ready and allow you time to hire someone else."

"What will Dorchester think?" Ned glanced toward where the duke spoke with Baron Ralston.

"I will tell him that Wallace will be arriving shortly.

Now if you will excuse me, I wish to speak with His Grace's wards."

As Sara approached the boys, Edward narrowed his eyes at her as if she would force him to eat jellied eel. She settled into a chair next to the sofa and noticed a smudge of white frosting on the collar of Jacob's coat. "Did you enjoy the wedding cake?" she asked both boys.

Edward shrugged.

Jacob nodded enthusiastically.

She took his hearty nod as an opening. "Is vanilla your favorite flavor, Jacob?"

"Yes, but I like chocolate as well. I especially like to drink hot chocolate—"

His words were cut off by his older brother giving him a jab in his ribs with his elbow.

"Ouch! Why'd you do that?" Jacob rubbed at his side.

She knew why. Obviously, Edward was determined that they not become close. Nor did he want his younger brother to befriend her.

The duke, who was still engaged in conversation with Nina's husband, glanced at them, then approached. "Edward, did you hit your brother?"

"No, Cousin Ian." Edward stared at her as if challenging her to contradict him.

And honestly, she didn't know what to do. "I'm sure he didn't mean to. Did you, Edward?"

The older boy responded with another shrug.

Next to her, the duke's nostrils flared. "When Lady Sara speaks to you, Edward, answer her. Do not shrug. Now what do you say?"

"No, I didn't mean to elbow him."

"As discussed, we will see you in a few days," Dorchester said, peering from one child to the other.

Sara's gaze jerked to her new husband. What did he mean, see them in a few days? They'd not discussed a honeymoon. "Are we going somewhere?"

"No. The boys are going to spend a few days with Julien at his town house. I thought it best you have some time to adjust to your new surroundings."

That comment actually sounded thoughtful. It also made it sound as if he thought the boys would not make the transition for her easy, but she was determined to win them over.

Jacob bounced on the seat. "Lord Dartmore's house? Is his stepdaughter, Mary, home?"

"No, she is visiting her grandmother."

The child's lips turned downward, reflecting his disappointment.

"Are you ready to leave, boys?" the earl inquired, walking up to them.

Edward slipped off the couch and gave Sara a less-than-charitable look.

"Thank you, Julien," Dorchester said.

Lord Dartmore turned to her. "It was a lovely ceremony, Your Grace. I wish you and my dear friend a long and happy marriage."

"Thank you, my lord." Sara forced a smile and wondered if such a thing as a happy marriage could be possible between her and Dorchester.

A gambler who knew all the facts would place his wager against them. For the hundredth time, she reminded herself that she would control her funds. Money that would allow her to continue her studies, but as she looked at the unsmiling man she'd married, she tried not to worry that she'd just made the biggest mistake of her life.

* * *

Though the wedding reception had ended hours ago, Ned had insisted she and Dorchester stay and eat dinner with him and Louisa. Now, with a light rain welcoming the night, Sara sat with Dorchester in his carriage as they headed to his Richmond residence. With the windows closed, the pleasant scent of his cologne, a mixture of citrus and spices, teased at her nose.

From the corner of her eye, she glanced at him sitting next to her. In the closed-in space, he seemed even larger than he had when he stood next to her.

The vehicle turned, causing it to sway, and his shoulder pressed against hers for a moment. A bolt of awareness shot through her body.

Tonight would entail more than the press of their fully clothed bodies. That thought caused her heart to give a slight flutter. The same type of flutter she experienced when she entered a ballroom. She still hadn't given him his answer regarding the type of marriage they would have after they consummated their union. She didn't like the idea of him having a mistress, but that left only one course of action.

A memory from when she was a child floated to the forefront of her mind. She remembered Aunt Beatrice and Grandmother the week before Beatrice was to marry. Though she'd sat a good distance away in the drawing room of her grandparents' country home, playing with her dolls, Sara had overheard their low voices.

"Now remember, Beatrice, you have a duty to your husband in the marriage bed." Grandmother patted Beatrice's hand as if consoling her.

"But what you've told me I must do seems so odd," Beatrice said.

"Yes, it's an unpleasant task. A woman's cross to bear. A proper, well-bred woman does not experience the same fever for the act that a man does, yet she must stoically tolerate it. Just lie on your back and let him have his way. If you are lucky, it will be over quick enough."

"How often do I need to do that, Mama?"

"He shall be quite content if you let him do it at least once a fortnight."

A bump in the road pulled Sara from her memory. Once every two weeks. Surely she could lie on her back every two weeks and act very stoic while Dorchester had his way with her. "I have decided about the type of marriage I wish us to have."

In the dim compartment, he held her gaze. "Do tell."

"There will be no mistresses."

"You know what that means?"

"Yes. Of course. You can visit my bed once every two weeks."

They passed a streetlamp and the light briefly illuminated Dorchester's clearly shocked expression.

Sara fought the urge to pat her cheeks to confirm she'd not grown a hairy wart.

"Once every two weeks?" he repeated, his voice laced with obvious disbelief. "Might I ask how you came up with this *schedule?*"

Why in the world did he sound so irate? Was that too often? "I have heard that it is a reasonable amount of time."

"By whom?"

"My grandmother."

"She told you this?"

Heat singed her cheeks. "No, she has long passed. I once overheard her giving advice."

After a moment of silence, Dorchester mumbled something that sounded like a death threat to his friend Julien; then he reached into his pocket and pulled out two gold sovereigns and handed one of them to her. "During each two-week period, we can hand in our coin for an extra night. Is that agreeable?"

"I'm sure I won't need an extra night. Once every fortnight should suffice." Yet, as she spoke those words, she couldn't stop herself from replaying how her body had reacted to Dorchester's touch at the masquerade ball. That memory remained imprinted on her mind as did the feel of his kisses and the way his tongue had stroked hers. She closed her hand around the coin. Like her insides, the cool metal grew warm.

"Is that agreeable?" Dorchester repeated.

"Yes."

He mumbled something again, then turned his attention to the window and remained silent for the remainder of the journey.

Upon entering the house, Dorchester introduced Sara to several members of the staff before the gray-haired housekeeper, Mrs. Pullman, showed her to her bedchamber.

A large tester bed with a carved headboard dominated the space.

Noticing how Sara stared at it like it was a gargoyle, Mrs. Pullman had smiled at her like a benevolent old aunt before she exited the room.

That had been over an hour ago. Now Sara wore a frivolous silk-and-lace nightgown she'd allowed Madame

Renault to convince her to purchase instead of the white cotton one she'd initially chosen.

As Sara waited for Dorchester to enter her bedchamber, she twisted her hands together as a nervous bubble burst within her stomach. Her husband hadn't lived the life of a saint. He was probably used to women who were experienced. Surely he would understand a virgin such as herself would be nervous.

The renegade thoughts going through her mind didn't help her anxiousness. What if she giggled when he stepped into the room? What if she couldn't stop. Again, she reminded herself how she'd not giggled when he'd kissed her at Lord and Lady Farnsworth's masquerade ball. Though, with his tongue exploring the recesses of her mouth, that would have been difficult. But even afterward, she'd not giggled. Nor when he'd called on her and offered marriage. Not even then.

But this would be different. It wouldn't be them conversing. It would entail more than kisses. They were going to get naked and . . . Her confidence withered a quick death.

Gracious! She glanced around the room. It was too bright. She would be completely exposed. She peered down at her silk-and-lace nightgown and cursed Madame Renault for convincing her to buy such a frivolous concoction.

Footsteps moved closer to the door that connected her bedchamber to Dorchester's room. She darted toward the bank of windows and pulled the heavy curtains closed, blocking out the moonlight. As she ran toward the bed, she kicked off her slippers and made a running leap onto the mattress. Then sitting with her back pressed firmly against the wooden headboard, she pulled the covers to her waist, then lowered the wick on the gas lamp on the bedside table.

A sturdy knock sounded on the connecting door. "Might I come in?"

Sara's heart beat fast. "Yes."

The door swung open and Dorchester, dressed in a navy robe, stood at the threshold. The light from his bedchamber highlighted him, making him look like a giant. A very broad-shouldered, virile giant.

Chapter Eight

Sara's gaze drifted down Dorchester's body from his head to his bare feet. Even in the gloom, she could see his skin exposed between the velvet lapels of the navy robe he wore. He appeared completely naked underneath the garment.

She swallowed hard. With her stomach clenching, she twisted sideways and turned off the bedside lamp, leaving only the light streaming in from the open door behind him. Perhaps darkness would help her—a kind of anonymity, like what the mask provided at the ball.

How utterly foolish. Tonight, in this bed, there would be no true anonymity between them. "Would you mind terribly closing the door behind you?" she asked, pleased her voice remained steady.

"If I do that, we won't be able to see a thing."

Yes, that was the point.

As if he read her thoughts, he turned and closed the door, shuttering them in complete darkness. As he moved toward the bed, the light sound of his footsteps made her think of how softly a lion would move toward its prey. She heard him stumble.

"Damnation. What did I just step on?" he grumbled.

"Most likely one of my slippers. Take care. There is another one. Though I'm not sure where it landed."

"Sara, if we are going to continue doing this in the dark, I suggest you clear a path to your bed beforehand."

"Yes—" Her agreement caught in her throat as his hand touched her waist.

"Ah, there you are."

She nodded even though she realized he most likely couldn't see the movement. Cooler air swept over her as he tossed the covers downward. She experienced a slight dip in the mattress when Dorchester settled beside her, bringing with him the light, pleasant scent she associated with him.

His hand, which had temporarily left her waist, returned. "Are you aware of what transpires in the marriage bed? Or do you need me to explain it to you?"

She knew. She'd overheard her sister chatting and giggling with her friends, and she had studied the reproduction of insects. "Your Grace, I might not be experienced, but I do understand what occurs. I am an entomologist, and though there are distinct differences between the way humans and insects reproduce, there are also similarities in reproduction."

"Really? Do you know if they garner pleasure from the act?"

She opened her mouth to answer him, and her words caught in her throat as his mouth touched the corner of her lips, then made a warm path to the spot below her ear.

"You're not sure?" he asked, pressing tiny kisses to the sensitive skin.

She tried to center her mind away from what he was doing and re-center it on the question he'd asked, but she couldn't recall what it was. If he would stop kissing her, she believed it would come back to her. "About?"

He paused. "Insects and gratification?"

Ah, yes, now she remembered. "I'm not sure. It's quite difficult to communicate with an insect." It was also extremely difficult to communicate with him while he kept pressing his mouth to her skin.

"True." His lips brushed against hers before the contact became firmer, yet still tender. Skillfully, his mouth coaxed hers open, and he deepened the kiss. The slide of his tongue stroking hers answered the question about whether he would kiss her like he had at the masquerade ball.

Though she'd planned to lie still, as her grandmother advised a proper woman should, she was finding it difficult. She knotted her hands in the sheets, forcing them not to seek the heat of his skin.

"You'll find it more enjoyable if you relax." His tongue touched her earlobe before he gently pressed his teeth into the soft flesh.

She'd read about the mating of lions. They licked and bit each other. At the time, she'd thought it odd, but the way Dorchester nibbled at her ear was making her grow exceedingly warm.

His mouth returned to hers, and he kissed her in that same delicious way that involved their open mouths. She loosened her grip on the sheets and twined her hands around his neck, giving in to the need building within her, tearing her reserved intentions apart like a landslide does to the compacted earth beneath it.

As if her actions pleased him, he made a noise of approval, a growl that said more than any word could convey. Then his hand slid from her waist to capture the weight of one of her breasts, while his thumb stroked the tip of her nipple through the silky material of her nightgown.

The more he touched her with his mouth and hands, the deeper she was sucked into a spiraling vortex that made her mind immune to everything else besides physical touch. It made her want to explore his body further, as he was exploring hers. She was a scientist after all. Eager to learn. She slipped her hands under the lapels of his robe to skim them over his chest. His skin was hot and delineated with muscles.

As if her actions surprised him, his thumb stroking her nipple stilled. Obviously he'd not expected such a bold move from her. She'd not expected it either. Nor the fact that she, a woman who'd been sitting firmly on the shelf, could shock the all-powerful Duke of Dorchester, a man lauded for his skill with women.

Dorchester's fingers worked the small pearl buttons that lined the front of her nightgown. One by one, he slipped them loose with the skill of a man who'd undressed women before. Cool air drifted over her breasts as he brushed the garment off her shoulders and down her arms, leaving the gauzy material pooling at her waist.

She reached for the sash of his robe and untied it.

He shifted, and she realized he was removing the garment.

For a moment, Sara wished she'd not turned the gas lamp off. She wanted to see him. Every inch of his naked body.

His breath ghosted across her ear. "Now, your turn." His fingers deftly worked to draw the nightgown pooling at her waist over her hips, then down her legs. The action had caused her to shift downward, so she lay on her back.

He stretched out beside her. One of his hands settled

on her ribs, then almost maddeningly slow, it moved up. Her nipples puckered in anticipation. Then his hand cupped one of her breasts. She almost jumped when she experienced the wet tip of his tongue teasing at her nipple.

"Oh." She uttered the single syllable.

"Does what I'm doing offend you?" he asked, his voice raspy.

She swallowed, trying to moisten her mouth, which had grown dry. "No. Not in the least. It feels . . ."

"Yes?"

"I'm not sure how to explain it. But perhaps, if you did it again, I might find the proper word."

Sara believed she might have shocked him again, because for a moment he didn't move. Goodness, she wished she could see his face. See his reaction.

He bent down and drew his tongue over the tip again. "Have you found the word to describe it?"

It felt like pure bliss. Wet and warm and utterly intoxicating. But she would not tell him that and boost the man's amour propre with extravagant fawning. "It's quite becoming."

"Becoming?" His breath puffed against her now-damp nipple. "That's an interesting way of putting it."

Before she could respond, he drew her breast farther into his mouth.

An odd pulse beat between her legs as her body and mind further tumbled into the swirl of need and want.

He lavished her other breast with the same decadent attention as his hand drifted downward—his palm a smooth slide of skin against skin that seemed to ignite each nerve it traveled over. His hand settled between her thighs and brushed against her sex.

Sara curled her toes to stop herself from squirming from

the raw need unfurling within her. She would never look at two butterflies as they mated in the same way.

"I don't hear you breathing," Dorchester said.

Realizing she was holding her breath, she exhaled.

"Sorry if I startled you. I needed to make sure you are ready."

Her body was extremely ready. Eager.

He shifted, and the next thing she knew, he was braced over her with his hands placed by the side of her head and his hips and something much firmer was settling between her legs.

"Would it make you feel more at ease if you positioned me at your opening?"

Did he mean for her to take his manhood in her hands? Sara liked the idea of possessing some control. Without answering, she reached out and curled her fingers around it. The texture was like silk over steel. She ran her hand down his length.

He sucked in a breath.

"Do you like that?" she asked, startled by her own inquiry.

"It's very becoming," he replied, using her own words.

She smiled and applied a bit more pressure, while she slid her hand up and down his length several more times. In the darkness, she heard his breathing increase.

He lowered himself to her and she positioned him between her slick folds.

"It might hurt, but I promise it will get better," he said.

She experienced a sharp pinch of discomfort, then slowly, inch by inch, he sank deeper into her, stretching her to accommodate him.

He rocked into her, and she thought it an odd, yet pleasant feeling. The more he moved, the more an unfamiliar sensation grew within her. In the darkness, his mouth met hers again. The kiss added to the physical pleasure building in her.

Within a short time, it culminated in almost unimaginable sensation. Wave after wave of it consumed her before slowly ebbing away.

Confusion followed as she tried to grapple with such a physical reaction to another person's touch. She felt as if she floated. Sated and still confused, she opened her eyes and, though it was dark, she could feel Dorchester staring at her. Then he began moving again, and she realized that his body was reaching for the same physical sensation that had come over her.

He rocked into her several more times, then tensed before he collapsed beside her.

Chapter Nine

Sara awoke to a bright, single beam of light streaming around the edge of the closed curtains, along with the feel of a heavy arm draped over her bare stomach. Keeping her body still, she turned her head slightly and studied Dorchester's countenance. She had thought perhaps he would look different while sleeping—that the hard, yet beautiful, angles of his face would be softened, but he still looked fierce in sleep.

She'd believed she would awake to find him gone. But he slept beside her. The breaths moving in and out of his lungs were even and deep. She was thankful for that. She wasn't sure what she would say to him. Or more importantly what he would say to her after their night of consummating their marriage. Not once, but twice. The second time, she'd been sleeping when Dorchester had drawn her from that state with his touch and the warmth of his body.

Slowly she scooted sideways.

His arm slid off her, and he shifted slightly.

Fearing he'd wake, she froze. When he didn't move again, she stood and padded to the armoire, grabbed her clothes, and quickly darted into her bathing room where she washed and dressed.

When done, Sara opened the door, unsure of what she would find. But thankfully Dorchester was still asleep. She wondered if he normally rose late. Many members of the nobility did. Louisa didn't usually get up until one in the afternoon. Ned rose near noon, but her brother wasn't a man of industry.

On almost silent feet, she slipped into the corridor and made her way to the morning room, trying not to think of everything Dorchester and she had done to each other last night in her bedroom. Yet, the memory of him settling between her legs, as his mouth kissed hers in that tantalizing way, seemed hard to banish from her mind.

Of course, she had touched him for purely scientific reasons, needing to grasp the understanding of copulation. Yes, that was the only reason. It had nothing to do with the pleasure the act brought her.

Oh, nonsense! Who was she kidding? She'd enjoyed it tremendously. She had not simply laid on her back as she had planned. She'd been full of lust and want.

Dorchester hadn't seemed to mind her behavior. In fact, he'd encouraged it, but he was a wicked libertine. Her grandmother's words replayed in her head. *A proper, well-bred woman does not experience the same fever for the act that a man does.*

A wave of heat warmed her cheeks. Now that she understood the act, next time she would behave with more restraint. Next time she would keep her hands to her sides. She would not skim her palms over nearly every surface of his body or slip her hand up and down his manhood. Though truthfully, the feel of it had fascinated her. Everything about last night had left her panting. She wouldn't do that either. No, next time would be different. She would behave as her grandmother had instructed her aunt. Just lie on her back. The way a proper woman should.

She entered the morning room to find the butler standing next to the long sideboard, which was topped with chafing dishes.

"Good morning, Jeffers." Sara smiled brightly at the man who looked as stiff as a block of granite.

"Good morning, Your Grace," he replied, his voice and face devoid of emotion.

She picked up a plate and placed a scone, marmalade, and two eggs on it before sitting at the round table in a chair that faced the garden. Today the sun was bright, and she was anxious to explore the flora and see if she could scout some species of butterflies.

"Orange juice, madam?" Like a specter, Jeffers appeared at her side, holding a carafe.

"Thank you."

He filled her glass and backed away, as quietly as he'd appeared.

"Jeffers, did His Grace tell you I'll need a sizable room for my studies?"

"He did, madam."

"I would be ever so pleased if it overlooked the gardens."

"Very well. I think I know of one that will suit your needs."

"Thank you." She glanced at the French doors, anxious to finish her meal and step into the garden before Dorchester entered the room. "Does His Grace usually sleep in late?"

"No, madam."

Then she needed to hurry. She had nearly finished her scone when she saw what looked like a Papilio machaon butterfly flittering near the window—a species rare to this part of England. With an exclamation of pleasure, she shoved the last bite of her scone into her mouth and jumped to her feet.

"Is something the matter, Your Grace?" Jeffers asked.

"I believe I spotted a species of swallowtail butterfly that is rarely seen in this part of England." Only a few of her items had been delivered with her trunk of clothes, but she was sure her nets were among them. "Jeffers, do you know where my butterfly nets are?"

"I had a footman put them in the storage room next to the kitchen. I'll go get them."

"No need. I can get the one I wish to use." She dashed out of the room, and as fast as her feet could take her, she moved belowstairs. She passed a laundry room, a larder, and an empty servants' hall. Then what looked to be the butler's quarters. She peered through the next open doorway to find the housekeeper sitting behind her desk.

"Your Grace." The woman bounced up from her chair as if assisted by a spring mechanism.

"Mrs. Pullman, could you direct me to where the storage room is?"

"Of course, madam."

Hearing the clicking of shoes on the flagstone flooring, Sara turned to see the stone-faced butler moving toward them. "I would have gotten them for you, Your Grace."

She smiled at him. "Yes, I know you would have, Jeffers, but I have several and wished to choose a specific one."

After being shown to where her items were, Sara darted outside.

* * *

Half-asleep, Ian instinctually reached out for the warmth of Sara's body. Last night had been unbelievable. His wife had acted so responsively to his bedding that he'd almost forgotten the situation that had brought them to this marriage.

As his hand slid across the cool sheets, he realized he lay alone in Sara's bed. He opened his eyes.

Good Lord, had he dreamt last night? Dreamt how receptive she'd been to his touch? Dreamt the way her hands had explored his body?

No, not a dream. He was in her bed, not his. He hadn't planned on staying, believing they would consummate the marriage, and he would return to his own bedchamber. He recalled how, before entering Sara's room, he'd hoped she would not be frightened and cry virgin tears. But she'd been an equal participant. He could still remember her soft sighs of pleasure and awakening during the night to find her sleeping body snuggled up to his. He'd rolled her onto her back and, once again, buried his hard length into her slick folds and lavished in her welcoming warmth.

Perhaps surprises did come in small packages. If he and Sara shared nothing else, they at least were compatible in bed. Which was a blessing, considering he had said he would remain faithful. And he had meant it. Whatever his shortcomings, he believed in fidelity in marriage and had hoped Sara would choose it as well.

He glanced toward the bathing room, listening for sounds, but there were none.

She'd left.

A burst of something akin to agitation shot through him. Why? Because he left women's beds; they didn't leave him. Or they hadn't before. He had always made sure to please his partners, asking women to teach him what they liked. Initially, he had done it for purely selfish reasons. He'd wanted Isabelle to know that while his father lay pumping his seed into her, for the sole reason of begetting his spare, she would hear the gossip that Ian was a skilled lover. But somewhere along the way, he'd realized that hearing a woman's breathy voice as she climaxed was another form of satisfaction. Perhaps it was nothing more than male pride.

But Sara had left.

Well, so much for my male pride. His wife had knocked it down a peg with little effort at all.

He possessed half a mind to go find her. Tell her they weren't done, especially if he had to wait a bloody fortnight unless he used his coin. He mumbled an oath. Perhaps enjoying her body the second time meant he'd already used his coin. No, a night with each other was just that— a whole night. And the morning. Ian tossed the sheets off and stormed toward the door; then realizing he was naked, he turned back to the bed and grabbed his robe from where it lay tangled in the sheets.

He could still recall the feel of Sara's hands slipping under the garment before she'd reached to untie his sash so she could explore the rest of his body.

As he pulled his robe on and tied the sash, he thought about how it would look if he tracked her down and demanded she return to her bed. He'd look desperate. The Duke of Dorchester was never desperate. He was cool and aloof. Then why the hell was he so agitated? What had he expected? For Sara to fawn over him as if he were some god because he had brought her to climax not once, but twice?

Grumbling over his train of thoughts, he strode to the

door that connected this bedchamber to his. He would bathe and take his time going down for breakfast.

An hour later, Ian entered the morning room to see only one place setting on the table. Had Sara already eaten? Damn that woman. Where was she?

"Good morning, Your Grace." Jeffers bowed his head.

He glared at the butler standing by the sideboard with its plethora of chafing dishes. "Where is my . . . wife, Jeffers?" Even though last night had been most surprising, the word *wife* almost stuck in Ian's throat like a broken chicken bone.

"She is in the garden."

Jeffers had been in the family's employ for years. Ian wasn't sure if he'd ever seen the stoic butler crack a smile, yet he would have sworn the man's eyes glinted with humor.

Not sure what that meant, the hairs on the back of Ian's neck stood on end. He strode to the French doors and peered out the mullioned glass. Beyond the terrace in the manicured gardens, a movement caught his eyes. Wearing a drab brown dress, Sara reminded him of a little sparrow, a dunnock, fluttering about. She made an abrupt stop, turned around, dashed a few yards left then right like a windup toy that moved back and forth.

I've married a madwoman. He glanced over his shoulder at the butler. "What in God's name is she about?"

Jeffers stepped next to him. "While eating breakfast, Her Grace said she saw a swallowtail."

"And what in blazes is that?" Ian frowned.

"She said it was a type of butterfly. She seems to have an affinity for them."

Yes. He remembered her saying she was an entomologist, and hadn't Julien said she collected insects or something similar? She'd also stipulated she needed a spare room for a study. His gaze followed her around for another minute as she continued darting around the garden chasing something so small, he couldn't see it from this distance. She lifted a net in the air and almost stumbled.

Ian's heart skipped a beat.

As if oblivious to how she'd almost fallen, she righted herself and continued dashing across the gardens with her blasted net in the air. If she fell and snapped her neck, the gossip sheets would spin some nefarious tale about how he'd quickly found a way to get rid of her. They'd probably accuse him of tripping her.

He threw open the French doors and stormed outside onto the terrace, intent on dragging his careless wife back inside before she harmed herself or broke her neck. With ground-eating strides, he moved across the terrace, then took the stairs down to the gardens. Sara was so busy looking at the sky, she didn't seem to realize the fountain with the mermaid Atargatis was straight ahead of her. If she didn't change direction, she would tumble straight into the water, if she didn't fall and crack open her skull first.

He called out her name, but with the splashing of the fountain, she didn't appear to hear him or was simply like his wards and chose to ignore him.

She was only a few feet away from the fountain when he came up behind her and wrapped an arm around her waist, lifting her off her feet.

With a gasp, she glanced over her shoulder.

Her startled expression shifted to one of undisguised

outrage. "Why did you do that? I was about to catch a rare swallowtail."

Ian had a feeling if he didn't remove the long-handled net from her hands, he might find it whacked against his skull. He set her down and gently pried it from her white-knuckled grip. "You were about to topple into the fountain, and I didn't feel like fishing you out."

"I was quite aware of where I was. One would have to be deaf not to hear the water spouting out of the fountain." She tipped her head back and searched the sky before returning her glower to him. "Now you've scared it away, you . . . you overbearing man!"

He'd been called many things over the years. Things much worse than *overbearing*. He ignored the comment and looked for the butterfly. Seeing a small green one, he pointed to it and handed the net back to her. "Why don't you catch that one?"

She followed the direction of his finger. "Because that is a common brimstone. It is not unusual to see them, but that swallowtail is a rare sight in this part of England. And he was so lovely that I wished to temporarily place him in a jar so I might sketch him."

Ian was tempted to ask how she knew it was a male, but he tossed that question away. He really didn't care.

He motioned to the fountain with a jerk of his chin. "The way you were swinging that net, you might have chipped off Atargatis's nose."

"I would not have." Her full lips flattened out as her gaze shifted to the mermaid fountain. "Isn't Atargatis the mermaid who killed her husband?" The glint in her eyes conveyed she thought the woman a genius.

"No. She killed her lover, not her husband."

She mumbled something under her breath.

Probably her desire to kill him, but he was going to wipe that sanctimonious expression off her face. "She killed him because she was too great a lover for him. Have a go at it, darling. Let's see if you can do me in."

Her mouth parted and her cheeks grew red.

Ian could remember the taste of her mouth and the sounds of pleasure she made while kissing. He was half tempted to close the distance between them and kiss that tart look off her face.

Instead, he spun on his heel, took the steps to the terrace, and returned to his breakfast.

"Abominable man," Sara grumbled as she paced back and forth in her bedchamber. How dare Dorchester act as if she were a madwoman without a smidgen of sense. She stopped and twisted her hands together. Perhaps she *was* mad. That would explain why she'd agreed to marry the man.

She could not understand why women were drawn to him. No matter what she'd told her brother, she did find Dorchester handsome, but he was also aloof, cynical, domineering, and sullen. Perhaps women fell at his feet because of what her sister had said—that he was as rich as the queen. That had to be the reason. Nothing else made sense.

Her gaze shifted to her bed. Unbidden, an image of their bodies tangled together flashed in her mind. She shoved the memory aside and slumped into the upholstered chair in the corner of the room. As she rested her head against the chair's feather-stuffed back and stared at the ceiling, she recalled what he'd said at the fountain of the mermaid

Atargatis. *She killed him because she was too great a lover for him. Have a go at it, darling. Let's see if you can do me in.*

Wicked, scandalous man.

Someone knocked lightly on her door.

Sara stood and smoothed out the skirt of her chestnut-colored day dress. "Yes, come in."

A tiny maid with ginger hair stepped into the room and bobbed a curtsy. "Your Grace, Mr. Jeffers asked me to inform you that a dray has arrived with the rest of your belongings."

Wonderful. Her butterfly collection, books, and journals were here. Excitement sent a tingling sensation through her body. She hoped nothing had been damaged on the ride from Mayfair to Richmond. Butterflies were delicate, as were the glass-and-wood cases they were stored in.

"Where is Jeffers?" she asked, moving toward the door.

"He's directing the men as to where the boxes should be placed."

"And where is that?"

"On the second story of the west wing, Your Grace."

"Thank you." She impulsively clasped the maid's hand and gave it a squeeze.

The woman's eyes grew as large as a new moon, and Sara realized the inappropriateness of her actions, but she was too delighted to care about propriety. Her collection was here.

She stepped into the corridor, pivoted left, then right. She was on the second story but had no inkling as to where the west wing was. Or even what wing in this monstrosity of a house they were in now. "Where is the west wing?"

"That way, Your Grace." The maid pointed past the open

landing above the massive stairway to a wide corridor beyond an arched doorway. "Through there."

"Thank you." Sara turned around. "What is your name?"

"Nellie, madam." The maid gave a slight smile, then nervously averted her face and stared at the colorful navy-and-red runner that ran down the length of the corridor.

"Well, thank you again, Nellie."

Almost running, Sara dashed through the archway. Footmen were using a back staircase to haul her collection into a room close to the end of the corridor. She stepped into the room to find the butler directing the men to set the boxes on a long table that ran under a bank of three tall windows. There were already several crates on the floor.

As if she were Medusa and capable of turning them to stone, they froze. Everyone except Jeffers, who gave a stiff bow. "Your Grace."

"Hello, Jeffers."

"Does this room suit your needs, madam?"

Cheerful yellow walls captured the bright light streaming through the bank of windows that overlooked the gardens. She smiled. "It's absolutely perfect."

Sara thought she heard a relieved sigh from the footmen who had pulled themselves out of their frozen state. Had they thought she might yell and stomp her feet if displeased? She knelt in front of one of the crates on the floor, pried open the lid, and pushed the packing straw aside. She couldn't halt the sound of delight that escaped her lips when her gaze settled on the glass display case that held her prized *Siproeta stelenes*.

The green-and-black butterfly, with a sizable wingspan, had been sent to her from South America. It was one of her favorites. She clasped the case to her chest. This was why she'd married Dorchester. The fact that she could keep her collection and fund her studies. That and that alone.

Sara suddenly realized that the room had grown quiet again. She glanced over her shoulder to see Jeffers and the footmen staring at her. While still holding the case, she carefully scrambled to her feet. "This butterfly is from South America. It is commonly known as a malachite butterfly because its striking green color reminds people of the mineral. The underside of its wings are brown and green. Isn't it simply lovely?"

The footmen nodded and in unison mumbled their agreement.

One young man stepped closer. "Is that what is in all these crates, Your Grace? Butterflies?"

The butler cleared his throat and speared the young footman with a deadly glare. She could only presume he thought the young man impertinent, but Sara loved sharing her collection.

"Yes. That and my drawings and journals." She turned to the butler. "Jeffers, I'd like to hire a woodworker to build shelves on the far wall. Would you happen to have the name of one?" Now that she had her own money, it pleased her to know that she could pay for the materials and not have to ask her husband for the funds as she'd had to do with her father and brother.

The butler's face remained without expression. "Dorchester Hall has a carpenter on staff."

"Oh, how delightful." She gently set the encased malachite butterfly back in its crate and placed the lid back onto it. "Could you direct me to where I might find him?"

Jeffers blinked. "You do not need to go to him, madam. I will go see Mr. Brown and instruct him to come to you."

"Thank you, Jeffers," she said, before kneeling in front of another box.

Standing in his home office, Ian leaned over his desk and examined the drawings of the steamer that would be placed in service soon. Over the next few years, he and Julien planned to retire several vessels from their Magnus Shipping fleet and replace them with more efficient ones.

The new steamer's sleek design and screw propeller, along with its compound engine, would allow it to make the trans-Atlantic journey quicker than the other ships in their line. It was also fitted with auxiliary sails to take advantage of wind when necessary and possessed boilers that required less coal and manpower.

He rolled up the drawing and sat at his desk to look over a letter that had arrived from his land agent in Baltimore, where he and Julien hoped to open a second shipping office. He withdrew a piece of paper from the tray and began his response.

A loud *thump* sounded in the room above him.

Ian's fingers flexed against the pen, and he glanced at the ceiling heating grate. Over the last hour, he'd heard a racket coming from up there.

Another *bang* caused the gas pendant light in the center of the room to sway.

How can anyone think with all this ruckus? Fingers tightly gripping his pen, he marched into the hall as a footman carrying a wooden crate moved past him in the corridor. "What's going on up there?"

The servant turned to him. The color drained from the

man's face. "H-Her Grace is setting up her collection of butterflies."

"Does her collection also include a pachyderm?"

The man's eyes grew wide. "I—I don't believe so, Your Grace."

"Then what is all that noise?"

"Some of the furniture is being moved about to make room for the crates."

"Tell Jeffers I wish to speak with him."

Another bang rattled the teardrop crystals on the wall sconces in the corridor.

Gritting his teeth, he mumbled an expletive. "Never mind. I'll handle this myself."

"Yes, Your Grace." At a fast clip, the man darted up the stairs.

Ian returned to his desk, tossed the pen on the blotter, and stormed out of his office.

Chapter Ten

Ian took the stairs two at a time. As he reached the room directly above his office, he saw the footman he'd spoken to a minute ago. The man was profusely apologizing to Sara as he picked up several thick tomes that had fallen when the footman had obviously dropped the crate he'd carried upstairs.

"Your Grace, please forgive me for my clumsiness," the servant said, nervously peering at Sara.

"Do not worry over it." She smiled. "You're Archibald, aren't you?"

"Y-yes, madam." The footman's already flushed face turned a shade redder.

"As you can see, nothing is broken. The box only contained books on entomology that I reference in my studies." She picked up one of the books and placed it on a table.

Ian stepped fully into the room and noticed two other footmen who were stacking crates on every available surface, including several chairs. *Good Lord. How much stuff does the woman possess?*

Sara's gaze veered to him. "Your Grace, thank you. The room is lovely."

Though her eyes sparkled with pleasure, her voice sounded businesslike—not as warm as it had sounded when she'd spoken to the footman. He supposed she remained vexed about the incident with the swallowtail at the fountain and his rather bold challenge that she try to *do him in* as the mermaid had her lover, during a robust round of sex.

"It's also directly above my office, and the noise up here is distracting." He surveyed the two footmen. "Leave us."

Without a backward glance, they hurried out of the room.

The footman who had said his name was Archibald was still repacking the crate he'd dropped. Ian cleared his throat and arched a brow.

The man set the last tome into the box and scurried out of the room.

"How much longer will this noise be going on?" Ian asked.

"That was the last of the crates, so it should be much quieter for the time being."

The hairs on his neck stood on end. "What do you mean for *the time being?*"

"I wish for your carpenter to build display shelves and bookcases there." She pointed to the far wall.

At that moment, Jeffers and another man stepped into the room. He supposed the fellow with the butler who wore a loose white linen shirt, trousers held up by braces, and a boilerman's cap was his carpenter.

Ian realized his expression must resemble the devil's because the carpenter's Adam's apple bobbed convulsively in his throat as he pulled off his cap and crushed it between his fingers.

"Jeffers," Ian said. "I wish to talk to you in my office."

"Yes, Your Grace."

As Ian walked toward the door, Sara called out, "Thank you again for such a lovely room."

At the threshold, he spun back around to tell her she would have to go to another room. His regard shifted to the butler and carpenter; they both seemed to be holding their breaths as if waiting for an explosion.

Damnation. He wasn't cruel. He only wished for some peace and quiet while in his office. Was that such a terrible thing to want? Without saying anything, he pivoted and made his way back downstairs.

In his office, Ian settled behind his desk and glared at Jeffers. "Why, in God's name, did you give her the room directly above my office?"

"Her Grace asked for a room that overlooked the flower garden and hoped it would be large enough to hold her collection. That room does, and you had said to give her what she asked for."

"Yes, but I'd not thought that Her Grace's collection was so large or that it would cause such a commotion. Move her collection to another room."

Normally, the butler would have answered yes, then spun on his heel to follow Ian's request, yet the man stared at him as if he wished to say something.

"Is there a problem?" Ian held the butler's gaze.

"No, Your Grace." Jeffers turned and left the room, closing the door behind him.

Ian picked up his pen and continued writing his letter to the land agent in Baltimore.

He'd nearly completed it when the door to his office

swung inward. He glanced up to see Sara looking like a miniature Amazon warrior.

He recalled the last time someone had barged into his office without knocking. Sara looked nearly as put upon as the nanny had, though not as disheveled or muddy. His wife looked rather feisty, and something within him reacted to her.

Ignoring his reaction, Ian leaned back in his chair. "I'm used to people knocking before entering my office."

Without responding, she stepped into the room and closed the door behind her with a less-than-delicate hand. "Why must I move to another room?"

He pointed to the heating grate in the ceiling. "Because you are making too much noise for me to think."

"I don't hear a sound."

"That's because you are down here, not up there causing a commotion."

"Your Grace—"

"We are married, Sara. You should call me Ian."

"I think addressing you by your given name might be too intimate."

He gave a low laugh. "More intimate than what we did last night?"

Her cheeks turned a fetching shade of pink. "Yes, but that was . . . well, business."

Business? The woman was determined to shred his pride. "Why are you so resistant to moving to another room? There must be a half dozen that you could use."

"But do they have such a large bank of windows, overlooking the flower garden's sizable plantings of lavender and astilbe, which is sure to attract butterflies?"

He really didn't know. He rarely walked in the gardens, and though he could probably point out lavender, he had no inkling what astilbe looked like. Instead of admitting he didn't know, he waved a hand in the air. "Very well, you may remain there, but tell the carpenter to hire a couple of men to help him, so your display shelves can be built with all expediency."

"Thank you." She turned on her heel, and as her fingers clasped the door handle, Ian spoke. "I have a business meeting in town, so I won't be home for dinner, but I'll be home later so we can take care of *business,* if you wish."

She pivoted around. "Business?"

He realized the moment she comprehended what he meant, since her cheeks turned red.

"You wish to use your coin so soon?"

"I'm giving you an opportunity to try to do me in."

She stared at him for a long minute. "I've never thought myself particularly lucky, but by chance, do you suffer with a weak heart?"

"No."

"Too bad," she said, and exited the room.

Why, the minx. He couldn't stop his grin.

He was signing his name to the letter he'd written when a large bang from upstairs reverberated through the room as if someone had dropped one of Sara's large tomes on the floor. He had the oddest feeling it was his wife, and she had done it on purpose to grate on his nerves.

When trying to woo potential customers, Ian and Julien always conducted business at the Fontaine Hotel on Broad Street instead of at Magnus Shipping's dockland offices in the East End. The lavish, private dining rooms boasted crystal chandeliers, gilded dining chairs, and costly silk wallpaper. While negotiating contracts, the atmosphere, fine French cuisine, and exemplary wine lulled potential customers into a state of contentment that was beneficial to business.

Sadly, the two gentlemen meeting him and Julien today would not be as impressed with their surroundings. Lord Ralston and Lord Talbot, the owners of Langford Teas, were used to the finer things.

Ian stepped into the private dining room, and the three men sitting at the round table glanced up. A puzzled expression settled on Julien's face.

His friend and partner stood and moved toward him. "I wasn't expecting you. I thought you'd be spending the evening with your new bride."

"Have I ever missed a meeting before?"

"No, but you've never been married before."

"We have business that needs attending to." *Business.* He would never say the word again without replaying what his wife had said to him today. But was she so wrong? Hadn't he offered her a business relationship? Wasn't that what he wanted?

He needed to forget about his own thoughts, along with his wife's comment, and carry on with this meeting to acquire the contract to be the sole shipping exporter for Langford Teas.

As Ralston and Talbot stood, Ian reached out to shake their hands.

Two hours later, with a signed contract in hand, Ian took a sip of his brandy and smiled at something Julien said, though he wasn't quite sure what. His mind was wondering if Sara was in bed waiting for him.

As Ian lowered his glass, he realized Lord Ralston's astute gaze was on him. During the meeting, he'd come to grasp how shrewd and savvy the baron was. He'd negotiated one of the best shipping contracts Julien and Ian had ever offered.

"How is Sara?" Ralston asked.

"She is well." Ian forced a smile.

"Your wedding invitation caught us by surprise. Sara had not mentioned to Nina that she had become secretly betrothed."

The look in Ralston's eyes clearly revealed he knew the tale was a farce. Ian wondered how much the baron was privy to, especially since during the wedding breakfast, Ian had felt Lady Ralston's gaze on him while Sara was talking to her.

Ralston handed him an envelope. "Nina asked that if you attended tonight's meeting that I give you this letter for Sara."

He took the missive and put it into the inside breast pocket of his coat. "Of course. I'm sure Sara will be pleased to receive it."

"Ralston," Julien said, pulling the baron's attention away from Ian. "Talbot was telling me that you both are planning to build a larger warehouse near the docks."

"We are. We've hired my brother-in-law Anthony Trent to design the interiors. It won't be completed for a couple of years, but we are hoping that our tea sales in America will be a boom for our business."

Ian hoped so as well since the exporting of Langford Teas would also increase Magnus Shipping's profits.

After Lord Ralston and Lord Talbot left, Julien clapped a hand on Ian's shoulder as they made their way outside the hotel. "Let's hope Ralston and Talbot are successful in selling the Americans their tea. More money in their pockets will mean more money in ours."

Ian nodded.

"You seem a bit distracted, Ian. Thinking of your new wife?" Julien grinned.

"You of all people know it isn't truly a love match, so why would I be thinking about Sara?" But throughout the meeting, instead of his mind centering on the business at hand, he'd become preoccupied with the *business* he wished to conduct when he returned home. "I was wondering what mayhem my two wards were inflicting on your staff while you are here."

"They have behaved remarkably well."

"Really? I bet they are leading your servants on a merry chase and turning your residence into utter chaos."

"They have been perfect angels."

"Ha! Now I know that is balderdash."

Julien smiled.

"I appreciate you watching over them, but for your own sanity send them home."

"Let them stay a little longer."

"Are you sure you don't mind?"

"Of course not. My house is too quiet with Evie and Mary in the country."

"Well, it's your sanity. Hopefully, I won't receive a letter from your butler informing me you've been admitted to Bedlam."

"That's doubtful. Now go home and spend some time with your new wife."

Ian rubbed the coin in his pocket. He had every intention of doing that.

Chapter Eleven

Sara spent the evening sorting through the boxes containing her books and butterfly collection, trying to make sure nothing had been damaged.

As she opened a crate, she watched Mr. Brown as he measured the wall in her new study and sketched up a drawing of the shelves he would begin building tomorrow.

Occasionally, he would mumble something, remove the pencil tucked above his ear, and adjust the drawing.

"Your Grace?" He walked over to where she was sitting on the floor, going through another crate.

"Yes, Mr. Brown."

He handed her the sketch he'd made. "Is this similar to what you envisioned?"

The drawing revealed cabinets on the lower one third of the wall with shelves above that reached the ceiling, topped with an intricate crown molding. "That's perfect, sir. Exactly what I pictured in my mind."

A broad grin stretched across the man's face. "Then tomorrow the lads and I will start them."

"Wonderful."

He peered around the room at the number of still-unopened crates. "Do you wish for some assistance?"

"No, Mr. Brown. You should retire. I imagine you will have a busy day ahead of you."

"Well, if you're sure, madam, then good evening."

After the carpenter left the room, Sara scrambled to her feet and moved to another crate to check the contents. The sky outside the bank of windows had turned from sun-drenched to dark over an hour ago, but Sara was determined to make sure none of her collection had been damaged in transit from her family's Mayfair town house to Richmond.

"Madam." Mrs. Pullman stepped into the study. "Do you wish to eat in the dining room, or would you prefer a tray sent up?"

The idea of sitting in the cavernous room by herself held little appeal. "Mrs. Pullman, I'll eat in here." She pointed at the long table under the window.

Staring at the table, the housekeeper blinked as if wondering where a tray would fit on the crowded surface. "Very well, madam."

Two hours later, having eaten her dinner, Sara opened the last crate, while her mind shifted back to how she'd referred to what Ian and she had done in their bed as *business*. She wasn't sure why she'd called it that. Surely, it hadn't felt like business. But he'd made a deal with her, and referring to it that way dispersed most of the emotional entanglements, leaving just the physical pleasure.

She'd heard the rumors about him. How the coldhearted duke left broken hearts in his wake. She was determined not to become one of them. Plus, there was more to love than physical pleasure. So much more. Even she understood that.

I'm giving you an opportunity to try to do me in. His words, spoken like a challenge, replayed in her head. What did he expect her to do? Twirl? Kick her legs up in the air like one of the acrobats she'd seen at an East End theater? The only way she'd *do him in* was if she accidentally kicked him in the head.

She grinned at the absurdity of her thoughts.

Next time, she might challenge him to try and *do her in*.

The only problem with that was he might be capable of doing it. She thought of the scandal sheets. *The new Duchess of Dorchester suffers apoplexy while in bed with her new and very skilled husband. Don't fear, gentle readers. It is said she was found with a smile on her face.*

Sara gave herself a mental shake. It was time to stop mulling over this. They had a marriage of convenience—with no room for emotional entanglements. Business. Yes, that's what it was. And tonight, if he visited her bed, she would try not to tangle such physical pleasure with any strong emotions. That would be a fool's bargain. And no matter what some people thought, she wasn't a fool.

Plus, she wanted to be proper as her grandmother had said a woman should be. Not wicked like the man she'd married. She forced her focus back on the crate and removed the straw packing. Everything remained intact. On weary legs, she stood and removed her spectacles. Bits of straw speckled the skirt of her gown. She brushed them off and glanced around the room, envisioning what it would look like in a few days.

Sara tucked a loose strand of hair behind her ear and headed to her bedchamber. In truth, she was beyond tired. She stepped into the room, placed her glasses on the bedside table, kicked off her shoes, and fell back onto the thick mattress. Staring at the ceiling, she wondered when Ian would arrive home.

If she were honest with herself, she'd admit she'd opened every crate as a distraction from what would transpire when he returned. Releasing a tired sigh, she let her eyes drift closed. She would rest for a minute before she slipped on her nightgown and waited for the wicked scoundrel she'd married to visit her bedroom.

No sooner had Ian stepped into his entry hall when his butler rushed forward.

"Is my wife in the drawing room, Jeffers?"

"No, Your Grace. She worked in her study all evening and retired to her bedchamber a short time ago."

Good. He and Sara were about to conduct a *business meeting.* Ian took the steps two at a time and entered his bedchamber. He removed the sovereign that had felt as if it was burning a hole in his pocket throughout the evening and set it on his bedside table. Then he quickly undressed and slipped his robe over his naked body. He was about to pick up the coin when someone knocked on his door.

"Yes," he snapped.

His valet entered the room. "Just here to pick up your garments, Your Grace." Adams stepped up to the chair where Ian had tossed them, and one by one meticulously lifted each garment as if he were handling a Qianlong vase. Had the man always been this slow? Ian released an impatient breath.

He noticed a slight smile turn up the valet's lips.

Good Lord, the man thought him anxious to be with his wife.

Bloody hell. Was he acting eager to bed a wife he'd never wanted? He reminded himself it was to establish whether everything he recalled from last night had been real. The woman who ran around his garden during the day, looking as prickly as a stinging nettle bush, was nothing like the woman from last night. Most likely, he'd turned a rather pedestrian round of lovemaking into some earth-shattering event that was a figment of his imagination.

Perhaps he would read, then go to bed. He picked up the book on financial record keeping from his night table and settled into the upholstered chair by his hearth. He could always bed his wife tomorrow. Or wait a fortnight, minus one day.

The valet collected the last garment, and Ian noticed the man's lips twitch.

"Have you developed a tic of some type, Adams?"

Though the smile on his valet's face withered a quick death, humor remained in his eyes. "Not that I'm aware of, Your Grace." As the valet always did, he checked the pockets of Ian's clothing and withdrew Nina's missive to Sara. "I found a letter addressed to Her Grace in your coat pocket, sir."

Damnation, he'd forgotten about the letter. He held out his hand for it and placed it into the pocket of his robe.

"Good night, sir." Adams stepped out of the room with Ian's garments draped over his right arm.

As soon as the door clicked closed, Ian realized he held the book upside down.

Bugger it! No wonder the man had grinned like a ninny.

Standing, he tossed the book onto the chair-side table and strode to the door that connected Sara's room to his. He'd give her the letter and leave.

He rapped his knuckles against the wooden surface.

No answer.

His bare foot impatiently tapped against the carpet. Was she waiting for him to enter? He inched the door open and stepped into the room. Unlike last night, moonlight streamed through the parted curtains, sending shades of gray light into the bedchamber.

As he moved toward the bed, he realized his wife was sleeping. She lay on her side, above the bedcoverings with her hand curled under the pillow. Her breaths were a gentle steady sound, moving in and out of her lungs. He almost laughed. Here he'd spent all evening distracted and antic-ipating joining Sara in her bed and come home to find her sound asleep, still dressed. Had she fallen asleep waiting for him, or had she not given a singular thought to him joining her tonight? His self-esteem wanted it to be the former.

For a long minute, he stared at her. Well, mostly he stared at her full bow-shaped mouth. He'd thought such a sensual mouth seemed so out of place on her, yet if every-thing he recalled from last night had truly happened, it seemed rather fitting.

Ian took the last step that separated him from the bed and noticed a piece of packing straw in her hair. He re-moved it, grabbed the quilt from the foot of the bed, and draped it over her. He was halfway to the door when he remembered the letter. He moved back to the bed, set it on the bedside table, and left.

In his room, the gold coin reflected the light from the bedside lamp, causing it to sparkle and taunt him. Uttering an oath, Ian opened the table's drawer and tossed the sovereign inside. He would wait the damnable fortnight if that was what Sara wanted. He would not beg like a dog after a bone.

Chapter Twelve

The following morning, as Sara dressed, she repeatedly glanced at the door that connected her room to Ian's. Had he come to her bedchamber last night only to find that she'd worked herself up into such a state of exhaustion that she'd fallen asleep still wearing her clothes?

Someone had placed a quilt on her. Had he done it?

Ha! Doubtful. She couldn't see Mr. Grumpy giving a fig about her comfort. Surely, it must have been a maid who'd come to check on her.

She was about to head down to breakfast when she noticed a letter on her bedside table. Picking it up, she recognized Nina's swirling, flowery script right away. The absence of a stamp meant it had been hand-delivered.

Someone knocked on the door.

"Yes, come in."

A maid, dressed in a dark gray uniform with a white pinafore, stepped into the room and bobbed a curtsy. "Pardon me, Your Grace, but Mrs. Pullman wishes to know if you would like to take your breakfast in your room today?"

"No, I'll eat in the morning room." She lifted the letter

in her hand. "I see there is no stamp on this. Do you know who delivered it?"

"No, madam." The maid slipped out of the room.

Sara sat on the bed and opened the letter. Nina reiterated that she thought Sara looked lovely at her wedding, and how she believed Sara's marriage to Ian would bring her true happiness. Sara wished she possessed Nina's confidence. In truth, she would be pleased if they could accomplish something as simple as not snarling at each other. She slipped the missive into the top drawer of her dresser, then headed downstairs.

She entered the morning room to find her husband sitting at the round table reading a newspaper. Like yesterday, the butler stood by the sideboard as still as one of the queen's guards.

"Morning," she said.

"Your Grace." Jeffers inclined his head.

Ian peered over the edge of the paper, briefly stood, and grunted a response.

Taciturn man. Well, she didn't care. The sun was streaming through the windows, revealing the beauty of the morning. She would eat her breakfast then explore the library before venturing outside. She would not let one grumpy duke ruin her day.

She walked to the sideboard and placed fresh fruit, a scone, and clotted cream in her dish. As she moved to sit, Jeffers appeared to pull out her chair.

"Orange juice, Your Grace?"

"Yes. Thank you."

The butler filled her glass, then soundlessly stepped back as if he were an apparition.

Ian lowered his paper and looked at her, then at the food

in her dish. "If you wish for something special to be made for breakfast, you have only to tell Cook."

"This is perfect. I love fresh fruit." She forked a piece of pineapple and plopped it into her mouth.

He nodded, then the newspaper went back up like a barrier.

Sara glanced out the bank of windows, hoping she would see the swallowtail butterfly again. Wondering if Edward and Jacob would enjoy searching for it, she returned her gaze to Mr. Grumpy. "When will the boys be returning?"

He lowered the newspaper, revealing a startled expression. As if he thought she most likely wished they would not return. He turned to the butler. "Jeffers, excuse us for a minute."

"Yes, Your Grace." With his back straight as an arrow, the butler exited the room.

"As I said, I thought it best you have a few days to adjust to your new surroundings without the boys being here."

She understood what he was saying. That he expected that they would not make it easy for her. But she also understood that they most likely acted out over all the changes that their parents' deaths had brought about. "It cannot be easy for them. Being orphaned and uprooted. Might I ask what happened to their mother and father?"

"Both became ill within a few months of each other." The hard angles of his face softened.

"Oh. How tragic."

"It was." For a long moment, he stared at her. It reminded her of the way her father used to stare at her, along with the way her siblings did. As if they couldn't quite figure her out.

Ian stood. "If you'll excuse me, I have work to do in my office, then a meeting with Julien at Magnus Shipping."

Sara watched as Ian's long-legged strides moved him toward the door. She released a slow breath, reiterating that she would not allow Mr. Grumpy's vacillating temperament to ruin such a bright, sunny day.

At the threshold, he pivoted around. "I almost forgot. Did you see the letter Lord Ralston gave me to give to you last night?"

Goodness, she'd slept so soundly, she'd not heard him come into her bedchamber. She hoped she hadn't been drooling, or worse, snoring. "Yes, I saw it. Thank you. I did not know that you and Lord Ralston engaged in business together."

"Magnus Shipping will be handling the exporting of Langford Teas products to America. Now if you'll excuse me." He walked out of the room.

She picked up her orange juice and almost drained the glass dry before slathering clotted cream over the corner of her scone.

So Ian had come to her room, only to find her asleep. Could that be the reason for his grumpy mood?

She almost laughed out loud at such a delusional thought.

The stealth butler suddenly appeared at her side. Startled, she nearly dropped her scone. When had he returned? She needed to get him a cowbell or a pair of squeaky shoes.

"More orange juice, Your Grace?" Jeffers asked.

"Thank you."

The butler refilled her glass.

"Jeffers, do you know if Mr. Brown has arrived to start building the display shelves in my study?"

"Yes, madam. He has already begun working. And he's brought two helpers."

Good. Perhaps that would make Mr. Grumpy happy.

Bang, bang, bang.

In his office, Ian gritted his teeth.

His fingers clenched tighter onto his pen as he stared at the heating grate in the ceiling. The hammering in Sara's new study above his office was beyond distracting. He couldn't think. He should have insisted she find another room.

How bloody long is this going to last? He strode out of his office, made his way up the stairs, and marched into the room.

Sara wasn't there, but the carpenter and two young men assisting the fellow turned and stared at him, their hammers halting in midswing.

All three looked as if they wished to flee, or perhaps leap out the windows.

Ian forced the scowling muscles in his face to relax. "How long will it take to complete these shelves?"

"A-about a week, Your Grace," the carpenter said.

A week! That was seven days too long. "Could it be completed sooner if you hire another man?"

The carpenter nodded. "Yes, Your Grace."

"By all means, then do so."

"I'll go see to hiring someone right now."

As Ian left the room, he heard the old man instructing the two lads on what to do while he was away.

Ian stepped into his office just as the *bang, bang, bang* of the hammering began again. He needed quiet to think.

He gathered up his business correspondence and several ledgers and headed to the library.

He stepped into the room and immediately heard humming. He glanced up at the bookcases on the balcony that circled the library. And there she was, his new wife, who was causing more havoc in his house than he wished.

She was running her fingers over the leather bindings. A touch that somehow seemed like a caress, reminding him of how her fingers had explored him. Ian tossed that memory from his mind and wondered why he obsessed over it. The only answer that came to him was how unexpected her inquisitive touch had been, like a painter's brush against a canvas, soft yet determined.

Sara stopped humming and read a book's title out loud. She was still wearing the simple brown dress she'd donned at breakfast. But he realized there was a distinct sensuality to her movements when she thought herself alone.

He cleared his throat.

She spun around. Her eyes looked like large tea-colored pools behind the spectacles she wore. They seemed to settle on the ledgers in his hand. She removed her glasses, slipped them into her pocket, and made her way down the spiral staircase. "Are you going to be working in here?"

If he wanted to be able to hear himself think, it appeared he had little choice. "Yes."

As if reading his thoughts, she offered a sympathetic look. She motioned to the bookshelves. "Do you know if you have any books on entomology?"

Ian set the ledgers down on the desk. "I'm not sure, but I don't believe so."

Disappointment flashed in her expression before clearing. She gave a weak smile and stepped closer to him.

"Thank you again for letting me stay in the room that overlooks the gardens. The view is wonderful."

"You're most welcome." He moved around to the other side of the desk and pulled out the chair.

She pointed to the ceiling. "The mural is magnificent. Do you know who painted it?"

He glanced up at the painting where cherubs, who held instruments, flew in a blue sky with white clouds. "Frederick Armstrong."

"Oh. He died at a young age, didn't he?" Sadness took over her expression.

"Yes."

"I remember reading about him. He was compared to several of the great Renaissance painters. Wasn't he struck by a carriage while walking across the street in front of his studio in Soho one night?"

"Right after he finished painting this. Over thirty years ago." Ian had read about the painter as well. The driver never stopped to offer assistance. Armstrong was left for dead.

"Such a tragedy." She returned her regard to the ceiling. "I bet as a child you spent hours imagining yourself flying up there in the clouds."

He'd not had that luxury. If his father had found him doing such a whimsical thing, he would have paid the price with either a birch rod or leather strap to his arse. "No, I never did."

She tipped her head to the side, and he thought perhaps he saw pity in her eyes. No one pitied him. He was a duke.

"Well, I'll let you get to your work."

As Ian watched Sara move toward the door, he realized she hadn't picked out a book yet. He was half tempted to remind her of that fact, but he didn't wish to be distracted.

And he begrudgingly admitted that his little sparrow of a wife in her drab brown dress fluttering around the library would distract him.

He glanced at the mural and peered about the room. Sitting in here always brought back memories from his childhood. When darkness took over the sky outside, the library had always filled with shadows, obscuring the beauty of the mural. But he didn't mind because it was in those shadows where he could not be observed. He'd always waited until everyone had taken to their beds, leaving the house quiet except the ticking of the clocks. Then he would sneak into the library, leaving the scary world he'd found himself in for another happier one and find solace in the pages of the novels.

It had been years since he'd taken pleasure in a book of fiction. Maybe because he didn't need to escape the life he now lived. Yet, he remembered the simple pleasure reading had brought him. He made his way to one of the tall bookcases and removed a Robert Burns book of poetry.

As if it were only yesterday, he heard his father's voice resonating in his head like the tolling of a bell in a belfry. He heard the *whack* of the leather strap striking his backside. *"Boys don't read poetry. If I ever catch you reading such flowery dribble again, I'll hit you even harder."*

That day, like all the others, Ian hadn't cried, knowing such a transgression would cause his father's temper to become more intense. Emotions such as those were a weakness. That realization had been drilled, along with beaten, into his head and body, and now he found them difficult to show. And Isabelle, the one woman he'd opened his heart to, had stomped on it by marrying his father.

Feeling his chest growing tight, Ian set the book back onto the shelf and slowly let the air out of his lungs to the

count of five and drew another breath in just as slowly—
a trick he used to calm himself when younger. A trick he
hadn't had to use in years. His father was dead, so why did
he feel the need to do it now?

Perhaps it was the fact that he'd managed to get himself
leg shackled to a woman he barely knew. A woman who
would change everything about his life, removing some of
the control he possessed. Some of the control he relished
to obtain as a child and now thought one of his most valu-
able assets.

Chapter Thirteen

After entering the massive dining room for dinner, Jeffers informed Sara that her husband had not returned from his meeting at Magnus Shipping and had sent word not to wait for him.

She stared down the length of the massive twenty-foot dining table, then at her porcelain plate, now loaded with food by an army of footmen who had paraded in and out of the room. Somewhere between the first footman and the last, she'd lost most of her appetite wondering if it was only shipping business her husband was conducting.

Shoving that thought from her mind, she glanced at Jeffers who stood like a centurion next to the mahogany sideboard, his face its usual stoic mask.

The butler rarely showed emotions. He was worse than her husband. At least Ian raised his eyebrows in that haughty way of his, and sometimes she noticed the slight twitching of his lips, along with the occasional smile, but Jeffers was the most mechanical person she'd ever met. As a scientist, she'd conducted experiments. Feeling devilish, she decided it was time she did one on the man.

"Jeffers," she called out.

He pivoted slightly and peered at her. "Yes, Your Grace."

"I think there is a bug in my food."

The butler's rigid expression slipped. Slack-jawed, he darted toward her end of the table, looking as if the world was coming to an end.

He was only a couple of feet from her when she forked a piece of mushroom and lifted it in the air. "Forgive me. I think I'm mistaken. I believe it's a mushroom. What do you think?"

He stopped dead in his tracks and blinked at the piece of food on the tines of her utensil. His stoic mask fell back into place. "Yes, madam, it is definitely a mushroom."

Back ramrod straight, he walked back to his place, guarding the sideboard as if someone might slip into the room to steal the three-hundred-pound piece of furniture.

She forked a piece of carrot and lifted it into the air. "Jeffers, can you tell me what is on my carrot?"

He blinked several times again, then walked to where she sat. "I believe parsley, madam."

"Yes, I think you are correct."

He'd just returned to his guarding spot when Sara eyed him again. Before she could say anything, he moved back to where she sat. "Yes, madam?"

She grinned. "Sorry, Jeffers. I fear I must be bored and perhaps a bit out of sorts. Usually, my sister chats away like a magpie when we eat. The quiet is unsettling. Perhaps when Edward and Jacob return, their chatter will make me feel more at home."

"They usually eat upstairs with their nanny."

"But since they do not have one at present, I thought upon their return they could eat in the dining room."

The butler winced slightly.

"Should I be frightened of them?" she asked, half joking, half serious.

"No. I have a feeling if anyone can handle them, you might be capable of the task."

"Really? Why is that?" She tipped her head to the side, eager to hear his response.

"Because of the way you handled them that day you came to visit."

"I'm not sure what you mean."

"Mr. Conners, the head gardener, stood only a short distance away. He saw Edward place a worm in your palm. You didn't scream or become hysterical. You handled the situation quite well. If I might be so bold to say, madam, myself along with the other members of the staff are hoping you can tame them. For your benefit as much as ours."

People rarely put their belief in her—well, at least not the members of her family. The butler's words were refreshing. She suddenly felt like a peacock who should spread its feathers. She also felt the sudden weight of accomplishing such a task on her shoulders. She drew in a deep breath and released it.

"Might I ask where you were born, Jeffers?" Sara inquired before the butler could return to his place standing next to the sideboard.

"A small seaside village in Cornwall."

"Do you have family?" Gaining her appetite back, Sara drew the carrot off her fork.

"Most of my family has passed on, but I do have a sister."

Sara finished chewing and swallowed. "Does she live in Cornwall?"

"She does." Once again, his stiff-upper-lip expression faltered, and longing deepened the already cavernous wrinkles on the butler's face. "I haven't seen her in years, but we write to each other."

"Why don't you go and visit her?"

"I am needed here, madam."

"You are very important to the running of this house, but I bet you are just as important to your last remaining family member. It might be difficult, but I'm sure we could hobble along, and upon your return you would be appreciated more because even His Grace will have realized how paramount you are." She winked. "That's when you ask him for a raise in your salary."

This time a genuine smile turned up his lips. "I will think about it, Your Grace."

Sara realized in that short span of time, she'd gotten to know more about the stoic butler than her own husband. And wasn't that a sad fact indeed?

Ian arrived home to find the house quiet. It seemed an oddity until he remembered that Edward and Jacob remained at Julien's.

Jeffers stepped into the entry hall.

"Has Her Grace retired?" he inquired.

"An hour ago, sir."

Did Ian hear a tinge a censure in the butler's voice? Believing he must be wrong, he stared at the butler's face; it looked as unreadable as always. Surely, he was mistaken. His wife probably was pleased when he was not about.

"You might as well head to bed, Jeffers, I have something I need to do in my office." Having a wife meant he needed to make changes to his will. His valet was most likely upstairs waiting for him. "Tell Adams to retire as well. I'm not sure how long I'll be."

Ian stepped into his office. This late at night, there would be no distracting hammering drifting through the ceiling's grate. After turning up the gas lamp on the desk, he sat and removed a piece of parchment from the paper tray.

As he pondered exactly what changes he should make if he predeceased Sara, his gaze settled on the painting of Iris House that hung on the wall. His mother had lived there during most of Ian's life, not here at Dorchester Hall with him and his father. Ian was his parents' third child, the previous two having been stillborn. In father's eyes, mother had failed him by only having one healthy child, so she'd been cast aside and sent to Wiltshire to live.

Occasionally Father had visited Iris House, and since his father held no great affection for Mother, Ian presumed several more attempts at begetting a spare took place, obviously all unsuccessful.

Ian supposed his mother felt relieved to be free of her callous husband. And if that freedom meant leaving her only surviving child, it had been a sacrifice she'd been willing to make. For years, while growing up, he'd wondered if his mother had comprehended what would befall him while under his sire's tutelage. Father had been incapable of love. Cruelness had dripped from the man's pores, poisoning the emotional range of everyone around him. When younger, he liked to imagine his mother hadn't comprehended what he would be subjected to, but deep down he realized she surely must have known.

Confirmation came on her deathbed. While at university, he'd received a note from the housekeeper at Iris House, stating his mother was gravely ill and wished to see him.

Ian knew she must be dying, since she'd never asked to see him before, and the one time he'd run away to visit her, he'd received a severe birching by his father after being caught at the train station. Over time, he'd grown bitter over her abandonment and never tried again—not until he'd received that note.

The woman he'd found lying on her deathbed at Iris House was only a shadow of the woman he recalled. In his memory, she'd been lovely with dark hair and startling blue eyes as crystal clear as the Mediterranean Sea, but the frail woman with cloudy eyes looked nothing like his memory.

She'd placed her frail hand on his cheek, and whispered in a low, barely audible voice, "God forgive me, I'm sorry."

To this day, he wondered if she feared for her own internal soul or his, or if she truly felt regret for leaving him with that monster, yet he'd held her hand until she drew in her last breath. Afterward, he'd gone outside and into the parkland at Iris House and found the gardens full of colorful spring blooms, contradicting the darkness of what had transpired inside. In an odd daze, he'd sat on a garden bench and stared at the vibrant colors until he'd heard footsteps on the flagstone path.

He'd glanced up to see the housekeeper standing beside him.

"This was her doing." The woman motioned to the profusion of flowers and budding plants.

It appeared his mother had poured all her love into the garden. He wanted to feel angry at her for abandoning him, but he realized then that she had been as much a victim of his father as he had been.

As he'd stared at the housekeeper, tears had burned the

backs of his eye, yet none fell. He believed that well had dried up a long time ago—beaten out of him.

The unwelcome whizzing noise of a birching rod cutting through the air and the *whack* it made when it contacted with his backside echoed in his memories.

With a quick jerk of his head, Ian pulled his now-unfocused gaze away from the painting and returned his attention to the list of changes he wanted made to his will. He might have trouble showing deep emotions, but he knew right from wrong. When he visited his solicitor tomorrow, he wanted to make sure if something happened to him that Sara and his two wards would live a comfortable life. Sara would like Iris House, especially the gardens. The property wasn't entailed, so she could inherit it if he predeceased her.

After jotting that down, along with some other changes, Ian folded the paper and tucked it under his blotter.

The following morning after dressing, Sara stood before her bedroom window and gazed out. The bright sun foretold that within the hour the hot rays would dry up the morning's dew that lingered on the spikey blades of grass, leaves, and petals. The heat from the sun would also bring out butterflies.

Though she had a meeting at the London Society of Entomologists later this morning, before she left, she wished to search the garden for the Papilio machaon butterfly— that was rarely seen in London.

She was about to turn away from the window when a movement to the far left of the formal gardens caught her attention. Ian stood in an open field practicing archery. He removed an arrow from the quiver, positioned it in his bowstring, and pulled it back. It sailed through the air and struck the center of the bull's-eye.

Jeffers, who stood several yards to the left of the target walked up to the arrow and pulled it loose, then returned to his place a safe distance away.

Ian reloaded and shot another arrow, striking the bull's-eye again.

She had always wanted to try her hand at archery. Without much further thought, she raced from her room and down the stairs, hoping her grumpy husband would allow her to try.

Mrs. Pullman glanced up from where she was instructing a maid. The housekeeper's eyes widened. "Is something the matter, Your Grace?"

"No, everything is fine." She made her way to the French doors in the morning room. Once outside and past the manicured gardens, she hiked up the skirt of her brown dress so she could move at a fast clip as she made her way through the copse of trees and to the field. As she neared the clearing, she smoothed the skirt of her dress and patted the bun at her nape to make sure it hadn't come loose.

Ian loaded another arrow and drew his arm back. He was dressed in gray trousers and a white shirt, rolled up on his forearms. The muscles there bulged as he drew the arrow back and took aim.

Jeffers spotted her. "Good morning, Your Grace."

Ian released the arrow, and it completely missed the target, sailing above it. He grumbled something under his breath. "Is there something you need, Sara?"

"No, I . . . Well, yes, I wondered if I might try my hand at the sport."

He studied her with his startling blue eyes. "You're a skilled archer?"

"No, but that doesn't mean I cannot learn."

"I fear my bow is too large for you."

"How about if I step closer to the target?"

"I don't think that would make a difference. It's rather heavy."

"I'd like to try anyway." She tipped her chin up, wondering if Mr. Grumpy would refuse her.

He held her gaze for a long moment. "Very well."

She followed him as he moved several paces closer to the target.

He handed her the bow and an arrow.

Goodness. It was heavy. She tried not to cringe at the weight.

Ian watched her as if waiting for a reaction. She would not give him the satisfaction. When she said nothing, she thought she witnessed a spark of admiration in his eyes as he explained the mechanics of positioning her hands and loading an arrow.

"Now pull the arrow back and aim."

Sara did as instructed. She didn't want to admit it, but between the weight of the bow and the tension on the bow's string, her muscles burned to keep it steady. She'd only pulled it halfway back when her grip slipped. The arrow took a wobbly flight and sailed through the air toward Jeffers.

The butler scurried out of the arrow's path and squatted low to the ground. She'd never seen the man move so fast. Standing, Jeffers touched the top of his head as if worried she'd taken off a strip of his gray hair.

"Sorry, Jeffers," she called out.

Ian was staring at her as if contemplating taking the bow and arrow from her hand. "Have a care, darling. Good butlers are hard to find."

Sara frowned. "Is that all you care about? That you'd have to find another butler?"

"No. The uniform would be ruined as well."

Startled by his thoughtless comments, her mouth gaped.

But as Ian bent to retrieve another arrow from the quiver, she noticed his lips twitch.

Why, the scoundrel was only teasing.

"I think it might be best, Jeffers, if you move farther away," Ian said. "Perhaps take shelter behind a tree."

Though she narrowed her eyes at Ian, Sara did think that might be wise.

Ian handed her another arrow.

As she positioned it, he stepped behind her. His chest pressed against her back as he covered her hands with his and drew the arrow back. The warmth from his body enfolded her and his spicy scent filled her nose.

"Now set your gaze down the length of the arrow," his velvety voice whispered warmly against her ear. "Do you see the trajectory it will fly?"

"Yes," she answered, suddenly feeling breathless.

"Is it pointed at the center of the bull's-eye?"

He'd positioned it perfectly, but she was having trouble concentrating with him touching her. She glanced over her shoulder. With him leaning down, their mouths were mere inches apart.

His gaze dipped to her lips.

Her heart skipped a beat.

He inched closer to her, and she thought he was about to kiss her, but instead his mouth moved to her ear. "If you don't look ahead, Sara, you might actually hit Jeffers this time," he whispered.

Heat warmed her face. She peered at the target and stared down the length of the arrow.

"Ready?" Ian asked, his warm breath drifting over the back of her neck.

"Yes."

The arrow flew in the air and struck only a few inches from the bull's-eye.

Smiling, Sara turned around to see Mr. Grumpy smiling as well.

"Well done."

"Might I try again?" she asked.

He nodded and withdrew another arrow, but sadly this time he didn't help her, and it agitated her that she wished he would.

After several more tries that all missed the target, Sara handed the bow back to Ian. "Thank you for the lesson. I have to get ready for a meeting at the London Society of Entomologists, but if you do not mind, might I join you again next time you practice?"

He looked baffled, perhaps because she had shown little skill. But it didn't mean she could not improve.

"If you wish."

As she strolled away, she called over to Jeffers, still hiding behind the large trunk of a tree. "I'm leaving, Jeffers. It is quite safe to come out now."

Ian stared at the slight sway of Sara's hips as she walked away. He should be more irritated than he was that she wished to continue insinuating herself into the time he spent practicing his sport. Yet, if honest, he would admit, he'd enjoyed watching how she nibbled her lower lip as she aimed her bow, along with the way her eyes lit up as she waited to see if she would hit the target. And though she'd only struck it the one time he'd helped, she had not given up. There was a great deal of determination in his wife. It reminded Ian of himself. It reminded him of how, after his father had married Isabelle, he was determined to make a name for himself and surpass anything his father had achieved.

He recalled Sara's comment to him the first time they had spoken. "*If I want my father's benevolence, I must wear such an atrocity.*" He understood how it felt to be under someone else's control. He also knew what it felt like to be out from under that person's thumb. The glorious taste of freedom. Had his desire to give her that played a role in his decision to ask her to marry him? He tossed that thought away and realized Jeffers was watching him watching her. Instead of the butler's normally stoic expression, the man wore a broad smile that showed his teeth. In all the years the fellow had worked for him, Jeffers had smiled so rarely, Ian had wondered if the man even possessed teeth. Yet, he was grinning like a ninny showing a full mouth of rather large ones.

"What do you find so humorous?" Ian narrowed his eyes.

Jeffers's smile slipped away. "Nothing, Your Grace. Nothing at all."

Chapter Fourteen

After her archery lesson, Sara stood in her bedroom and studied her reflection in the cheval glass, especially the brown dress she wore. Her sister's cutting words about how Sara dressed no better than a maid replayed in her head. She opened the armoire and viewed the dresses she'd purchased from Madame Renault's shop.

Someone knocked on the door.

"Yes, come in."

Wallace, the lady's maid she'd shared with Louisa, stepped into the room.

"Hello, Wallace. When did you arrive?"

"Just a short time ago, Your Grace." The lady's maid glanced around the well-appointed room. "Oh, madam, your room is lovely."

She agreed. The walls were painted in a sky blue, while the floral and damask bedding looked fit for a queen. "Yes. It is quite lovely."

"I wish to thank you, madam," Wallace said.

"For?" Sara blinked.

"Mrs. Pullman gave me my own room next to the maid's quarters. She said you requested she do so."

Sara smiled. Wallace had once told her she'd never had her own room, that growing up she'd shared a room with five sisters. "I'm glad you're pleased."

"Are you going out?"

"Yes. I have a meeting at the London Society of Entomologists."

Wallace stepped beside her and peered at the gowns.

Sara lifted the sleeve of the shimmering copper day dress. Though the cut wasn't much different from most of her other day dresses, the taffeta material's sheen reflected light and the cuff and hem had delicate cream stitching. "What do you think of this for my meeting?"

"It's perfect. The color will bring out the hazel of your eyes."

Would it? She'd rarely thought about such things and wondered if Ian would think so. She inwardly chastised herself for harboring such thoughts—for even caring what he would think.

An hour later, bathed and wearing the copper day dress, Sara made her way downstairs. She patted at the loose topknot Wallace had coiffed her hair into. She wasn't used to the lady's maid fussing with her hair. In the mornings, Sara normally pinned it into a bun without Wallace's assistance. However, without Louisa taking up the lady's maid's time with her demands, the woman had all but insisted.

When she stepped into the entry hall, Jeffers's eyes widened slightly.

She would take his reaction as approval, and though she didn't think of herself as vain, she felt a rush of pleasure.

"Your new carriage is waiting, Your Grace."

"New carriage?" she echoed.

"Yes, madam. It arrived this morning." He opened the door, revealing a shiny black vehicle.

She gave a small squeal of delight. A noise her sister and brother would call undignified. Almost overwhelmed by such a gift, she glanced over her shoulder to the corridor that led to the library. She was tempted to run into the room and thank Ian, but her delight withered a bit as she realized that the opulent equipage had been gifted to her so people would believe he truly was a besotted and loving husband and not the glowering, and mostly indifferent man she'd married. She shouldn't worry about thanking him, yet . . .

She bit the inside of her cheek. "Is His Grace in the library?"

"No, madam. He left only a few minutes ago for some business he needed to attend to at Magnus Shipping, along with a meeting with his solicitor."

A husband who cared about his wife would have told her about the carriage in person. She walked outside, and a coachman, dressed in black livery and top hat, opened the door.

"Thank you." She smiled.

"You're most welcome, Your Grace."

"Might I ask your name?"

"Jasper, madam."

A few minutes later, they'd passed the gatehouse and were on the road. Leaning her head back against the squabs, Sara plucked off her gloves and ran the tips of her fingers over the nap of the thick, sapphire-colored velvet that covered nearly every surface of the interior. Since she traveled alone, she slipped off her shoes and stretched her legs out so she could curl her silk-clad toes into the plush fabric.

As the carriage moved closer to central London, the traffic grew thicker. The smell from a bakery mixed with the stench of horse manure as they drove past a street sweeper. The carriage turned onto St. James's Street and swayed ever so slightly before it righted itself with the smooth precision of a vehicle equipped with costly springs.

They moved past several gentlemen's clubs. Most of London's clubs did not see fit to allow women to attend. They were bastions of the male hierarchy. And though the London Society of Entomologists did allow women, there were still those men who believed that constituted a grievous error.

The carriage slowed as it neared the society's Georgian building.

Hastily Sara reached for her gloves and shoes and slipped both on.

"Whoa," the coachman called out, and the vehicle rolled to a stop. The man jumped down from his perch, opened the door, and flashed a broad grin.

"Does she handle well, Jasper?"

"Ah, Your Grace, she's a peach for sure. Smooth as a kitten's fur."

Smiling at the coachman's pleasure, Sara stepped onto the pavement. "My meeting should be no more than a couple of hours."

"Very well, Your Grace."

As she made her way to the society's entrance, someone called out her name.

She turned to see Henrietta Bailey, moving at a fast clip, waving her arm in the air. The woman, like Sara, had joined the society a few years ago and been met with the same opposition by several of the more conservative male members who believed women should be home painting watercolors and stitching needlepoints.

"Sara." Henrietta smiled brightly. Her gaze drifted over Sara's new day dress. "Is the gossip true? Are you now the Duchess of Dorchester?"

It appeared the news of her wedding to Dorchester was already spreading through Town. "Yes. I'm sorry I did not invite you. It was a small gathering."

"Oh, I would have been honored to attend, but that is quite understandable." The woman held her gaze for a long moment, and Sara realized Henrietta wanted to ask her more questions. She either thought Sara a fool for having married such a scandalous man or brilliant for having snagged the most eligible bachelor in England. Or she was simply baffled by it all. Yes, that was probably it.

"I wish you and His Grace many long years of happiness," Henrietta said, breaking the silence stretching between them.

Sara would settle for them not grumbling at each other. But she was more or less free to do as she pleased, and she had a shiny new carriage to convey her to the London Society of Entomologists' meetings. Whereas her brother would have scoffed at her attending and made her hire a cab.

Henrietta lifted several sheets of paper. "I've written a lecture on the benefits of ladybugs in a horticultural setting. I hope Mr. Graham will read it today."

Reginald Graham was the society's president and had welcomed them with open arms. Sara suspected that he was also a bit enamored with Henrietta, who appeared oblivious to that fact. The gentleman read many of the lectures submitted to the group, but especially those written by the female members, since some members subjected them to derisive looks when they stood at the podium. It was only after others applauded that Mr. Graham mentioned who had written each essay.

"Henrietta, why don't you read it?"

"Me?" The woman instantly paled. "I'd be subjected to the glower of several male members."

"Mary Plum read her lecture on leaf insects last week."

"Yes, and only half the room applauded her findings, and if her spectacles were not so thick, she would have seen how several members closed their eyes and took a nap, while others acted bored. And someone in the back of the room kept letting his flatulence out."

Sadly, Henrietta was correct even though Mary's lecture had surpassed any other given that day.

They walked into the building and immediately saw George Young, who was not young at all, but one of the curmudgeons who didn't care for the female members and was quick to show it. Instead of his normally formidable scowl that usually stated they were persona non grata, a broad smile settled on his face.

Startled, Sara turned to Henrietta who was peering at her with a perplexed expression that caused the woman's brows to raise high on her forehead.

"Do you think he is in need of new spectacles and doesn't realize who we are?" Sara asked.

"I'm not sure, but his smile is rather frightening."

Still grinning broadly, the man moved toward them. "Ladies, I am beyond pleased you could join the meeting today."

Baffled, Sara blinked.

With a sweep of his hand, Mr. Young motioned to the chairs in the front row. "Why don't you sit there?"

"Thank you, sir." Sara peered at the ceiling to make sure there wasn't a booby trap consisting of pails of sand or something more odious that might come crashing down on their heads once seated.

They had no sooner taken their seats when Martin Grayson, another member who was less than enthusiastic about female members, approached.

"Your Grace, I read your findings on the life cycle of the yellow swallowtail and found it enthralling."

"Thank you, sir." She glanced at Henrietta after the man walked away. "What's going on? The man usually snarls at us."

"He called you 'Your Grace.' Like me, they have heard the news that you are the Duchess of Dorchester now. Married to a man who wields a great deal of power. A man who has been a benefactor to several of London's societies. Last month he gifted the Royal Horticultural Society a rather substantial sum."

Sara hadn't known that. She felt her face heat. She knew so little about the man she'd married.

Henrietta glanced around the room. "They hope you have your husband's ear, and this building is in dire need of repairs."

True, the building's interior plaster cornices were crumbling and several of the chimneys no longer functioned. Plus, the roof had several leaks that were dealt with by putting pails under them.

Mr. Graham stepped into the lecture hall and hurried over to them. "Hello, Lady Sara." The man's ruddy cheeks reddened further. "I mean, Your Grace." His regard shifted to Henrietta, and he smiled brightly. "Hello, Miss Bailey. I hope you are both well. Do you have some new findings you wish me to read for you at the podium?"

Mr. Graham leaned close and spoke in a low voice. "I think you will find the members more receptive today if you wish to present the information yourselves."

"You should give it a go, Henrietta," Sara said.

The woman nibbled her lower lip. "Yes, after the meeting is called to order, I'd like to stand at the lectern and read my newest findings on ladybugs, sir."

"Very well, Miss Bailey." Mr. Graham grinned.

After the man walked away, Sara grabbed her friend's hand. "Bully for you."

"If it goes off without the men in attendance snarling at me, it will because I am your friend. Otherwise they would all but wish to throw tomatoes at me."

Close to an hour later, as Henrietta completed her lecture, Sara smiled. So far it had gone off without a hitch. Only one time had two gentlemen sitting behind Sara started talking loud enough to be disruptive. She had turned around and raised her eyebrow in that arrogant way her husband did, and both men had snapped their mouths closed.

"And in conclusion," Henrietta said, "my study showed that the addition of ladybugs reduced not only aphids but other species of soft-bodied insects that cause destruction of crops."

When Henrietta gathered up her papers from the lectern, Sara realized only a handful of those in attendance were applauding. Sara swiveled in her chair and eyed both George Young and his cohort, Martin Grayson, who were not applauding.

"That was a wonderful essay, wasn't it?" she prompted.

Both men nodded and started clapping enthusiastically.

Chapter Fifteen

A green sign with gold lettering that read NEWTON AND NEWTON, SOLICITORS AND NOTARY PUBLIC hung above the door of Ian's attorney's office in Kensington. The elder Newton had suffered apoplexy nearly a year ago, leaving Ian to deal with the man's young son and partner, Miles.

As soon as Ian entered the office, the secretary seated at his desk stood.

"Your Grace." The fellow rushed to open the door that led to Miles Newton's office.

Ian entered the office to see the solicitor with his head bent over some legal document. The man's ginger hair and pale skin were highlighted by the light streaming through the windows.

Newton glanced up, bounced to his feet, exhibiting even more exuberance than his secretary.

Though the solicitor possessed a rather nervous nature, the man had proven himself beyond competent.

"Your Grace, as I said in my missive, I would have come to your residence." Newton motioned to one of the high-backed leather chairs that faced his desk.

"No need. I had business in Town." Ian sat. "I need to make a few changes to my will."

The man folded his thin frame into his chair. "I have already set aside the amount you want bequeathed to your two wards. Is there something else?"

"Yes. I need to add my wife."

"Wife?" The man's pale gray eyes widened. "I—I didn't know you had married. My felicitations, Your Grace." The man stuttered as if it was him who'd been caught in the parson's noose.

"Don't worry, Newton. It's not contagious."

The man's cheeks reddened. "Forgive me. I just thought . . ."

"That I would never marry?"

"Yes, I guess that's it, sir."

Ian hadn't thought he would marry either. He nodded and removed two pieces of paper from the inside breast pocket of his coat. He handed the contract Sara had had drawn up stipulating that the money she brought into the marriage was hers alone. "My wife's funds are to be kept separate from my own, and I wish to make sure that if I predecease her, my will states they will remain that way."

"I can add a codicil to the will."

"No. I think it best you draw up a new will, since that isn't the only modification I want made." Ian handed him the second piece of paper. "Should I predecease my wife, I want her to inherit Iris House, my estate in Wiltshire, which isn't entailed. She is also to be named guardian of my two wards and given the amount I have written down."

The solicitor's eyes widened. By the startled look on the man's face, one would have thought Ian had decided to foolishly bequest the sum to a house plant, but Sara was due the funds if she was to be tasked with raising the two hellions.

"Is there a problem, Newton?"

The solicitor glanced up from the paper. "No, Your Grace."

"As you see, Lord Dartmore is to remain the executor of my estate, along with having the option to purchase my investment in Magnus Shipping and any other businesses we are jointly involved in. I want this will ironclad. I don't wish anyone to contest it." By anyone, he meant Isabelle. A sudden knot formed in the back of his neck, and Ian fought the urge to rub at it.

"And the duchy's entailed properties will go to your young brother and heir?"

The question seemed odd, since the man knew Ian could not make changes to the entailed property, only what wasn't entailed. "Yes, unless my wife has a son."

As if nervous, the young solicitor picked at the skin around his index finger while he read over the papers Ian had handed him. Newton seemed more jumpy than usual. Perhaps his father had taken a turn for the worse. "How is your father doing?"

Newton glanced up. "He has shown some improvement."

"I'm glad to hear it." Ian stood. "Message me as soon as the new will is drafted."

The solicitor sprang to his feet.

Ian shook his hand. "Good day, Newton."

As Ian climbed back into his carriage he wondered if Sara knew about his young half brother—Isabelle and his father's child—the duchy's presumptive heir. She hadn't known about his two wards. He had a feeling she spent most of her time studying insects instead of listening to the gossips.

After traveling from his solicitor's office to the docklands, Ian's carriage pulled in front of Magnus Shipping. He leapt down from the vehicle. The scent of the Thames drifted in the air.

He stepped into the building and took the stairs up to the first floor, where offices were filled with shipping clerks. At the end of the hall was Julien's office. His secretary wasn't at his desk, so Ian knocked at the door and stepped in. His gaze settled on Julien's blotter, overflowing with ledgers, invoices, and correspondence. The man was a business genius, but Ian always wondered how he found anything.

His friend and partner stood at one of the tall windows, peering out. Julien glanced over his shoulder. "The *Calypso* came into port last night."

Ian stepped next to him and looked at the docks. From where they stood, the tall masts of the *Calypso* were visible. After the new ironclad vessel from Scotland arrived, the ship would be sold. "Have you found a buyer?"

"Not yet. I think I'm feeling a bit nostalgic."

He understood. Selling the vessel would be bittersweet. It had been the first ship they had bought, but the new ironclads were the future. "Is the new ship still on schedule?"

Julien moved back to his desk and sat. "Yes. We will need to take the rail up to Scotland before it makes the journey to London."

Ian leaned against the sill. "Any word from Floyd on him selling us his ironworks?"

Julien pulled on his chin. "No. Do you want his company?"

"You know the answer to that."

"Then perhaps you need to be seen about with your new wife and play the devoted husband."

He'd been thinking about that as well.

"I've heard that the man enjoys joining the promenade of carriages in Hyde Park during the late afternoon at five o'clock. Why don't you take your bride for a carriage ride there? It might help the situation."

He abhorred driving through the park. But his friend was right. If he wanted to appease Floyd's morality, the man needed to see him with Sara, playing the devoted husband.

After going over several contracts with Julien, Ian returned home and stepped inside Dorchester Hall. As usual, Jeffers met him in the entry hall.

"Has Her Grace returned from her meeting at the London Society of Entomologists?"

"Yes. She is in the garden."

Hopefully, Sara wasn't swinging her oversized net wildly about and putting the fountain of Atargatis in danger of losing her nose or an appendage. Ian stepped into his office and sat at his desk. A flash of copper became visible behind a manicured hedge. Was that Sara? Curious if it was her, he stood and moved to the window, hoping to get a better view. Seeing nothing, he grasped the casing and shifted closer. After several uneventful minutes, he grumbled. What was he doing wasting his time, staring out the window? He had work to do, yet he reminded himself what Julien said about Floyd riding in Hyde Park, and his friend's suggestion he take Sara there. He would ask her.

With a resigned sigh, he strode from his office, out the morning room's French doors, and onto the terrace. Once down the granite steps and into the garden, he glanced around. Not seeing Sara, he headed down a path and spotted her.

Well, not all of her. Only her derrière, sticking out from under a cropping of bushes.

"Sara?"

"Yes." She didn't sound at all embarrassed by the fact that he'd found her crawling on the ground.

"Might I ask what you are doing?"

Shuffling backward, she scooted out from under the shrubbery, stood up, and brushed the grass and dried leaves off the skirt of her dress. Instead of one of her brown dresses, she wore a day dress that sparkled like a buffed copper penny and matched her eyes.

"The wind from last night must have tipped a bird's nest." She pointed to the top of the bush where it leaned precariously at a forty-five-degree angle. "I saw an egg on the ground. It must have fallen out. I was trying to retrieve it to see if it survived the fall."

Sara was perhaps the only woman he knew who would crawl on the ground to retrieve a fallen egg. He stepped forward and removed a dried leaf from her hair, which had all but come loose, leaving several long brown shimmering strands trailing over her shoulders and back.

Her eyes widened.

He held the brittle leaf up.

She gave a self-deprecating smile and patted at her fallen hair and pulled out another dried leaf. "Any more?"

He circled her, feeling more like a predatory animal, since her disheveled appearance made him feel rather randy.

Good God! What was it about his little wife that caused him to think like a green lad seeing a woman naked for the first time? And dash it all, she wasn't even naked, but rather alluringly rumpled. He wanted to toss up her skirts and press tiny kisses to her thighs as he made his way to the sweet spot between her legs. Needing a distraction, he squatted in front of the bushes and scanned the area.

"Do you see it?" She crouched next to him and pointed. "It's right there."

"Hmmm," he said, wondering if now that he saw it, she expected him to retrieve it. And why the bloody hell had he even squatted down to look for it?

He remembered. A distraction from his randy thoughts.

"Do you think you can reach it?"

That query answered his question about whether she would expect him to retrieve it. He should have stayed in his office. Releasing a gusty breath, he crawled farther under the bush and bit back an oath when a lower branch poked him in the head.

"Hello, Jeffers," Sara said cheerfully.

Ian twisted his body and glanced over his shoulder at the butler's legs. The man probably thought he was going mad. Perhaps he was. Perhaps lack of tupping one's wife caused such a state.

"Madam, is His Grace in need of assistance?" Jeffers inquired.

"I think he's nearly reached it."

"It?" the butler echoed.

"An egg. It tumbled out of its nest and His Grace is trying to retrieve it. Isn't that sweet of him?"

"Yes, madam, very sweet."

Ian heard the smile in the man's voice. Cursing under his breath, he crawled farther into the underbrush.

Another set of feet walked up. By the look of the worn boots, Ian figured it was one of the gardeners.

"Your Grace, Mr. Jeffers. Is that His Grace under there? Does he need any help?" the man asked.

"No, Mr. Conners," Sara said. "I believe His Grace has it all under control. But if you could get a ladder, that would be helpful."

"A ladder?" both Jeffers and the gardener repeated.

"Yes, if the egg isn't damaged, His Grace is going to place it back in the nest."

He didn't recall offering to do that.

"I'll be right back, madam." The gardener's retreating footsteps crunched against the pebbles.

Ian stretched his arm out. The blasted egg was only an inch away. "I've just about. . . . There. I've got it."

"Is it broken?" Sara crouched down and peered at him.

"It doesn't appear to be." Arse first, he backed out from under the bushes.

Seeing the egg, Sara smiled broadly at him like he was a warrior. "Thank you."

He smiled back, then remembering Jeffers's presence, blanked his expression and turned to the butler who was grinning and showing his teeth again.

"Is there something you find humorous, Jeffers?"

"No, Your Grace."

Just then, the gardener returned with the ladder and positioned it next to the bush.

"Thank you, Mr. Conners. Now His Grace can return the egg to the safety of its nest." Sara said it like he would be restoring semblance to a world slipping off its axis.

He climbed onto the ladder under Sara's, Jeffers's, and the gardener's watchful eyes and placed the egg in the nest, then straightened it. Once back on the ground, he turned around to see three smiling faces.

Good Lord, his life was turning into utter chaos and his wards weren't even here. What would it be like when they returned?

"If you'll excuse me." He strode away, trying to look dignified, even though he assumed he had leaves and twigs in his hair and the knees of his gray trousers were filthy.

Ian made his way into the house and up the stairs. The wide-eyed glances he received from servants confirmed he looked a bloody mess. He stepped into his bedchamber to find his valet placing neckcloths into the highboy.

Adams turned to him, and his eyes widened as he took in Ian's disheveled appearance. "If I didn't know better, Your Grace, I'd think you'd been crawling on the ground."

He *had* crawled on the ground. Without answering, he kicked off his shoes, began stripping off his clothing, and marched into his bathing room.

The manservant followed him, picking up the garments. "Are you going out, sir?"

He was tempted to return to Magnus Shipping, find Julien, and strangle the man. *Find a wife who is a help-mate. Lady Sara seems a sensible woman.* His friend's words replayed in his head.

"Sir?" Adams peered at him.

"No. I'll be staying home this evening." While crawling on the ground he'd forgotten to ask Sara about going for a ride in Hyde Park tomorrow. He unbuttoned his trousers and drawers, tossed them aside, and turned on the faucets that worked the shower bath he'd had installed last year. Normally, he would wait for the water to heat, but instead he stepped into the tub and under the cool spray. Hopefully, it would revive his sound judgment, which he obviously had momentarily lost when he'd decided to crawl on the ground like a nincompoop.

Chapter Sixteen

At dinner, Ian stared down the long length of the dining room table to where Sara sat at the other end. Several minutes ago, she'd called Jeffers over and asked the butler about his sister. Ian hadn't even known the man had a sister. Now she was chatting about Cornwall and how she'd once visited Penzance and found the scenic beauty of the Cornwall coastline breathtaking.

With each word Sara spoke, Jeffers's normally rigid posture relaxed, and he flashed his large-tooth smile. In all the years Jeffers had been employed in this household he'd rarely shown a smile. But that made three times this week, which was probably more times than the butler had smiled in a decade.

Ian stared at them for several more minutes before shoving a piece of roasted potato into his mouth. Let them chat away. He didn't care. He didn't wish to be part of their conversation.

Then why do you feel agitated? an irritating voice in his head asked.

Because he liked peace and quiet while he ate. It allowed him to think about the day's events regarding his businesses and what plans he had for them, along with what holdings he wished to acquire. Just like Sara had disturbed the peacefulness in his office and infringed on his archery practice, she appeared intent on disrupting his meal. *But you enjoyed her presence when you practiced your archery,* that irritating voice reminded him. Remembering how the normally unflappable Jeffers had hidden behind a tree caused Ian to chuckle.

He glanced down the length of the table to see both Sara and Jeffers staring at him. Ignoring them, he shoved another piece of potato into his mouth, then lifted his wineglass and took a sizable mouthful.

"Ian?"

He glanced up to see Sara waving her hand at him. "Yes?"

She set her hand to her ear. "What?"

"I said yes."

"This is foolish." She picked up her plate and moved halfway down the table and sat, so that only ten feet separated them. "This is much better. Screaming will cause us to get sore throats."

Did that mean they would be expected to converse? So much for his solitude. "Yes, much better," he replied, forcing a smile.

"Definitely. I'd like to thank you for the carriage."

"You're quite welcome."

"It was glorious riding in it, especially since I used to have to take a hansom to my meetings at the London Society of Entomologists."

"Never your family's carriage?"

"Definitely not. My brother thought my going there was a waste of my time."

He frowned. No wonder she'd agreed to marry him. He lifted his glass and drained it dry.

Noticing Ian's empty wineglass, Jeffers picked up the carafe from the sideboard and refilled it. Instead of the smile he'd flashed at Sara, the man frowned. He was half-tempted to ask him why. But he knew the reason. It was a rare event when Ian indulged in a second glass of wine. It was especially unusual for him to indulge in a third with his dinner. Or perhaps this was his fourth. An excessive amount if he couldn't recall exactly how many he'd downed. He curled his fingers around the stem of the glass, lifted it a fraction, then thinking better about it, set it back down. He peered at Sara again—watched how her lips moved as she slipped a length of carrot into her mouth. A wicked thought entered his mind.

Damnation. The excessive amount of wine he'd consumed had turned his brain into licentious mush. "Sara, when did you last visit Cornwall?" he asked, hoping to distract his randy thoughts. Something he seemed to need to do on a regular basis when near his wife.

Her startled gaze shot to his. "When I was sixteen."

"So it's been a while?"

Sara narrowed her eyes.

Bugger it. Did she think he was calling her old? The prickly woman. He hadn't meant it that way. "Perhaps we could take the rail there one day." He rubbed at the back of his neck, while wondering why he'd suggested that. He frowned at his wineglass; he'd definitely swilled too much. He wasn't the only one startled. Both Sara and Jeffers became so still, one would think they'd spotted the snake-haired gargoyle that turned one to stone.

Sara blinked. "I . . . I would very much enjoy that. Soon

the warm air from the Continent will cause the migration of butterflies to the county."

Good God. Had he just made an assignation to go butterfly watching? Ian drew in a fortifying breath. He stood before the wine caused him to say something else that would bring him more regret. "If you'll excuse me, I have work that needs attending to."

He was halfway down the corridor when he remembered he'd once again forgotten to ask Sara about going for a ride in Hyde Park. He'd do it tomorrow. If he returned to the dining room, after overindulging in spirits, he might offer to do something even more foolish than offer to take her to Cornwall to search for butterflies.

Instead of going to his office, Ian headed to the library. He wasn't sure why since the carpenter and his helpers had quit for the day. Perhaps it was because he didn't wish to hear Sara milling about in the room above him. The woman distracted him more than he wished to admit. And sometimes it had nothing to do with the noise she made.

Once again, he wondered why.

Bloody hell, he knew exactly why. He wanted to bed her again. And he was too stubborn to hand her his coin.

After her husband's abrupt departure at dinner last night, Sara had eaten breakfast in her room. She did not need to subject herself to Ian's taciturn moods in the morning.

Though his invitation to go to Cornwall had almost left her speechless, she doubted they would actually go. She studied her reflection as Wallace styled her hair and tried not to fidget as the lady's maid worked the curling tongs on several wisps of hair she'd left out of Sara's bun. She had to admit the style was rather flattering.

"How are you settling in, Wallace?" Sara asked.

"The staff is quite friendly, especially Mrs. Pullman."

"I'm glad."

Wallace set the curling tongs down. "All done, madam."

"Thank you."

Curious to see the progress in her study, Sara exited her bedchamber and headed down the corridor. As she walked by an open doorway, she heard two maids chatting inside the room.

"I heard the duke was as mad as a badger 'cause Her Grace insisted on making changes to several rooms in the house."

Changes to several rooms? Sara's steps faltered. Not true. She'd only wished for the display shelves to be built in her study. She had no desire to change anything else.

"Aye, I heard she created such a ruckus above His Grace's office, he moved into the library to work."

That *was* true. But he would only be inconvenienced for a few more days. And how could anyone mind working in such a lovely library?

"Do you think he truly loves her?"

"I doubt it. She's rather plain looking. Not at all the type of woman I thought he'd marry."

She had tolerated enough of their gossip. Sara stepped through the doorway and cleared her throat.

Both women spun around.

"Your Grace," they said in unison, bobbing curtsies.

"Might I ask your names?" Sara raised a brow, mimicking the way Ian arrogantly raised his.

"Mabel," the redheaded maid answered, her reply so low it was almost inaudible.

"Katherine," the other said, her eyes bright with unshed tears.

Obviously, they thought she intended on having them dismissed.

Sara forced a smile, deciding it might be better to try to make friends with the staff than alienate them. "Thank you. I'm terrible with names, and I'm trying to learn everyone's."

Both maids blinked.

"Carry on," Sara said, and continued down the corridor. As she did, she agitatedly plucked at the cuff of her sleeve. Perhaps she should have reprimanded them. What good would it have done? Servants gossiped. She stepped into her study. Seeing the progress on the shelves caused a wave of pleasure to filter through her body, making her momentarily forget about the gossiping maids.

Mr. Brown and his three helpers, who were sawing wood and hammering, stilled. A nervous expression settled on the carpenter's face. Was he worried she would not like the shelves? He had nothing to fear in that regard. They were turning out even lovelier than the drawing he'd shown her.

"They are absolutely perfect, Mr. Brown."

The carpenter's tense posture eased. "Thank you, Your Grace. We shall be done in a couple of days."

The words the maid said about the noise and Ian's displeasure echoed in her head. They were building them as fast as they could to try to tame Ian's displeasure.

"Well, I'll let you get on with your work." She exited the room and saw Jeffers.

"Excuse me, madam, His Grace wishes to know if you might spare him a minute in the library."

"Tell him I'll be there after my stroll in the garden."

The startled expression on the butler's face conveyed he thought her mad for not immediately running off to speak with Ian. Her husband might cause fear in others, but she would not allow the man to cow her. She'd grown up under her father's dominance and then her brother's. She would not permit that to happen here. For once in her life, the bargain was not one-sided. Ian could not hold her money from her. She had made sure the marriage agreement was worded to her exact liking. Plus, if he wanted his business partners to think this was not a marriage of convenience but a love match, he could not banish her to one of his country estates. She finally wielded some power, and it felt beyond glorious.

Ian glanced at his pocket watch. He'd sent for Sara over an hour ago, and she'd yet to show up. Jeffers had informed Ian that his duchess would speak with him after her stroll. His wife, whom he'd thought would be more biddable, was proving to be anything but. Yet, hadn't she proved that to him on the day he'd asked for her hand, and also on that long-ago night in the library? He'd actually admired that little mulish tilt of her chin when she said he should apologize for implying she was a Peeping Tom.

He glanced up from the ledger he was distractedly mulling over as Sara entered the room.

"You wish to speak with me?" she asked, brandishing that defiant tilt of her chin.

"Yes." He stood and motioned to one of the chairs across from his desk.

She tucked her skirt behind her and sat, then primly folded her hands in her lap, drawing his attention to them.

Unbidden, the memory of her skimming them over every inch of his body on their wedding night flashed in his mind. Her hands had felt as skilled as those of any lover he'd ever had. Everything about that night seemed a contradiction about his wife.

His gaze shifted back to her face. "I wanted to inform you that Julien has sent word that Edward and Jacob will be staying at his residence for several more days."

The disappointment on her face surprised him. "That is a shame. I am most eager for their return. I should very much like to get to know them better."

He'd come to the conclusion that Sara possessed exceptional intelligence; she'd proven that when she'd bartered with him, but she didn't seem to grasp the situation that lay before her. Namely, that the boys might try to terrorize her, and she could not quit as each of their nannies had. They had made a bargain and he intended to hold her to it.

"They might not make this easy on you when they *do* return."

"I realize that. Was there anything else you wished to discuss with me?" Sara shifted as if she intended to rise.

"Yes. I wondered if you would like to go for a carriage ride later this afternoon in Hyde Park."

"Oh. Is this to be our first performance as an adoring couple?"

"Yes. Do you think you can manage that?"

"I've seen enough women make cow eyes at you that I think I can mimic their tomfoolery."

"You sound jealous."

"Ha! Never. Anyway, it is your performance we should be concerned about."

"You don't think I can act head over heels in love with you?"

"No. Not if you continue to arch your brow in that arrogant way you seem to favor." She lifted a brow, mimicking the expression.

"I am a duke. I am supposed to look that way. And I can act so devoted it will curl your toes."

"Doubtful."

"You wish for proof?" He stood and walked around the desk.

Her lovely hazel eyes grew round. She stood as if intent to make a quick escape. "You don't need to do that."

"No. I insist." He ran the back of his fingers over her cheek before placing a finger under her chin to tip her gaze up to his so he could demonstrate that he could look at her as if she'd captured his heart.

Sara's breath quickened. Her tongue darted out, glistening the surface of her sultry mouth.

He'd only intended to act as if she enthralled him by looking into her eyes like a lovesick lad, but now he wanted to kiss her. He inched closer and brushed his lips against hers.

Sara made a little sound—similar to a sigh, but more grounded in pleasure. One of her hands skimmed up his chest, the pressure firm as if she wanted to gauge the delineation of his muscles underneath his shirt and waistcoat. The fingers of her other hand flexed against his hip.

Digging his hand into the hair at the back of her head, Ian coaxed her mouth open and tangled his tongue with hers.

She responded by making another noise of pleasure. This one more like a purr.

Something dark and lustful uncoiled in him. He fought the temptation to knock everything off his desk and make love to Sara on it. What was happening? He'd only planned to show her how he could play the besotted husband—do nothing more than stare into her eyes with the look of a smitten man, yet something sparked between them. Something he couldn't quite explain.

Yes, he could. It was lust. Nothing more.

He forced himself to step back. Then with an air of indifference he did not feel, he tugged at the cuffs of his shirtsleeves and rounded his desk, putting the piece of furniture between them. "Do you need any more proof that I can play the besotted husband?"

His little sparrow of a wife smiled. "No. Do you need any more proof that *I* can?" She grinned and headed toward the door.

What? Was she implying she'd felt nothing when they'd kissed? That she'd been acting the whole time? She was the most exasperating woman.

"We'll leave at four-thirty," he said, fighting the desire to stalk after her, toss her over his shoulder, then carry her upstairs like a Neanderthal.

"I'll be ready," she said, as cool as a cucumber.

Chapter Seventeen

As they traveled from Richmond to Hyde Park, Ian glanced at Sara, who sat as far away from him as the seat allowed. She'd changed into a topaz-colored day dress and wore matching gloves and a parasol. She looked rather fetching. However, since they'd sat in the carriage, she practically hugged her side of the vehicle.

"I guess the performance hasn't started yet." He cocked a brow, then realizing the affectation smoothed out his expression.

"What?"

"If you sit any farther away, you might as well join my coachman on the box."

She gave a brief nod and shifted only fractionally closer, as if an invisible person sat between them.

"Now you are sitting as if we are betrothed and not married."

"There is a difference?"

"Yes. Betrothed women know that the watchful eye of the *ton* will censure them if they sit too close. Married women will not be judged so harshly." He reached out and, clasping a hand on her hip, pulled her closer. Close enough that even with the roof of the carriage lowered and the slight breeze, he could smell the pleasant clean scent of her skin.

"I'm practically on your lap," she said, her hazel eyes wide.

"No. That would surely be frowned upon. Your leg is merely touching my thigh." It was hard to believe that the pious woman sitting next to him today was the same woman who'd returned his kiss earlier in the day. And he bloody well didn't believe she was acting. And neither had she been acting on their wedding night. She clearly enjoyed sex, but somehow morphed into a prickly woman during the day.

As the coachman drove the vehicle into Hyde Park, Sara frowned. "I didn't expect it to be so crowded."

"You've never visited the park during this hour?"

"No, I usually visit earlier in the morning when searching for butterflies."

That made sense since, if she swung her butterfly net while people were promenading, she might injure those near her.

"Are we here to impress someone specific?"

The minx was too smart by half. "Bertram Floyd. Julien and I want to buy his ironworks company. He was a friend of your father's, wasn't he?"

"Yes."

They drove through the park at a turtle's pace, garnishing more than their fair share of attention and greetings. Sara appeared calm, proving that her nervousness truly centered on dancing.

A woman called out Sara's name.

They turned to see her sister and brother riding horseback on Rotten Row.

Ian noticed the slight tensing of Sara's body as Hampton

and Lady Louisa pulled their horses close to the carriage. He also noticed the critical eye Louisa cast over Sara's dress as if judging her before turning her gaze to him and flashing a coquettish smile.

After they said their greetings, Hampton engaged him in conversation about the weather and the House of Lords. However, Ian found his attention drawn to what Louisa was saying to her sister.

Each of her compliments was flavored with a slight insult. At present, she was telling Sara how the gown she wore was quite pretty, but the color washed her sister's complexion out. The more Ian heard the younger woman talk, the more agitated he became. Having heard enough, he affectionately clasped Sara's gloved hand in his as if he couldn't bear to not touch her. Then while still conversing with Hampton, Ian began slowly rubbing his thumb over the exposed skin at Sara's wrist above the edge of her glove.

As he expected, Sara's siblings' gazes focused on the action.

"Darling," Ian said, turning to her, "we really need to get going. I have a very romantic dinner planned with oysters, strawberries, and champagne." He wondered if Sara and her siblings realized that every food he'd mentioned was considered an aphrodisiac.

His wife's cheeks reddened, while her brother's eyes widened, revealing they both were quite aware.

On the other hand, Sara's sister looked rather confused at the combination. "Sara doesn't like oysters," Louisa said.

"Not true," Sara replied. "Since marrying Ian, I cannot get enough of them."

Brava, Ian thought, and almost let loose a bark of laughter.

As they drove away, he noticed Hampton whispering to his sister and saw her mouth gape.

A smile settled over Sara's full lips, and she twirled her parasol. "You know that was rather wicked."

"But you enjoyed it, didn't you?"

"Tremendously. Thank you."

"You are most welcome."

He was used to complimenting women, usually with an ulterior motive, but he suddenly realized he did wish to let Sara know her gown suited her. "You look very nice today. That shade suits you by accentuating the color of your eyes."

She blinked and her cheeks flushed, causing him to wonder if she'd ever been complimented.

"Thank you. My sister said that I dress no better than one of your maids."

Her sister thought too highly of herself. She should have half the kindness Sara possessed. Surely, he could not envision Louisa crawling under a bush to try to save an egg. Then again, a couple of days ago, he could not have seen himself doing it either.

Having not spotted Floyd, they headed back to Richmond.

"Will you be eating dinner at home this evening? I realize I know so little about you. If you wish members of the *ton* to believe we are in love, I think we should learn more about each other."

She had a valid point. "Yes, I'll join you for dinner."

That evening, Ian walked into the dining room to find Sara had shifted two seats closer to where he normally sat at the head of the table.

Jeffers, standing by the sideboard, sported another silly smile.

"Either the table is shrinking, or you keep moving," Ian said, sitting.

"Well, if we are going to learn more about each other, we cannot be screaming down the length of the table. In fact . . ." She got up, picked up her soup bowl and utensils, and sat next to him. "There. That's even better."

Ian reached for his glass of wine, then remembering that the last time he'd overindulged he'd offered to go butterfly watching in Cornwall, he hastily set the glass down.

A footman stepped into the room and ladled soup into their bowls. After he stepped away, Ian watched as Sara spooned some into her mouth, then licked her lower lip.

His cock twitched.

"Where should we start?" She tipped her head sideways and waited.

He dragged his mind out of the libidinous cavern it had slipped into again and focused on a question. He realized though Sara looked in her mid- to late-twenties, he didn't know her exact age. "How old are you?"

"Twenty-eight. Yourself?"

"Thirty-two."

"Ah, you were more firmly on the shelf than I was. So I saved you from becoming the male version of an old maid."

Jeffers snickered.

He frowned at the man. "Unmarried men are rarely labeled in such unflattering ways."

"And why do you think that is?" Once again, she peered at him with her large hazel eyes.

"There are many injustices in the world and that is another example of one."

Obviously pleased with his response, she flashed a broad smile.

"Your turn," he said.

"Why do you work so hard?"

Well, he hadn't expected that question. He didn't believe anyone had ever asked him that besides Julien. He glanced at Jeffers. The man looked away. The butler knew why. After years of being made to feel as if he were lacking in his father's eyes, he worked to prove him wrong. Yet, he'd accomplished that years ago before his father's death. So why did he continue? Perhaps he needed to prove it to himself.

He was saved from answering at that moment by another footman entering to remove their soup bowls and another who served the next course.

After they left, Sara said, "You haven't answered my question about why you work so hard."

"I like having control over my finances."

She nodded, but Ian had a feeling she realized it was only a partial truth.

It was his turn to ask a question. "What made you interested in studying entomology, specifically butterflies?"

"My mother would take me with her to visit garden exhibits. My father and siblings had little interest in accompanying her, though I loved going. I realized how important something as simple as a bee is to this world. I find it utterly fascinating."

"And why specifically butterflies?"

"Because they are too beautiful to ignore. Graceful. Colorful. Perhaps . . ."

"Yes?"

She shook her head.

Her hesitance to continue made him wonder if she was

about to say they were everything she believed she wasn't. But he'd seen her when she thought herself alone—the sensuality of her movements. She was more like a butterfly than she realized.

"What did your father think about your interest in entomology?"

She seemed to ponder the question before turning her face more fully toward him. "He wished I would be more like my sister. Interested in painting and playing the piano and burying my head in fashion magazines instead of scientific papers."

"I'm sorry," he said, genuinely meaning it. He knew what it was like to feel one didn't live up to one's father's expectations. Though he wasn't quite sure if anything he'd done would have made a difference where his sire was concerned.

"You've asked more than one question. My turn," she said, interrupting his thoughts. "Have you ever been in love?"

He looked over at Jeffers again.

The man nodded and, without saying a word, left the room.

Sara noticed the butler's departure and drew her brows together. "Ah, you have secrets that you don't wish even your trusted butler to know."

Jeffers knew. He'd worked in this house when Ian had arrived home from university to find his father had attained a special license and married Isabelle. Isabelle who had promised to marry him. Who'd spoken of her great love for him. Who, in truth, had only wanted the title and was not willing to wait until Ian attained it.

The playful look in Sara's eyes evaporated. Somehow

his intuitive wife knew it had not ended well. "You don't have to answer."

He wasn't sure why, but he wanted to answer her. "Yes, I loved someone. A long time ago. In fact, it feels like a lifetime ago." Briefly he averted his eyes. "Have you ever loved someone, Sara?"

"No."

She was lucky. He wanted to tell her so, but it seemed an odd thing to say about love to one's wife.

For the third day in a row, they rode through Hyde Park, hoping to meet Bertram Floyd. But there was still no sign of the man. Floyd seemed as elusive as the butterfly Sara searched for.

Sara swiveled on the carriage seat and faced him. "Are you quite sure Mr. and Mrs. Floyd drive through the park at five?"

Ian was starting to wonder if Julien was misinformed. However, the more Ian thought about it, the more he couldn't envision the stoic Floyd driving through the park. "That's the time Julien stated."

"He doesn't strike me as the type of gentleman who would enjoy riding through Hyde Park," Sara said, echoing his own thoughts.

Had Julien lied to him? Why? A thought settled in Ian's mind. A manipulative one on his friend's part. After he dropped Sara off at home, he was going to visit Julien and get some answers.

As they pulled out of Hyde Park, a carriage with both Lady Randall and Lady Cleary passed them.

Damnation. Bad enough when one happens upon an ex-lover, more disconcerting when it was two together.

In unison, their gazes settled over him before shifting to Sara.

His wife's cheeks flushed. She remained quiet as they drove back to Richmond, mostly staring out her side of the vehicle. The wind had picked up and Ian pulled out the lap rug from under the seat and spread it across her legs.

"Thank you," she said, briefly looking at him.

When they pulled in front of Dorchester Hall, Ian stepped out and offered Sara his hand. "I need to visit Julien. If I've not returned before dinner, please don't wait for me."

"You're going to Lord Dartmore's?" she asked as if hoping to reveal whether he spoke the truth.

He realized what she wondered—if he really intended to visit Lady Randall or Lady Cleary. He didn't. "Yes, I have something I need to discuss with him."

Ian's carriage stopped in front of his friend's grand stuccoed residence. He marched up to the town house and struck the lion-head knocker against the door several times.

The butler, who was as ancient as Jeffers, answered and stepped aside. "Your Grace."

"Is he home?"

"Yes, he's in his study."

Without waiting for the butler to announce him, Ian headed down the hall, wondering why the house was so quiet if Edward and Jacob were there.

He stepped into the study to find Julien sitting at his desk.

"What brings you here?" Julien smiled.

Still wondering why the house was as quiet as a

monastery with his hellions in it, Ian glanced around. "Where are the boys? You haven't tied them up somewhere?" Ian asked jokingly.

"Of course not. Nothing so diabolical. I've only locked them in the larder."

Ian's heart skipped a beat. "Good Lord, Julien, tell me you're bloody joking."

His friend's smile widened. "Relax, old boy. They're upstairs playing cards with my under-butler. They're skilled for such young lads. Did you teach them?"

Understandable why Julien would think that. After Ian's fallout with his father, he'd used his skill at the card tables to raise the funds he needed to become a partner in Magnus Shipping. "No. Most likely their father, Finley, taught them."

Julien shook his head. "Well, they are only betting for biscuits, so no harm done, but I think Jacob would be ahead if he hadn't eaten half of his." Julien motioned to a chair across from his desk. "What brings you here?"

"I wish to ask you something."

"About?" Julien moved to the sideboard and poured two whiskeys.

Ian took the glass from him and sat, then leaning forward, he braced his forearms on his thighs, while holding the glass between his hands. "Bertram Floyd doesn't ride with his wife through Hyde Park, does he?"

"Is that a question or a statement?"

"An assumption."

Julien sat and took a sip from his tumbler. "I thought he did, but I might have been misinformed."

"Doubtful. If I know you, you've got men following the man and know every move he makes."

"True. I need to make sure he's not contacting other

possible competitors and pulling us like a fish caught by a hook, only to cut the line."

"Does he drive through Hyde Park?"

Julien picked up a pen and seemed to examine it before setting it back down and returning his gaze to Ian. "No."

"You lied. Why?"

"Because the fact that you and Sara are riding in Hyde Park will be mentioned in every drawing room. Surely Floyd will hear about it."

"That's not the only reason, is it?"

"No. I thought it would do you good."

"Damn you, Julien. I don't like being manipulated." His father had done enough of that. "Stop playing matchmaker."

His friend pressed the tips of his fingers to his chest. "Me? A matchmaker? Anyway, you are already married to Sara. The match is already made."

Ian took a large swallow of the whiskey, then stood and set the tumbler on Julien's desk. "Sara and I have made a bargain. Stop whatever you're thinking." Ian headed toward the door.

"I see the way you looked at her."

Ian spun around. "What are you talking about?"

"She intrigues you. When was the last time that happened?"

"I've been intrigued plenty of times."

"No, old chum. Your cock's been intrigued. Have you ever wondered why you only get involved with women like Lady Randall?"

"Because women like Lady Randall don't want much more from me than what I can give them in bed."

"I think there is more to it than that. I think you know that you could never fall in love with them."

"And you believe Sara is capable of making me fall in love with her?"

"She's different from the others. Remember that time we attended a garden party at Westfield's country house? Though nearly every woman wished for your attention, Sara was the only woman you asked me about. She was at the lake, helping the children sail their boats. Do you remember that?"

He did. "Bugger off!"

Julien grinned.

"Wipe that silly look off your face. I married her because I knew she would help with the boys. I married her because I knew some of our prudish business associates would turn their backs on us if I didn't."

"Ian, no one makes you do anything you do not wish to do. You need to ask yourself exactly why you married her."

Ignoring his friend's ludicrous insinuations, Ian continued to the door. At the threshold, he turned around. "I suggest you check on your under-butler. It might be quiet because those two hellions have tied the man up. They did that to the first nanny I hired."

The grin on Julien's face dissolved. "You're kidding, right?"

He arched an eyebrow and strode out of the room.

As Ian made his way home, he thought of what Julien had said. His friend was going mad. He'd not married Sara for any other reasons than he'd stated. Yes, he admired Sara's kindness and intelligence, but that was it. Grumbling, he shoved thoughts of his wife away. His mind quickly settled on the boys. He suddenly regretted not taking Edward and Jacob with him. In truth, he missed the hellions.

Good Lord. What was wrong with him?

He should go to Clapton's Boxing Club and have some

sense knocked into him He slid open the glass front panel in his carriage. "Fletcher, take me to Clapton's."

"Yes, Your Grace," his coachman replied.

After winding through the streets of London, they arrived to find the place closed. Ian uttered a blasphemy. Needing to squash the fidgety energy coursing through him, he gave his coachman a different address. An address to a place he hadn't visited in years.

Chapter Eighteen

The East End was full of questionable activities. Opium dens, illegal gambling hells, along with houses of ill repute where flagellation was practiced. And then there were the underground boxing clubs where one could engage in a bare-knuckled brawl if one were so inclined.

Ian's carriage pulled up to an alley between two brick buildings, and he stepped out of the vehicle. At the end of the dark alley was a green door with chipped paint. He knocked three times, waited a few seconds, and knocked again. As he did so, he wondered if the code and the question one asked to gain admittance had changed over the years.

A small wooden door set inside the massive door opened, revealing a man with a crooked nose. "What's your business?"

"I wish to know if you have the time of day."

The man held his gaze for a long minute, revealing that the question one asked had most likely changed. The fellow's dark eyes drifted over Ian, then he closed the small door. Ian was about to knock again when he heard the click of the bolt being slid back and the door opened. He stepped inside and moved down a long corridor to another door. He opened it and immediately heard the boisterous crowd inside. The place smelled the same as it had years ago—a mixture of sweat and ale. His gaze shot to the ring where two men were throwing punches. One man was dragging his feet as if ready to collapse.

He hadn't visited this establishment in years, but it looked the same. The people gathered here were a mixture of those privileged and those not, but mostly those who were a bit rougher around the edges.

The fellow wobbling in the ring took a facer to his jaw, then folded to his knees before he hit the mat facedown.

The crowd cheered and the count started. When the felled bloke didn't rise, two men stepped into the ring to drag him out.

A man stepped up to the winner and lifted the big brute's fist in the air, declaring him the champion. "Anyone brave enough to challenge McCullum here?" the officiator asked.

Ian shrugged out of his coat and moved toward the ring.

After a late dinner, which Sara had eaten alone, she paced back and forth in her bedroom while staring at the door that connected her bedchamber to Ian's.

Had he really gone to Julien's, or had seeing Lady Randall and Lady Cleary made him regret the bargain he and Sara had made? Once again, she questioned if he had pledged fidelity, or if she had only made herself believe that. She replayed the conversation in her head. He'd said if they lived like husband and wife in every sense of the word, he would not take a mistress. That didn't exclude single assignations, did it?

She needed to know. She changed into her nightgown and settled in bed with a book on the various species of African butterflies. She would wait half the night if need be.

Hours later, Sara set down her book beside her in bed and glanced at the clock. Two in the morning. She would not believe Ian this time if he said he was conducting business, because the only *business* one conducted at such an ungodly hour was more than clear to her.

Hearing noise in Ian's room, she tossed off her bedcoverings and marched to the door. She curled her fingers to knock and, thinking better about it, lowered her hand and opened the door.

The lamp on the mantel sent shafts of light over Ian. He lay flat on his back on the bed. His coat and waistcoat were tossed onto a chair, while his shoes and socks were on the floor.

"Go away, Adams. I don't need your assistance," he said, his words slightly slurred.

Was he drunk? She stepped toward the bed. "It's not Adams."

He tipped his head up and peered at her in the dim room. "Go away, Sara."

She marched toward the bed and gasped at the sight of his bruised face and bloody, split lip. He looked to have been in a fight. She could not see either Lady Randall or Lady Cleary inflicting such wounds. Well, perhaps Lady Randall. No, not even she could do this. "Goodness, were you set upon by thieves?"

"Ha! Thieves I could have handled. McCullum was a

bit tougher. But I took the brute down. The problem was it took twelve rounds."

"You went to a boxing club?"

"Of sorts."

"You told me you were going to Julien's."

"I did. This happened after I left his residence."

"Some people think I'm mad. It appears you are as well."

"Then we are a perfect match."

Frowning, she dashed into his bathing room. Her gaze settled on the massive tub with a three-sided enclosure. She'd seen images of shower baths in advertisements. She pulled her gaze away from the fixture, grabbed a flannel, and wet it at the sink. She returned to her husband's side and dabbed the wet cloth over the blood at the corner of his lips.

He closed his eyes and flinched.

"Who is McCullum?"

"A beast of a man."

"I presumed that. And why were you fighting him?"

He shrugged, in the same manner Edward tended to do.

"Promise me you will never go back there."

"Sara . . ."

"Promise."

"Do you really care if I'm bruised?"

"Of course, I do."

"You said you don't like me."

"Well, I don't hate you either, and I would not want to see even my worst enemy hurt."

"I doubt you have enemies."

"The men at the London Society of Entomologists might not hate me, but they do not like that I am a member."

"Idiots," he mumbled.

She smiled. "You're a bit drunk, aren't you?"

"A bit."

"Will you remember this in the morning?"

"Even if I do, I won't admit to it."

"I didn't think you would. I'll go get some ice."

As she moved to step away from the bed, Ian's hand caught hers. "Just help me up. A warm shower bath will help."

She set her hand on his waist as he stood. "Lean your weight on me."

"No, I'm fine."

"Have you seen the bruises on your face? You're lucky you're still handsome."

"Am I handsome?"

"You know you are, and it appears even McCullum's fist could not ruin your face."

He grinned.

As they stepped into the bathing room and up to the shower bath, Sara noticed that inside the enclosure a pipe soared upward then bent, coming to an end with what looked like a faucet with holes in it. "I've never seen one except in advertisements."

"When the water rains down on you, it feels glorious on the skin. You're more than welcome to join me."

She released his waist. "You're drunk, and I don't want to take advantage of you."

"I'm not that drunk. Just a bit of ale to numb the pain."

"I think you're drunker than you realize. Your speech is slurred."

"Yours would be too, if McCullum had planted several facers on you." He bent and turned the faucet on, then moved a lever upward. As if raining, water poured out of the showerhead.

Fascinated, Sara stuck her hand under it. "It's cold."

"It takes a minute to warm." He fumbled with the buttons at the top of his shirt.

"Let me help you." Releasing a heavy breath, she started unclasping the buttons, exposing his rather impressive chest.

He lifted the garment over his head.

The light in the room seemed to gravitate to him, highlighting the masculine beauty of his body. On their wedding night, though darkness permeated the bedchamber, she'd known Ian's body was something to behold. Her hands had glided across skin pulled taut over firm muscles. Skin she'd touched. Kissed. Tasted.

Her mouth grew dry over the memory. She swallowed, attempting to relieve the parched feeling. Her gaze moved to where a thin band of hair trailed from his belly button to disappear under the waistband of his trousers. It fascinated her. She forced her gaze back to his chest where the beauty of his skin was marred with bruises.

Men. She would never understand them. Agitated at him, she started to turn away.

"Aren't you going to help me with the buttons on my trousers?" he asked.

She felt her cheeks grow warm. "No, you can unclasp them yourself."

One side of his mouth turned up into a lopsided grin.

Sara had a feeling that perhaps he wasn't as drunk as she thought. She moved to the doorway, telling herself not to turn around. But at the threshold, she glanced over her shoulder in time to see him remove his trousers and drawers, then step under the spray of water. His back was to her, and she allowed her gaze to slowly drift over his broad shoulders, narrow hips, and bottom, where tiny little white lines marred the skin. Scars. Barely noticeable, but still there.

As she slipped out of his bedchamber and into her room, she wondered what type of accident had caused them. But besides concern, her mind was also full of lust. A little pulse had beat between her legs as her gaze had taken in his muscular male form. She'd wanted to step up to him and run her palms over him. She'd wanted to open her mouth on his skin and let her tongue taste him.

Nibbling her lower lip, she opened the trinket box on her dressing table and peered at the gold coin he'd given her after their wedding. She'd thought it his arrogance that she should have a coin she could call in like a marker for a night of passion. She'd all but told him she would never use it. She picked it up and stared at the connecting door, while her grandmother's words about a proper woman replayed in her head. Grumbling, she tossed the coin back into the box. Besides Sara's desire to act proper, she didn't wish to fawn over Ian. She'd seen too many silly women do it. Women who didn't understand that he obviously could not offer them anything besides physical gratification. She would not let her lust overtake her sensible mind. Not today. Not tomorrow. Never.

Chapter Nineteen

After a restless night that involved dreams of Ian, Sara rubbed at her eyes. This morning, she'd decided to breakfast in her bedchamber. She realized she was avoiding Ian. Why?

She knew exactly why. It was because of the dreams she'd had after seeing him naked in the shower bath with beads of water glistening on his skin. Wicked dreams with him wearing a loincloth. Wicked dreams in which she'd scattered kisses over his bruised skin. Wicked dreams in which she'd used her teeth to remove the loincloth. She'd woken up to find drool on her pillow.

She could not stay sequestered away for the remainder of the day, especially since Mr. Brown would most likely finish the shelving in her study, and she wished to see the progress.

As she made her way to the west wing, she thought of the scars she'd seen on Ian's backside and wondered if a tutor or some headmaster had struck him when younger. Doubtful; he was a duke's son. Surely his parents would not have allowed such cruelty, leaving her wondering what type of accident had caused them. Shoving thoughts of her husband's rather fine derrière out of her mind, Sara stepped into her study and wrinkled her nose at the smell of the white paint being applied. Mr. Brown had been aghast when she'd told him she wanted the mahogany wood painted until she'd explained that the neutral background would help show off the colors of her butterfly collection.

"Long strokes, Martin. Try not to leave too many brush marks," the carpenter instructed his youngest helper.

"They look wonderful." Sara clasped her hands together.

Paintbrushes stilled. Mr. Brown and his assistants turned and grinned.

"You're pleased, Your Grace?" the carpenter asked.

"More than I can convey. Tonight I'm going to ask Cook to make you fellows a feast."

"You're too kind, madam." A smile lifted Mr. Brown's ruddy cheeks. He turned to the young men. "What do you say, lads?"

"Gorblimey, that would be swell." Martin grinned.

Mr. Brown frowned at the boy. "Watch your tongue."

For a second, Martin looked shame-faced, then his almost perpetual smile reappeared. "Forgive me, ma'am."

Mr. Brown pulled his severe scowl away from the boy and looked at her. "Madam, will you let His Grace know we will be done this afternoon?"

Searching Ian out was the last thing she wanted to do, but she reminded herself she couldn't avoid him forever. "Of course, Mr. Brown."

"Thank you, Your Grace."

As Sara made her way down the stairs to the library, hoping Ian was not home and had gone to Magnus Shipping, she silently scolded herself. She would simply enter the room and tell him he could return to his office later this afternoon. She would not think of how his body looked, and she certainly would not try to imagine him wearing only a loincloth.

She stepped into the library to find it empty, but he'd been there. A silver salver and tea service, along with a cup, confirmed it. She strolled up to the desk and her gaze settled on the cup with tea leaves clinging to the bottom.

Once, when in Soho, Nina and she had visited a fortune-teller who read their tea leaves. The woman, with leathery skin and gray wiry hair, had told them to each ask a question. Nina had asked if she would find true love, and the old woman had studied Nina's leaves and said she would. When it was her turn, Sara worried about asking that question and instead asked if she would always live in her father's house.

"No, you will live in a much grander home," the fortune teller replied.

At the time she'd thought the woman full of balderdash.

Sara stared at the tea leaves in Ian's cup. She remembered the ritual the woman had performed and lifted the cup and began it.

From the doorway, Ian watched as Sara appeared to examine the contents of his teacup with the same attentiveness he presumed she lavished on her butterfly specimens. Memories of how her eyes had widened as he'd lifted his shirt off last night replayed in his mind.

He also remembered Julien's foolish words. He was not falling in love with his wife. He felt lust for Sara. Nothing more. He'd only gone to the East End because he needed to burn off some steam. He watched as Sara swirled the upside-down cup before turning it over in its saucer.

He cocked his head to the side. He'd heard of people

who read tea leaves. Was that what she was doing? He should walk out of the room, but like everything else his wife did, this captured his attention. Unable to pull himself away, he folded his arms over his chest, leaned against the jamb of the door, and watched her.

For what felt like an eternity, but was most likely close to a minute, Sara stared at the upended cup before slowly rotating it three times while still upside down. Then, with a decidedly quick flip of her wrist, she turned it over and seemed to study the remaining contents as if they held the answer to some complex question.

He'd never been a superstitious man, but . . . "What do you see?"

Sara spun around and her eyes seemed to take in his bruised visage. "Does your face still hurt?"

"No." It did, but he didn't like the look in her eyes that said she was confused as to why he would do such a thing. "What exactly are you doing?"

"Nothing."

"All that cup spinning was for *nothing?*" He pushed off the wall and walked toward her.

"I was reading your tea leaves."

"What did you see?" he repeated.

"I don't think I should tell you. You might not be pleased with what the leaves revealed. You see, the question asked before one examines the leaves is most essential."

"Then I guess I should inquire as to what question you asked." He stepped in front of her, leaving only a foot between them.

She tipped her head back and gently touched his jaw. "You cannot tell me this doesn't hurt."

"It doesn't hurt."

"I don't understand you."

He didn't always understand himself. "Tell me the question you asked."

"Do you really wish to know?" The sudden, amused sparkle in her eyes made their hazel color lighter. Sara was more than anxious to reveal what she'd seen.

He'd play along. "Yes."

"Some believe that inside every human is also the power of an animal, whether that is the courage a lion processes, or the keenness of a hawk, or the strength of an elephant. I asked the tea leaves to show me the animal you are most simpatico with."

"It sounds like rubbish to me." He opened the ledger closest to him on his desk and flipped through several pages.

"At first I couldn't make out the shape, but now it is as clear as the bruises on your face."

Feeling foolish over that, he bristled. "Sara, I have work to do. If telling me what you see is the only way to get you to stop staring at my teacup, then by all means do so."

"I really believe it best I don't tell you."

The minx most certainly wanted to tell him; he could tell by the twinkle in her eyes. She probably wished to inform him he was some slithery reptile. "What do you see? A snake?"

"No." She gave a solemn shake of her head. "Not a snake. If you insist on knowing, I will tell you."

"Please do."

"Well, it appears you are a small fluffy bunny with adorable floppy ears."

"A bloody bunny." He scowled, causing his pummeled face to hurt.

"With floppy ears." The corners of her lips turned upward.

"Let me see the teacup."

"No. You're not skilled at reading tea leaves." She tucked it behind her back.

"And you are?"

"Extremely." She gave a small laugh. Not a nervous laugh. A genuine laugh that sounded rather sweet to his ears. He reached for the cup.

Sara stepped backward.

With each step she took, he followed. Their eyes never left each other's faces. Her back and lush derrière pressed against the bookcases, stopping her retreat.

Still holding his gaze, she let the teacup fall to the floor. It made a small *thump* as it hit the carpet. "Oops. I guess you'll just have to take my word for it."

"I think you dropped it on purpose."

"I would never do such a thing." Like a sly cat standing next to an empty birdcage, she grinned.

"I think you are lying." He leaned forward, set the flats of his palms against the wall at her shoulders, and breathed in the clean scent drifting off her skin. As always, it made him want to bury his face against her neck to draw the alluring scent deeper into his nose.

She shivered slightly.

Ian knew it wasn't from fear. Sara was becoming aroused, as he was. Before he could stop himself, he touched the tip of his tongue to the sensitive spot right below her ear.

She drew in a quick breath.

"Now tell me what you really saw, or I'm going to do something that will make you talk."

"Doubtful you could do anything that would make me tell you."

"I think I could. And you just admitted it wasn't a bunny."

Her tongue darted out to wet her lips.

His gaze settled on the movement and how her pink lips glistened. Right now, all he wanted to do was beg her to retire to her bedchamber so he could spend the remainder of the day with her. Both naked. He would call in his marker. To hell with his pride.

"If you don't tell me the truth, I'm going to toss you over my shoulder and carry you upstairs. Then I'm going to—"

The sound of screaming in the hallway cut off his words, and it was then Ian remembered he'd sent a note to Julien this morning asking him to bring the boys back today. Another indication that something was seriously wrong with him.

Jacob and Edward, followed by Julien, stepped into the library.

His friend's gaze took in the sight of how Ian was all but pressing Sara against a wall. A slow smile settled on Julien's face, quickly dissolving when his eyes saw the bruises as well. "Hello, Your Grace, Ian."

With flushed cheeks, Sara ducked out from under his arms, taking her clean scent and the heat radiating off her out of his atmosphere. "Hello, Lord Dartmore, Edward, and Jacob."

Ian had to give Sara credit. Though her face was flushed, she sounded rather calm while he was praying his randy anatomy would go flaccid.

"I would be pleased, Your Grace," his friend said to Sara, "if you would call me Julien."

"Very well. If you'll call me Sara."

Suddenly deflated, Ian turned around and stepped up to Julien and the boys. "I hope you were on your best behavior, lads."

"Egad!" Edward exclaimed. "What happened to your face?"

"Tripped," he said calmly, ignoring the way Julien was staring at him. "Did you both enjoy staying at Lord Dartmore's residence?"

"We played cards, and I won lots of biscuits." Jacob puffed out his chest.

"You also cast up your accounts." Edward crinkled up his nose.

"Yes, a sad fact indeed, but he feels much improved now," Julien said.

Sara gave the boys a tentative smile. "It is nice to have you home."

Jacob smiled.

Edward narrowed his eyes.

"I was about to go into the garden to search for butterflies. Would you both like to accompany me? I have a net each of you could use," she said.

As if the idea pleased Jacob, the youngest boy's smile broadened. But before he could respond, Edward spoke. "No, we have things we need to do." Edward tugged his brother out of the room.

Disappointment settled on Sara's face.

Julien was right. Sara was different from most of the women he associated with. Neither Lady Randall nor Lady Cleary would have wanted to spend time with the boys.

"I shall leave you both to discuss whatever business you

need to attend to. It was a pleasure seeing you again, Julien," Sara said.

"You as well."

Sara walked out of the room.

Damnation. Though Ian didn't wish to feel any emotions with regard to his wife besides lust, he felt her disappointment nearly as clearly as if it were his own. He followed her out into the corridor. "Sara."

She turned.

"Give them time. They will come around."

She nodded and started to walk away then spun back to face him. "Oh, I almost forgot. Mr. Brown will be done with my study today. You can return to your office."

He watched as she walked away. When he stepped back into the library, the silly look on Julien's face didn't escape Ian's notice. "Don't say a word, otherwise I'm going to drag you down to Clapton's Boxing Club."

"Looking at your face, I believe you already did go a few rounds, and your opponent got the better of you."

"No. I got the better of him."

"Really? Well, we don't have time to debate this."

"And why is that?"

"Our new ship is completed. We need to leave for Scotland."

Instead of collecting her net, Sara headed straight into the garden and took a gravel path she hadn't previously noticed. After ten minutes, moving at a brisk pace, she noticed the sun reflecting off a shiny surface, sending shards of sunlight twinkling through the leaves of the trees. Curious, she continued down the path. When she reached a clearing, she came upon a glasshouse that looked to have been abandoned. Various vines climbed halfway up the sides. Moss clung to the lower panes, but the glass structure appeared intact.

Sara walked around it, then pressed her nose to the glass to peer inside. A few clay pots stood on an old wooden table, but little else remained. The rusty hinges on the metal-and-glass door squeaked when she pulled it open. She stepped inside and glanced up at the sun streaming through the pitched roof.

She had always wanted a butterfly sanctuary, and this would be perfect. And it obviously had been abandoned long ago. She wondered why since it didn't appear to leak.

Footsteps caused her to spin around.

The head gardener pulled off his hat, exposing more of his weathered face and his balding pate wreathed with gray hair. "Sorry, Your Grace. I didn't mean to frighten you."

"No worries, Mr. Conners." She glanced around the glasshouse. "It looks like this hasn't been used in years."

"No, madam. Not since His Grace's mother used it."

"I was thinking it would make a wonderful butterfly sanctuary."

The man smiled. "'Twould indeed. The groundsmen and I could clean it up if you wish."

"That would be marvelous."

For the next half hour, Sara and the gardener talked about the plants she wanted brought into the glasshouse after the gardeners returned it to its original glory. Colorful and nectar-rich plants like snapdragons, asters, sedums, and mint would work well.

"Thank you, Mr. Conners," Sara said before heading back toward the house. She'd almost reached the terrace when she saw Ian.

Briefly, she wondered if he'd come looking for her to finish what they'd almost started before the children arrived. However, the concerned expression on his face told her that was not the reason.

"Is something the matter?"

"Julien has informed me that the ship we are having built has been completed. Both he and I need to go to Scotland to finalize the transaction and inspect the workmanship before it travels to London. We need to leave shortly."

"Edward and Jacob and I shall be fine. Go tend to your business."

His warm fingers wrapped about her hand.

The touch both startled her and felt comforting.

"Are you sure?" He raised a brow.

"Yes. Of course. I assure you I can handle two small boys."

An hour later, Sara, Edward, Jacob, and Jeffers stood in the courtyard to bid Ian safe travels. As soon as the carriage made its way down the long drive, the boys darted back into the house.

Sara wasn't sure why, but she experienced a sadness watching the vehicle move away. Why? Her husband was nothing if not taciturn at times, but at other times. . . She thought of how he'd clasped her hand and the look in his eyes when he told her he had to leave.

She was making something out of nothing.

"I'll be in the library, Jeffers, if I am needed."

The butler nodded.

"Also, I wish for Edward and Jacob to eat luncheon with me."

The butler looked as if he wished to say something, but kept his guidance to himself.

Once in the library, Sara searched the shelves, hoping to find books on entomology but after a while, she became distracted by the mural. She stood in the center of the room and viewed the painting. Her gaze drifted over the cherubs and the instruments each held. It was a shame Frederick Armstrong had died at such a young age; his work was breathtaking. Forcing her gaze away, she glanced at the mantel clock. It was almost time for luncheon.

Hoping she could form some type of connection with the boys, she made her way upstairs. Inside her bedroom, the sheer under curtains billowed inward from the wind kicking up outside. Sara wondered who had opened them, since a storm appeared to be brewing outside. She stepped into her bathing room. After she freshened up, she would close them.

Someone knocked on her bedroom door.

Sara peeked her head out of the bathing room. "Come in."

Wallace stepped into the room, carrying a basket with clean clothes. "Will you be going out today, madam?"

"No. I'm going to be having lunch with Edward and Jacob."

Wallace cringed. "I've heard some wicked stories about them, madam. Mrs. Pullman said they frightened off not one but three nannies."

Yes. Ian had told her that.

Wallace opened one of the dresser drawers and frowned.

"Is something the matter?" Sara asked.

"Madam, did you move your undergarments?"

"No. They aren't there?"

With a frazzled expression, Wallace shook her head. "They're gone, madam. All of your drawers are missing."

Gone? That seemed rather odd. Sara was halfway across the room when the wind outside blew one of the sheer curtains sideways and a movement in the birch tree caught her attention. She strode to the window and saw her drawers dangling like decorations on a Christmas tree. She sucked in a breath. Someone had tossed them out this window.

Wallace stepped next to her. "Goodness, madam, who could have done such a thing?"

"I presume Edward and perhaps Jacob, if his brother could convince him."

"Why, the little heathens!" Realizing what she'd said, the lady's maid momentarily slapped her hand over her mouth. "Forgive me, madam. I should not have said that."

She wouldn't scold the woman, since she'd thought something nearly as uncharitable.

Outside, Mr. Conners walked up to the tree. The gardener scratched the back of his head as he peered up at the unmentionables.

A rush of heat flooded Sara's face. She might not like to stand out, so she wore plain clothing, but she did like pretty things. Things that made her feel different than how everyone perceived her. Her corsets and drawers were trimmed with lace, embroidery, and ribbons, and though most were made of linen, she also enjoyed the feel of silk ones against her skin. But now Wallace and Sara weren't the only people who knew she wore such garments. Now they were on display.

She leaned out the window. "Mr. Conners!"

The man glanced up.

His face was as red as she imagined hers to be. "Would you please get a ladder and remove those garments."

"Yes, Your Grace."

By the time he'd returned with a ladder, several of the

gardener's helpers, along with a few staff members, were standing under the bows of the tree staring up. The breeze moved the leaves and the branches, causing the garments to flap in the air like colorful flags being waved in surrender.

Jeffers stepped outside. "Back to work."

Sara doubted the boys would have done that if Ian were home. They probably thought she would become hysterical and leave. They needed to know that whatever they did, she would not go away. They also needed to know she would not allow such a prank to go unanswered.

When younger, Ned had played tricks on her. She'd never gotten mad. No, she'd gotten even. And the boys were about to learn that as well.

While they ate luncheon, both Edward and Jacob kept glancing at her. Obviously , they thought they would see some reaction. Hysterics. Tears. Her storming from the house, promising to never return. Instead, Sara chatted happily with them, pretending she was oblivious to their antics.

Jeffers, on the other hand, stood by the sideboard with a scolding expression that he kept shooting at the boys.

By the end of the meal, Edward appeared confused, while Jacob looked relieved.

After the boys left the dining room, Sara glanced around the massive dining room. "Jeffers, while His Grace is in Scotland, I'd like to take all my meals at the smaller table in the morning room.

"Do you still wish Edward and Jacob to join you?"

"Yes."

The butler blinked as if he couldn't comprehend why. He drew in an audible breath. "Your Grace, might I be so bold as to offer an opinion with regard to Edward and Jacob's earlier behavior."

"Of course, Jeffers."

"If you allow them to behave in such a manner, without any consequences, they will do it again."

She stood. "Oh, I don't intend to allow them to get away with anything."

"But you said nothing to them."

"I don't think raising my voice at them or punishing them in some other way, such as banishment to their bedchamber, would hinder their next plot. In fact, I believe the latter would allow Edward more time to contemplate it."

"Then what do you intend to do?" The man's gray brows pinched together, wrinkling his forehead.

"I have a plan."

Jeffers's eyes grew wide.

"Don't worry, Jeffers. There will be no bloodshed. When younger, my brother, Ned, used to enjoy playing tricks on me. Instead of crying, I decided that two could play at his game. I responded with several pranks of my own. It is what I intend to do with the boys. Do you wish to hear my plan?"

Light sparkled in the butler's eyes. "Yes, madam."

She stepped up to him and in a low voice told him what she intended to do.

Jeffers grinned. "A brilliant idea, madam."

"Do you think I can get several staff members to help me pull it off?"

"They would be honored."

Chapter Twenty

Several of the servants who'd watched the boys scare off nanny after nanny, leaving the staff to watch over the hellions, were more than pleased to help Sara carry out her plan. Even Jeffers still wore an expression of pure amusement.

"Ready?" Sara asked Wallace and Peggy, the upstairs maid who tended to the boys' bedchamber.

Her cohorts in crime grinned broadly and nodded.

On the tips of their toes, they walked by the closed schoolroom door where Mr. Marks was conducting the boys in a lesson.

Once past the doorway, they stepped into Edward and Jacob's bedchamber. It was a cozy space with two tester beds with navy damask bedding. Several upholstered chairs scaled down in size faced a table outfitted with checkers, and a large wooden chest overflowed with toys. On the floor was the largest toy train set Sara had ever seen. Metal toy figures—a conductor, porter, and passengers, stood on the floor near it. A bookcase held children's books and game boards.

This would most likely have been Ian's room when a

child. Sara couldn't help wondering if the toys and books were from his childhood, but the tin figures, unlike the ones her brother, Ned, had played with, were still in pristine condition without a stitch of paint missing. In fact, everything, including the books, looked new.

Sara turned to the maid. "Peggy, did these things come from Edward and Jacob's home?"

"No, madam. His Grace bought all these toys after the boys arrived. There wasn't much in the room before. Only a bed, a desk, and a chair. Not even a candle or lamp."

"No toys?"

"Not a single one."

Sara nodded, wondering if Ian's toys were packed away in the attic. Shoving thoughts of toys away, she grinned at the maid. "Where are the boys' knickers kept?"

"Master Edward's are in this dresser, and Master Jacob's are in that one." The maid pointed to two identical mahogany nine-drawer dressers with shiny brass pulls.

"Let's gather every one of them up. Don't leave any behind," Sara said.

When done collecting the garments, they retraced their steps and, once again, tiptoed by the door of the schoolroom, then made their way belowstairs and into the laundry room, which smelled of tallow, lye, and starch.

A maid folding a tablecloth grinned, then bobbed a curtsy. "Your Grace."

"You know what to do?" Sara asked, dumping the handful of knickers she carried onto a long wooden table.

"Yes, Mrs. Pullman explained it all to me." The maid giggled.

Sara turned to the upstairs maid. "Peggy, you better head back upstairs. Let us know when the boys are done with their lesson."

"Yes, ma'am."

Sara turned back to the laundry maid. "Will you be able to get them all done before the boys complete their school lessons, bathe, and get dressed for dinner?"

"Yes, madam."

"I can help." Wallace took one of the white bibbed aprons down from where several hung from a wooden rail with hooks.

"So can I," Sara added.

The two maids looked at her as if she'd grown a second head. "No, madam, you cannot do that."

"Of course, I can. I have two hands."

"Kind of you to offer, Your Grace," Mrs. Pullman said, stepping into the room, but I'm here to help." Like Wallace, she took an apron from the pegboard and put it on.

"That makes four of us," Sara said, still determined to help.

The women gathered glanced at one another, but none argued.

Eager to get started, Sara unfastened the buttons at her cuffs, rolled up the sleeves of her brown dress, and waited for instructions on how best to accomplish what she'd ask them to do.

Within a short time, they were all laughing, while imagining the boys' reaction to Sara's plan.

When done, Sara, Wallace, and Mrs. Pullman returned to the boys' bedchamber and, with the help of Peggy, they placed the garments back into the drawers.

After they snuck past the schoolroom, and were making their way down the corridor, Sara turned to the housekeeper. "Peggy said all the toys in the room are new. Are His Grace's childhood toys in the attic? If so, I'd like to see if there is anything Edward and Jacob might like."

The housekeeper fiddled with the edge of her sleeve. "No, madam. There aren't any toys up there."

"Were they tossed out years ago?"

The housekeeper nervously tugged at her earlobe. "No, madam."

Something in the woman's expression didn't seem quite right. "Didn't His Grace have any toys?"

"I don't wish to lose my position, madam, nor speak ill of the dead."

The dead? Did she mean Ian's parents? "Whatever you say to me will be kept in strict confidence."

"The last duke didn't think his heir should have any toys. He thought them an idle waste of time. Time his son should be spending in the schoolroom."

"Not a single toy?"

"He had one toy. A tin figure his cousin Finley gave him. Finley was Edward and Jacob's father. Your husband kept it in his pocket, and when the old duke wasn't home, he would play with it. But when his father caught him with it, he destroyed the figure."

"Destroyed it? How?"

"He crushed it with his foot, then tossed it into the hot coals in the grate."

Sara gasped.

"After that, the old duke forbid Finley to visit again."

The backs of Sara's eyes burned. Though she'd never met Ian's father, she suddenly hated him. "What of his mother?"

"She didn't always live at Dorchester Hall. She moved to the country. It was said, she needed the fresh air for her health." Mrs. Pullman's tone clearly betrayed she thought that poppycock.

"You don't believe that was the reason?"

"He was not a kind father or a kind husband."

As Sara continued down the stairs, she experienced a pain in her chest. Her father had not given her much time, but he had not been cruel. It appeared she could not say the same about the old duke.

Ten minutes before dinner would be served, Sara entered the morning room, pleased to see she'd arrived before Edward and Jacob.

Jeffers, who was already standing beside the sideboard, grinned. He inclined his head. "Your Grace."

Though excited over her plan, since speaking with the housekeeper a sadness had settled in Sara's chest over what she'd learned about Ian's father. She thought of the scars on his backside. No. Surely a father would not do such a heinous thing.

"Is something the matter, Your Grace?" The grin on Jeffers's face dissolved.

Jeffers had been employed in the household even longer than Mrs. Pullman. Sara wanted to ask him about the old duke, but bit her lip and forced a smile. "No. I wanted to make sure I was in the room before the boys arrived."

"Understandable." He pulled out a chair at the round table, one facing the door, so when seated she would have an excellent view of the boys when they entered the room.

"Have you heard anything?" Sara sat.

At that moment, Mrs. Pullman stepped into the room, giggling like a young girl. Upon seeing her, the housekeeper placed a hand over her mouth and mumbled an apology. "Forgive me, madam. I did not know you were already in here."

"Don't apologize, Mrs. Pullman. Is your laugh due to what we did earlier?"

A gregarious smile returned to the woman's lips. "Yes, madam. The boys are dressed and should be down shortly. It's a comical sight for sure."

Sara grinned.

A few minutes later, the boys' grumbling could be heard as they approached the morning room. They stepped into the room, looking as if walking was a chore.

"Our knickers are as stiff as a board." Edward grimaced. "They practically stand up all by themselves."

"I can hardly walk," Jacob added, forcing one leg in front of the other.

"Sounds like too much starch. Who would do such a thing?" Sara theatrically placed a hand to her chest.

Both Edward's and Jacob's eyes widened when they suspected who that person was.

"Did you do this?" Edward asked angrily.

"Perhaps it was the same person who tossed my drawers out my bedroom window and into the tree."

Jacob shook his head. "No, it can't be."

"Why not?" Sara arched a brow.

"Because Edward and I did that."

Edward shoved an elbow into his brother's ribs.

Oof! "Why'd you do that?" Jacob narrowed his eyes at his brother.

Edward whispered in his ear.

Jacob's mouth gaped. "She tricked me into confessing!"

Sara motioned to the chairs. "Why don't you boys sit down?"

Grinning, Jeffers moved forward to pull out their chairs.

Both Edward and Jacob grimaced as they sat in their stiff garments.

Edward narrowed his eyes accusingly at Sara. "Admit it. You did this to our clothes, didn't you?"

"I did." She smiled. "Did you expect I'd cry when I saw my drawers waving like flags in the tree? I quite enjoy practical jokes. I especially like to do them after one is done to me. I think that is something you both need to remember."

Edward gave a slight smile. Sara had a feeling that he respected her a bit more than he had yesterday. Hopefully, that would be the end to the pranks, though she wasn't willing to place a wager on it.

Chapter Twenty-One

Five days had passed since Edward and Jacob had tossed Sara's unmentionables into the tree, and she'd responded by starching their knickers. They appeared to have come to some sort of truce. Well, really it was more like the boys avoided her. Though she still insisted that they take their luncheon and dinners together in the morning room. During those meals, she was able to draw Jacob into conversation, while Edward continued to mostly shrug his shoulders when she tried to talk with him.

Sara had hoped by the time Ian returned from Scotland she would have made some progress. But she wasn't giving up. Today, after their school lessons, Sara was determined to spend some time with them, even if it required bribery.

"Thank you, Mrs. McNeil," she said, taking the tin of lemon-flavored biscuits from the cook.

The plump, gray-haired woman, grinned broadly. Since Sara's prank on the boys, every member of the household staff seemed to hold her in high regard, including the two maids she'd caught gossiping about her.

"And you say that these biscuits are both Edward's and

Jacob's favorite?" Sara opened the tin and the scent of the lemon treats drifted to her nose.

"They're like a cat to cream when they see them, Your Grace."

"Then they might work."

The cook's brows drew together in query, as if she didn't understand why Sara wished to befriend them. As if she thought Sara would be pleased to not have to contend with the boys—that their avoidance was a blessing.

She might have her freedom in this house, but she wanted more—some type of connection. Some sense of family. These children might give her that. She made her way upstairs and outside where the boys were running about in the garden. Though the end of May, the weather was extremely warm.

As usual, Edward frowned at her.

Jacob's gaze zeroed in on the tin.

"I thought we could enjoy a treat together."

"I'm not hungry," Edward said.

"Not even for lemon biscuits?" Sara sat on a concrete bench and opened the metal container.

"Did Mrs. McNeil bake them?" Jacob licked his lips.

"She did." Sara lifted one and took a bite, then dramatically closed her eyes, and made a sound as if they were the most decadent thing in the world.

Jacob glanced at Edward, then as if he didn't care whether his brother agreed to join them, he walked over to Sara and sat next to her.

She passed him a biscuit and the younger boy began to gobble it down.

"Oh. I guess I'll eat one," Edward said as if he was doing her a favor.

Sara patted the bench next to her, and after he sat, she passed him a biscuit, then handed Jacob a second one.

By the time the three of them had finished half the tin, they'd been chatting away. Sara told them stories about the pirate Anne Bonny and both boys listened with rapt attention.

Edward stood and brushed the crumbs from his clothes. "Have you walked about the pond?"

"I have, but not with such explorers as yourselves. Would you like to take a stroll along the bank?"

Both boys nodded.

As they made their way there, Sara was startled when Jacob wrapped his small fingers around hers. A sense of hope that she could get the boys to love her lifted her spirits. She glanced at Edward, who trailed them. He was frowning at his brother. It appeared it would take more than lemon biscuits and her knowledge of pirates to win him over.

"Cousin Ian had the pond stocked. Do you like fishing?" Edward asked.

"I've never tried."

"We can teach you. There are fishing rods in the boathouse." A mischievous look settled on Edward's face. Perhaps her prank had not completely detoured the child from thinking he could get the better of her.

Jacob's eyes grew as large as saucers. She had a feeling the younger boy feared his brother was concocting a devious plan.

Once at the pond, Edward opened the door to the boathouse and came out a minute later with three rods, along with a tackle box. With a dramatic flick of his hand, he opened the lid.

Sara eyed the colorful lures, some with feathers and one

with wings that made it resemble a butterfly. They were quite lovely. "I'm excited to learn how to fish. I bet you both will prove to be excellent teachers."

For a minute, the impish look in Edward's eyes dimmed before it returned. "I'll get your rod ready."

Jacob's worried gaze kept veering from his brother to her. Another telltale sign that Edward was up to no good.

After attaching the lure, he pointed to an area where a dock stretched into the water. "That's the best area to cast your line."

Sara peered to where he pointed. The old dock looked rather rickety. Several yards farther up the bank stood a newer dock, its wood not yet weathered.

"I think I'll use that dock instead." She pointed to the less-aged structure.

Edward's expression fell.

"Do you boys know how to swim?"

Jacob puffed out his chest. "We do."

They moved to the new dock and cast out their lines.

They'd been there for about half an hour when Edward's sniffle caused her to peer at the child.

"My line is snagged," he grumbled, attempting to turn the knob on the brass reel.

The vulnerable expression, so different from the distrusting one he usually wore, tugged at Sara's heart.

He sniffled again.

Sara's gaze traveled out from the dock and over the pond's glimmering surface. There were a series of flat-topped boulders that stretched out from the bank and ended no more than a foot from where the child's line appeared to be snagged. If she unhooked it, Edward might be more inclined to accept her. Without further thought, Sara walked to the bank.

"I'll get it." She removed her shoes and stockings and, holding her skirts up so her hems wouldn't get wet, she stepped onto the flat top of the first boulder.

The sad look on Edward's face faltered and a slow smile turned up his cheeks.

For a moment, Sara wondered if she was being bamboozled. She shoved that thought from her mind and leaped to the next massive stone. She'd nearly reached where the line was caught when Edward started reeling it in.

"Look at that. It's not snagged anymore." He grinned.

Why, the little devil. She doubted it had been snagged to begin with. As she turned, her bare foot slipped on a patch of moss.

Off-balance, she tipped forward, then backward. With her arms flailing in the air, she landed in the pond, sending a spray of water upward. Since it was only waist-high where she landed, she brushed her wet, tousled hair out of her eyes to see the startled look on both Edward's and Jacob's faces.

As if he wished to save her, Jacob dropped his fishing pole and ran toward the bank.

Edward was still standing with his mouth gaping like a beached fish.

"I'm fine, Jacob," she called out, making her way to the dock. The closer she got to Edward, the more an expression of nervousness settled on his face.

At the dock, she raised her hand to Edward. "Would you be a dear boy and help me up?"

He clasped it.

"You did say you are an excellent swimmer, correct?"

His eyes grew wide, and he nodded. Knowing it wasn't deep, she gave his hand a tug and he landed in the water next to her. When he emerged from the surface, he stared at her with big brown startled eyes. "You did that on purpose!"

She feigned shock. "I would no more do such a thing as you would send me on a wild-goose chase to unhook a line that you claimed was snagged when it wasn't."

A slow smile turned up his lips.

Using the flat of her palm, she splashed him and laughed.

Grinning, Edward splashed back.

"I'm coming in," Jacob yelled, tossing off his shoes and socks before jumping into the water next to them.

"Wonderful to have you home, Your Grace," Jeffers said to Ian as he stepped into the entry hall.

It was good to be back at Dorchester Hall, Ian thought. The return train ride had seemed interminably long, but all had gone well in Scotland. The new steamer was a glorious vessel and would be arriving in London shortly.

Wondering if Sara was in her study and the boys in the schoolroom, Ian's gaze veered to the stairs. He'd thought about his little wife in her drab brown dresses. How she'd tended to his bruised face with such a gentle touch. He'd even dreamed about her while in Scotland. An erotic dream with her straddling him in his bed, riding him until they both found their pleasure. Sara's hair had been loose, cascading over her naked breasts. As she'd reached her climax, she'd tossed her head back. He'd awoken hard as a brick.

Ian shook himself out of his memory. "Are Sara and the lads upstairs?"

"No, they're outside. Last I saw, they were walking toward the pond."

Ian hoped that meant Sara had made headway with them. Instead of going upstairs to remove his traveling clothes, he headed toward the doors leading outside.

As he neared the pond, he heard screaming.

Good Lord! It sounded as if either the boys were trying to drown Sara, or she was trying to drown them. With his heart beating as fast as a racehorse's, he ran toward the bank.

The air in his lungs lodged itself in his chest as he saw all three in the water. He knew the boys could swim but wasn't sure if Sara knew how. Terrified, his heart stuttered in his chest as he dashed toward them.

As he got closer to the bank, he realized they were not drowning, but swimming and splashing water at one another. Edward's and Jacob's laughter drifted in the air. Sara's as well. When a young lad, he'd swum in the pond when his father wasn't home, but never completely dressed.

"What the blazes is going on?" he asked, his heart still beating erratically from the panic slowly dissipating from within him. After hearing the screaming, unimaginable fear had taken hold of him. Still unable to completely squelch it, he stepped onto the recently built dock.

All three stopped their splashing and turned to him. Rivulets of water dripped down their wet faces. Most of Sara's hair had come loose to trail over her shoulders.

"You're home." Sara swam closer to the wooden structure.

"Yes, and, by God, what are you all about? Have you all gone mad?"

"Well, it's nice to see you as well," she replied tartly.

"I'm waiting for an answer."

"An answer?" she echoed.

The sudden look in her eyes reminded him of the mischievous ones Edward got prior to one of his outlandish schemes. Before he could ask her again what she was about, she splashed him, sending water onto his clothes and down his face.

"That's what we're about."

Why, the hoyden! Sara had spent only a few days with the hellions, and she was already acting like them.

Ian ran his hand over his face, removing the beads of water and shot her a lethal stare.

As if she intended to splash him again, she dipped her open hand in the pond, while a devilish smile lit up her face.

"I'm warning you, Sara, Don't—" He swallowed the rest of his words, along with a mouthful of water when she brazenly splashed him again.

The boys laughed. Edward robustly, while Jacob's guffaws sounded unsure.

"Do that again," Ian said, setting his hands on his waist, "and I'll. . ."

"You'll what?" She giggled.

"I'll—" Another spray of water rained down on him.

That was it! She'd gone too far. He tossed her a menacing expression that he hoped conveyed more than any words he could utter and pulled off his shoes and socks.

The boys' laughter died away.

Sara's eyes widened.

Ian regretted the fact that he would not see her expression when he dove into the water and swam toward her.

* * *

Sara's mouth grew dry as Ian tugged off his socks and shoes. Surely he didn't intend to jump in the water. A wicked look settled in his eyes as he unfastened the gold buttons of his waistcoat. With that gleam in his eyes, she wouldn't toss away the possibility he might be contemplating drowning her.

Oh, why had she splashed him? Perhaps because the boys and she had been having a grand time together, and Ian had arrived with his surly expression and accusations of madness, ruining everything. And here she'd been anxious for him to return. She was a madwoman, indeed.

Ian tossed his waistcoat down, then undid the top buttons of his white shirt and pulled it over his head.

Her gaze traveled down his broad shoulders and muscled torso, then to that tantalizing thin line of hair that ran from his navel before disappearing into the waistband of his trousers. Her mouth grew parched. She had little time to contemplate her physical reaction before Ian moved to the edge of the dock and dove headfirst into the water.

For a moment, she feared that perhaps images of her life should be flashing through her mind instead of lustful thoughts. Her gaze shot to the boys. They appeared as startled as her with their wide eyes and gaping mouths. Surely Ian wouldn't drown her in front of them. Safety in numbers, and all that.

She searched the water. Where was he? She saw the water in front of her ripple only seconds before he came to the surface several feet in front of her.

She took a step back. "Now, Ian, don't do anything rash. I was only playing. I'm almost certain somewhere in our vows you promised to never drown me."

"Hmmm, I didn't realize our vows had been so specific." He took another step forward.

"Obviously, you weren't paying attention." Holding his gaze, she retreated, nibbling her lower lip. She twisted her body away from him and dove under the water. She was an excellent swimmer, but the weight of her wet skirts made kicking her legs difficult.

Ian dove underwater to follow her. His hand caught her ankle, stopping her escape.

Squirming she turned around to fight off his grip. Then he did something unexpected. While under the water, he wrapped his hand around her nape and kissed her.

She stopped squirming, hesitated, then returned his kiss, matching his intensity.

He pulled back. His hands went to her waist, and he brought them both to the surface.

Swiping her hair off her face, she stared at him. He looked as shocked as she felt. As if he hadn't realized his intention until he'd caught up to her.

Sexual tension sizzled between them.

"Does this mean you aren't intent on drowning me?" Her breaths were coming in quick bursts, and she wasn't sure if that was due to the energy she'd expelled trying to get away or because she was completely aroused.

"I think you can make amends in another way, if you wish."

Did he mean what she thought?

Before she could ask, he swam toward the boys and began splashing them.

Sara watched in amazement. Ian rarely interacted with the boys. It was as if he wasn't quite sure how to do so. It brought her back to what the housekeeper had said about Ian's father.

Grinning, Ian turned to her. The smile on his face disappeared. "You're shivering."

Was she? She hadn't noticed. Her mind had reverted to that heated kiss they'd shared under the water.

"That's enough, boys. I best get Sara inside before she catches a chill." He swam over to her. "Do you wish to make amends?"

Almost positive she understood what he meant, she nodded. If being a proper woman meant she could not enjoy joining with her husband in bed, she didn't wish to be proper.

She wrapped her hands around his neck and held his gaze. "I do."

Ian scooped her up in his arms and flashed a devilish smile, sending more goose pimples over her skin, along with anticipation.

Chapter Twenty-Two

As Ian carried Sara into the house, she found herself staring at his chest, specifically the beads of water that glistened on the muscled surface. She had the oddest urge to run her tongue over the droplets. Instead, she set her hand on top of the firm surface, which caused memories of their wedding night and the pleasure she'd experienced to drift through her mind.

The sound of the boys laughing, as they opened the French doors ahead of them, pulled her from her thoughts.

"I can walk," Sara said.

"Oh no. You're not getting away. I'm not a man who forgets or forgives easily, and you have a debt to pay."

She didn't want to get away. She wanted to pay his so-called debt but didn't want everyone whose path they crossed staring at them. No one would take a second look at Edward and Jacob darting through the house with their clothes dripping wet. The staff expected their questionable behavior. However, when they spotted a barefoot Ian marching through the house, wearing only his wet trousers and carrying her, also sopping wet and fully clothed, Ian and she would draw a fair amount of attention.

As they moved past two maids, the young women's eyes grew wide, and their mouths gaped.

"Are you sure you shouldn't put me down? We are making a spectacle."

Before Ian could respond, the housekeeper rushed forward. "Oh my! Did Her Grace fall into the pond?" The gray-haired woman narrowed her eyes at the two boys already making their way up the stairs.

"I slipped," Sara replied.

"Should I send for a physician?" Jeffers asked, stepping up to them, concern in his eyes.

"No. I'll see to my wife's needs," Ian replied, looking quite serious.

A shiver worked its way through her body at the dark tone in his voice, and for minute she hoped she hadn't misunderstood his intent once they got to her bedchamber.

"You don't believe in capital punishment, do you?" she asked after they were out of earshot of the wide-eyed housekeeper and butler.

A burst of laughter escaped his mouth. "No."

"So, I will like whatever you're about to do to me?" she asked in a low voice as he carried her up the stairs.

"If there is something you don't like, you only have to ask me to stop." He moved past her bedchamber door.

Sara gave him a questioning look.

"The shower bath will warm you," he said, obviously sensing her confusion. He walked through his open bedroom door and with the heel of his foot closed it behind them. As he crossed the bedchamber to the bathing room, Sara tried not to stare at the massive bed draped in paisley and brown velvet bed coverings. She also tried not to make a noise as she swallowed the air bubble that expanded in her throat.

"Let's get you out of your wet clothes before you become more chilled." Ian carried her into the bathing room and lowered her to the cool marble floor. His hands moved to the buttons lining her wet dress.

Did he mean to act as her lady's maid? Would he watch her bathe? She fought against the burst of nervousness growing within her. Yet, as his fingers worked at unfastening the buttons running down the bodice of her dress, anxiousness, powered by lust, overtook her discomfort. The front of her gown gaped open, and she helped him push her soaking wet sleeves off her shoulders and arms. The sopping garment landed on the marble floor with a wet *plop*.

His eyes seemed to take in her sky-blue satin corset with lace and bows. She knew what he was thinking. The garment was lovelier than her brown dress. Now Ian knew what most of the servants in this household knew—that she liked to wear unmentionables that were a contradiction to most of her dresses.

Though she'd been embarrassed when the servants found out, Ian knowing sent a shiver of delight through her.

With ease, he unfastened the clasps on her corset, reminding her that he had played lady's maid before. As if he liked this garment more than her dress, he laid it over the back of a chair instead of tossing it on top of the dress.

He turned away, and she wondered if he wasn't going to remove her last garments. The thought that he might not continue to undress her left her disheartened. With the removal of each garment, she'd grown warmer. More lustful.

"It takes a minute to warm up," Ian reminded her, turning the lever. Water sprayed from the showerhead. He turned back to her and pulled loose the ribbons at the top of her shift, then lifted it over her head.

Sara stood there in only her drawers, while she fought the urge to clasp her hands over her breasts. Instead of acting the shy maiden, she surprised herself by untying the blue ribbon that held her drawers at her waist. The weight of the wet garment caused it to slip over her hips and legs, then to the floor.

Ian's heavy-lidded gaze traveled over her. He closed the small gap between them and whispered, "A body like yours should be wrapped in brightly colored satin and silk, not wools and cotton in shades of brown."

Before she could respond, he scooped her up into his arms and set her in the tub. She knew she should feel self-conscious, but his seductive words about her body had bolstered her confidence, and she stepped under the water. Closing her eyes, she tipped her face up, allowing the crystalline spray to rain down on her.

"What do you think?"

"It feels wonderful," she replied, her eyes still closed. She was so involved in the feel of the water, it took her a few seconds to realize that Ian now stood behind her. He pulled her body back against his, and she felt the hard length of his erection. She turned around and let her gaze drift over him from his broad shoulders, down his lean hips to his protruding erection. When her gaze moved back to his face, he was intently looking at her. Did he think she would become squeamish and dart out of the room? No. A pulse that cried to be soothed beat between her legs. Before she could examine her thoughts, Ian framed her face with his hands and brought his mouth to hers. His kiss was hard at first, then it softened, and he coaxed her lips apart. She rubbed herself against him, trying to soothe the clawing need building within her.

One of his hands slid from her waist upward to cup her breast.

A moan of pleasure escaped her lips.

Slowly, almost maidenly so, he circled one of her nipples with his index finger before he cupped her derrière, lifting her up. "Wrap your legs around me."

She did, locking her ankles behind his back.

He bent his head to capture her nipple with his mouth.

Oh Lord. With the warm water raining down on them, while Ian's tongue lapped at her nipple, she thought she might climax from that alone. Her breathing grew heavy, sawing in and out of her lungs.

The next thing she knew, he'd reached behind her, turned the water off, and was carrying her into his bedroom.

Quick strides brought their wet bodies to his bed, and without pulling down the bedcoverings they tumbled onto the mattress, landing on their sides. His mouth met hers, firm and demanding.

Eager for what lay ahead, she answered with the same intensity.

His tongue slipped past her lips.

She savored the erotic way their tongues touched and tangled. This type of kiss made her wet with desire.

Ian rolled onto his back, taking her with him. Now she was on top. He pulled her upward, so her breasts were above his mouth. When he set his tongue against the pebbled tip of one, she closed her eyes and centered her senses on that single touch—wet and warm. A hum of pleasure eased from her lips.

"You like that?" he asked, his voice gentle.

"Yes." Her own voice sounded foreign. Low and husky. Perhaps from the yearning ache weaving through her body, making every nerve she possessed more aware than she could recall.

Ian moved his mouth to her other breast and did the same thing until she began panting.

Shifting positions so she lay beneath him, Ian braced his hands beside her head, bringing his face even with hers. His dark pupils were large in his blue eyes. He looked like a drugged man. It amazed her that she could do this to him. That she held such power. She'd never known what it was like to be desired. And Ian might not love her, but he desired her. In this realm they were equals. Never in her life had she felt like an equal. It wasn't one-sided. She desired him as well, especially after he'd showed his playful side at the pond. Though she couldn't explain precisely how she felt about her husband. He was so distant at times. But she believed it was his way of protecting himself. But from what?

"I want to do something to you."

His words tugged her from her musings. Her heart rate increased. "Something? Will it be painful?"

A slow smile turned up his sinful mouth. "No. I hope it will bring you pleasure. If you don't like it, you just need to tell me to stop."

She wanted whatever he alluded to. She nodded.

He propped two pillows against the headboard. "Scoot up and put your head on these."

She did as he asked.

He pressed a soft kiss to her mouth, then one to her neck. Next, each of her breasts. The press of his lips was so light, it made her want more. But she realized that it was meant to tease. To draw her yearning higher, and it worked. She subdued the urge to squirm with pent-up desire.

Ian's tongue dipped into her belly button, and when his

mouth moved even lower on her abdomen, she realized he was slowly trailing a path to her sex.

She quivered with both curiosity and apprehension about the unknown.

His lips pressed little kisses to the inside of her thighs. He stopped and looked at her. "Spread your legs."

She did so and watched as he settled between them. His mouth only inches from her sex. Now there was no question as to what he intended to do. Anxious to experience the pleasure he promised, she pressed her heels into the mattress and arched slightly.

"How you surprise me." His warm breath ghosted across the dampness between her legs.

She surprised herself. She recalled her grandmother's words about duty to one's husband in the marriage bed. This didn't feel like a duty. She loved the feel of Ian's body rubbing against hers. Loved his kisses. Loved every aspect of what they shared when in bed.

When Ian's mouth touched her sex, Sara almost bucked. The sensation, though pleasant, felt foreign, wicked, and sublime. She wanted to toss her head back and close her eyes, but watching Ian's head between her thighs added to the erotic experience, especially when he looked up at her and she saw the lust in his eyes before he dipped his head again and set his tongue against her. It was as if every nerve in her body now gathered in that spot where his tongue delved, stroked, and teased.

She felt herself climbing to that pinnacle of pleasure. Any minute it would overcome her, as it had on her wedding night. In the quiet room, she heard her breaths sawing in and out of her lungs, growing faster. As her climax overcame her, she pinched her lips tight to stop her scream, but could not stop her moan.

For a minute, she thought she floated as the pleasure washed over her. She was returning to the here and now when Ian settled his hips between her legs.

Her body welcomed him, pulsing around him, drawing him in.

His mouth found hers as he settled deeper into her.

She waited for him to move, but instead he held her gaze. "There will be no more coins or waiting a fortnight, agreed?"

She didn't want to wait a fortnight. She nodded.

Smiling, he moved in that rhythmic way.

As her hands traveled over his warm, damp skin, the little pulses in her body grew again and another wave of pleasure washed over her. He thrust once more then stilled, and she knew he'd found his pleasure as well.

Chapter Twenty-Three

Over the next several days, there was a shift in Sara and Ian's relationship. Ian visited her bed every night, but in the morning, she'd always awaken to find him gone. She would not lie to herself and say she did not enjoy their time in bed. She did. Tremendously. Their nights were full of passion, or perhaps *lust* was a better word for it.

But during the day, it was as if Ian worked at not growing closer to her. At one time, she had felt the same way—a strong need to keep her heart uninvolved. But lately . . . It wasn't because of what they did in bed together that had changed her mind about guarding her heart, it was the tenderness of Ian's touch and the occasional concerned looks he flashed at her. Brief, but there. Like his expression at the pond when he'd said he didn't want her to catch a chill.

However, as soon as she believed she was dismantling the wall he'd built up, he would place another brick on it. She thought about how he'd admitted to loving someone and realized that her husband who seemed so strong on the outside guarded his heart with a vengeance.

Last night before he slipped from her bed, she'd asked about the scars on his backside. He'd said he'd once fallen on a hot fireplace grate and burned himself. The way his jaw had tightened as he told the story made her wonder if that was the truth.

A knock on her bedroom door pulled her from her thoughts.

"Sara, are you in there?" Jacob called out.

She opened the door.

"Are you ready?" Jacob grinned.

"Yes." She picked up the three butterfly nets she'd set on her bed. It had taken Sara a great deal of convincing to get Edward to agree to go searching for the rare swallow-tail butterfly in the garden with her. Jacob, on the other hand, had quickly agreed.

"Where is Edward?" For a minute, she feared the older child had changed his mind.

"He's already in the garden waiting."

Well, that was a surprise.

A few minutes later, they meandered through the gardens. So far, they had only seen butterfly species common to this area of England.

"Stop it, Edward," Jacob said.

Sara glanced over her shoulder to see the older child had set his net over his brother's head. Before she could say anything, Edward removed it and grinned.

When the boy smiled at her, it was so unexpected, it made Sara want to smile back, but his devilment needed no encouragement.

"Is that it?" Jacob pointed to the sky where a butterfly fluttered over them.

"That's a monarch. It's lovely, but the butterfly we are searching for possesses yellow wings with black, blue, and red markings."

They walked past the manicured parts of the garden to

where there were fewer flowers. Sara was about to suggest they turn around when she heard what sounded like the mewling of a kitten. "Did you hear that?"

Jacob nodded. He bent and peered under the bush closest to him.

"No, it came from here." Edward scrambled onto his knees and searched the shaded area below the evergreen bush to his right.

The kitten made another noise.

"I see him!" Edward said. "He's white with gray spots."

Sara crouched and squinted into the dark underbrush. "Oh, he's lovely."

Edward reached for the kitten and held him up with its white belly facing outward. "Can we keep him?"

The hopeful expression on both boys' faces almost broke Sara's heart. She wasn't sure if Ian liked cats. "We'll have to ask your cousin Ian."

They frowned.

"Do we have to? We could hide him in the house." Jacob's eyes widened with hope.

"We can put him in the schoolroom," Edward said. "Cousin Ian never goes in there. Mr. Marks won't tell if you ask him not to."

They could, but she believed someone on the staff would eventually mention the kitten to Ian. No, it was best to ask. Though she could wait until Ian was in an agreeable mood. "Very well. For now, we can leave him in the schoolroom."

Both boys beamed with delight.

"But we'll need to take him outside several times a day." Sara scratched under the tiny kitten's chin.

His purr rumbled in the air.

"Can we name him Snowball?" Jacob ran his hand down the cat's back.

"I think that's a splendid name," Sara said.

Edward crinkled his nose, but seeing the hopeful look on his brother's face he agreed. "I'll sneak him inside." Edward tucked the kitten under his shirt.

After the boys made their way to the schoolroom, a pang of guilt settled in Sara's chest. She really needed to ask Ian about the kitten. No, she would not ask. She would simply inform him they had a new pet. This was the boys' house as well as hers.

She squared her shoulders and strode to his office to find the door open and the room empty. Well, she would tell him after her meeting at the London Society of Entomologists.

Sara had just stepped into her bedroom to get ready for her meeting when someone banged loudly on the door. She opened it to find Edward and Jacob, breathing heavily.

A tingling sensation moved through her body, causing an explosion of nerves in her stomach. "What is wrong?"

"Snowball wiggled out of my arms and took off." Edward bit his lower lip.

"We need to find him before Cousin Ian sees him," Jacob added.

"Yes. That would be for the best," Sara said, stepping into the corridor to help them search for the wayward kitten.

As Ian made his way to his office, something small and furry dashed down the corridor. Either he was hallucinating or that was a kitten. He started to follow it but the chatter in his office drew him to the room.

At the doorway, he spotted a set of legs sticking out from under his desk.

Edward's legs.

He presumed the lad was looking for the furball. His gaze pivoted to the settee where two people had their heads tucked under it. Easy to identify Jacob's small frame. Even easier to identify his wife's shapely and rather fine derrière, which was in the air since she was on her hands and knees.

His gaze slipped to her trim ankles, which were visible from where her skirt had ridden up the back of her silk-clad calves. One thing he'd learned about Sara was that though she seemed to hide behind drab colors in muted shades of brown, her undergarments were as seductive as a French courtesan's.

"Do you see him, Jacob?" Sara asked.

"No."

"He's not under here either." Edward crawled out from under the desk. He turned around and his eyes grew as round as the moon when he spotted Ian in the doorway.

Ian pressed his index finger to his lips, motioning to the child to remain mum, then he stealthily stepped up to the settee and cleared his throat.

Jacob sucked in a clearly startled breath.

Sara grew as still as a petrified tree.

"Might I ask what you are looking for in my office?" Ian crossed his arms over his chest, anxious to hear what fantastical response he was about to get.

Both Sara and Jacob scrambled to their feet.

"Dust bunnies," Jacob said.

He had to give the child his due for being quick with a response. "Really? I cannot imagine why."

"It's a game," Edward added. "We're trying to see who can find the largest one."

He peered at his wife. "Is that true, Sara?"

Unlike the boys, she appeared inept at lying, since she just stared at him, mute.

"*Cat* got your tongue?" he asked.

That made her eyes grow large. "You saw him?"

"Yes, he just darted down the hall. Edward, Jacob, I suggest you both go and find him."

They looked at Sara as if unsure whether to leave her alone with him.

Good God. Did they think him such an ogre? He would never hurt Sara. Never strike anyone as his father had him. Never. They had to know that by now after all their antics. "I would never do anything to harm either of you or Sara. You realize that, don't you?"

"Yes," Edward said without hesitation.

Jacob nodded.

He'd misread the look on their faces.

"We don't want you to scold Sara," Edward said. "We begged her to let us bring him into the house before asking you. So it's not her fault."

Ian felt almost speechless. Edward was sticking up for Sara. He wondered when the lad had become Sara's champion. Pleased, he smiled. "I promise I won't scold her. Now run along and go find that kitten."

"Go on, boys. See if you can track him down," Sara added, giving them a reassuring smile.

As soon as the boys walked out of the room, Sara stepped close to him. "Don't make them give the kitten away. They have lost so much."

"Did you get it for them?"

"No." She shook her head. "We found him while walking in the garden. He's a bit wild, which is not uncommon when a kitten is not coddled by its mother, but I'm hoping with the boys' love he might make a good pet."

He'd never owned a pet. At their country residence, the hounds were not allowed in the house, and Father forbid petting them, since he believed it made the dogs soft.

"I bet he'll be a great mouser," Sara said.

He released a long, drawn-out breath. "Very well."

"I *knew* you wouldn't make them give him away."

She was correct. He wouldn't have.

"I'll go tell the boys." With a broad smile, Sara tipped herself up on her toes and kissed his cheek before she darted out of the room.

Grinning, Ian sat at his desk and opened a ledger. As he wrote several figures onto the pages, he heard a low, rather creaky meow. The small feline slinked into the office with its head held high as if flaunting the fact that he'd ingratiated himself into Dorchester Hall.

"Of all the rooms in this house, it's my office you decide to hide in? I'm trying to work. Go away."

Ignoring him, the animal meowed again.

Damnation. The little beast was already distracting him. He had enough distractions. Namely his wife. He placed his hand over his cheek where she'd kissed him. It had been a sweet kiss. Nothing like the passionate ones they shared at night, which left him randy during the day and eager to join her in bed. It wasn't purely lust. Julien was right. Sara intrigued him, more than any woman had in his life. Yesterday, he'd found himself standing outside her study listening to her give a lesson on butterflies to Edward and Jacob. Her voice had sounded lyrical, and he'd fought the urge to step into the room so he could watch her animated face.

Something brushed against his legs.

He glanced under the desk to see the kitten. "You're still here? Shoo."

As if Ian's words held little significance, the cat squinted his almond eyes at him as though Ian was an imbecile who didn't realize who was in command of this situation.

Ian arched his brow at him.

Like everyone else lately, it seemed to have little effect on the furball.

"Aren't there some mice you can find?"

The kitten responded by sitting on Ian's shoe.

He had to admit the beast was rather cute with all that white fur. He glanced up at his open door and seeing no one about, reached down and ran his hand over the kitten's back.

The feline purred.

Ian rubbed him under his chin. "Don't get used to this."

Someone cleared their throat.

Ian hastily straightened to see Jeffers standing in the doorway. "I dropped my pen."

The butler's gaze shifted to Ian's hand where there was no pen; then the man had the audacity to flash his over-sized teeth.

"Is there something you want?" Ian flipped to a page in the ledger on his desk.

The butler shook his head. "No, I was helping look for Snowball."

Good Lord. Snowball. That was what they'd named the kitten? He would grow up emasculated with such a name.

He should have a strong name. Hercules or Zeus, or something in that vein.

"You haven't seen him, have you, Your Grace?"

"No." He hoped the kitten wouldn't be a traitor and make a noise, though he doubted the butler was believing any of the hogwash he was spouting.

The butler's grin broadened, but he said nothing and left the room.

As if the kitten realized it was safe to make a noise, he let out another creaky meow and rubbed up against Ian's legs.

"Very well, I'll pick you up, but only because I don't want you putting hair on my trousers." Ian lifted the kitten and rubbed him under the chin, causing the kitten to purr loudly.

Sara, Edward, and Jacob were searching the library for the kitten when Jeffers stepped into the room. "Madam, I think I know where the kitten is."

Relieved, she clasped her hands together. "Where?"

The butler walked up to her and in a low voice told her what he'd just witnessed.

Sara couldn't halt her laugh. "Edward, Jacob, you might as well return to the schoolroom. Jeffers has found him, and I will bring him upstairs in a bit."

They nodded.

As soon as they were out of the room, Sara turned to Jeffers. "Are you sure he was petting him?"

"Quite." An amused expression settled on the butler's face.

Smiling, Sara made her way to Ian's office. As she approached it, she heard him talking.

"You are such a greedy puss. Needing me to stroke you every few minutes."

Sara tiptoed to the doorway to find Ian staring down at his lap. "Did you find Snowball?"

Ian glanced up, looking like a child caught with his fingers plucking the marzipan off a cake.

"The little furball jumped onto my lap, and I was trying to get him off."

"Really?" She walked to the desk. The kitten was looking at Ian as if he were a god.

"Yes, really." He lowered the cat to the rug.

She'd never seen Ian blush, but a slash of red highlighted his cheeks. Feeling a laugh bubbling up in her chest, she attempted not to laugh, but couldn't help her grin.

"It's not funny, Sara. The animal will be a nuisance. I should never have agreed to allow him to stay."

"Do you wish him to be relegated to the stable?"

"No," he said rather quickly. "That wouldn't be fair. He is already used to the house."

The man was as transparent as a pane of glass. Whether he wished to admit it or not, he liked the kitten.

Snowball pranced over to her, and Sara scooped him up into her arms. "I hear you've been a naughty boy." She ran her hand over the cat's back. "Was that grumpy duke admonishing you?"

"I most certainly was." Releasing a heavy breath, Ian flipped to a page in the open ledger in front of him. "Is there something you wished to discuss? I need to get back to my work."

"Would you like me to leave Snowball so you can pet him some more?" Sara grinned.

"I told you, I was not petting him. He was bothering me." He flashed that cool look he was rather skilled at giving.

She was starting to learn it was an act. "I have a meeting at the London Society of Entomologists, so I will be leaving shortly."

"You do not need to tell me, Sara. You are free to come and go as you please." He returned his attention to the ledger, then glanced up. "Have we received any replies from the Governess and Nanny Association with regard to a new nanny for the boys?"

"None."

Ian rubbed at the back of his neck. "Perhaps I should run an advertisement in the *Daily Telegraph*."

"While in town, I'll see to it."

"You wouldn't mind?"

"No, not at all."

"Thank you."

"Are you sure you don't want me to leave the kitten?" She ran her hand over Snowball's back.

"No. Both of you out!"

Chapter Twenty-Four

After Sara changed into a brown and cream striped satin day dress that she'd bought from Madame Renault's, she walked out into the courtyard where Jasper waited with her carriage.

"Your Grace." The coachman bowed his head and opened the vehicle's door.

"Hello, Jasper. Before we go to the London Society of Entomologists, I'd like to stop at the Governess and Nanny Association on Weymouth Street."

"Yes, madam."

Sara had decided that instead of placing an advertisement again, she would visit the association who had sent the three previous nannies, but none since.

Once there, she entered the brick building to find a narrow room with a young woman sitting at a desk. "May I help you, madam?"

"Yes, I'm in need of a nanny."

The woman's gaze took in Sara's costly attire. "I'll see if Mrs. Reynolds can see you. Might I have your name?"

"Mrs. McAllister," Sara said, purposely omitting that she was the Duchess of Dorchester.

The woman motioned for Sara to be seated, then walked down a long hall.

A short time later, she returned. "Mrs. Reynolds can see you now. Please, come this way, madam." The secretary showed her to an office.

Mrs. Reynolds, a short, sturdy woman, stood and shook her hand. "What may I help you with, Mrs. McAllister?"

"My family is in need of a nanny."

"Well, we can surely help you with that. We have many skilled and eager women here. Now, can you tell me how many children and their ages?"

"Two boys. Ages seven and eight."

The woman wrote the information down.

"Might I ask your husband's occupation?"

"He is in trade."

"Will the nanny have a room of her own?"

"Yes."

"Very good. I have three candidates that I think would be perfect for the job."

"Wonderful." Sara beamed at the woman.

"Do you wish to conduct the interviews now?"

"That would be lovely."

The first two nannies seemed qualified. But the current one Sara was interviewing, Miss Georgiana Turner, who looked to be in her late thirties, seemed the most suitable. The woman possessed a jovial nature and had admitted to having been raised in a family with five brothers.

"Did your brothers ever play tricks on you?" Sara inquired.

"Yes. Do you have bothers, Mrs. McAllister?" Georgiana asked.

"I have one."

"Then you know they can be high-handed at times and act like tricksters, but I gave back as good as I got."

Mrs. Reynolds, who remained in the room during the interview, cleared her throat as if she didn't think the woman's response appropriate, but Sara thought it perfect.

"Miss Turner, might I ask why you are searching for new employment?"

"I served as nanny to a family with three boys, but they have all gone off to school. My employers offered me the job of housekeeper, since theirs was soon to retire, and though I had come to love the family, I wish to continue working with children."

"Here is her letter of recommendation from the family," Mrs. Reynolds said, handing Sara the letter.

Sara read over the glowing reference. "Would you be available to start in two weeks?"

"Yes, madam. I could start today if you wish," the nanny replied.

"No. Two weeks is fine. You see, I'm newly married, and I am getting settled with the boys, who are my husband's wards."

Mrs. Reynolds blinked as if a warning bell was going off in her head. "You said they are seven and eight?"

"Yes."

"Might I ask where you reside, Mrs. McAllister?"

"Dorchester Hall, Richmond."

A wave of ashen color lightened Mrs. Reynolds's complexion. "You are the Duchess of Dorchester?"

"I am."

The woman peered at Miss Turner. "Georgiana, will you leave us for a minute?"

As soon as the door closed behind the nanny, Mrs. Reynolds spoke. "Your Grace, we have already sent three nannies to Dorchester Hall. I hope you will forgive my boldness in what I am about to say, but the nannies informed me of the horrors they faced at the hands of those two boys. Mrs. Winterbottom said that a zookeeper should be sent to handle them."

Zookeeper? Anger bristled in Sara. "Obviously, Mrs. Winterbottom was not the right person for the position. I believe Miss Turner will be a perfect match. She grew up with brothers and is aware of how rambunctious they can be. I wish her to start in two weeks." Though Sara's stomach fluttered, she stood and gave the woman a look that she hoped made it seem like her decision was final.

Mrs. Reynolds stood. "Very well, Your Grace."

Delighted over her success at hiring a nanny who seemed a good match for the boys, Sara walked into the London Society of Entomologists to be greeted by the broad smiles of those in attendance. Men bounced up from their chairs and bowed as deep as Henry Irving after a performance at the Lyceum Theatre.

"Your Grace, so lovely to see you," Mr. Young said.

"We're so glad you could attend," Mr. Grayson added. The man grabbed her gloved hand and almost drooled on it.

She glanced around, wondering if they'd taken to drinking at the society, since this greeting surpassed the one she'd received at their last meeting.

She spotted Henrietta Bailey and Mary Plum sitting in the front row. Both women turned and flashed cheerful smiles.

Making her way through the almost fawning horde of

men, Sara sat next to her friends. "Have they been drinking? Before the meeting, did they visit that new gin palace?"

Henrietta chuckled. "You don't know why they are in such jovial moods?"

"I have no inkling."

"They are over the moon about the generous gift you and His Grace gave to the society."

Sara blinked as her mind grappled with what Henrietta had said.

Her face must have revealed her shock because Henrietta tipped her head to the side. "You truly didn't know?"

Before she could respond, Mary beamed at her. "Your husband must have wanted to surprise you with such a substantial gift. How utterly romantic."

She forced a smile. Both women peered at her as if they envied the love Ian must have for her, causing Sara to feel like a fraud.

Mr. Graham stepped up to where they sat. "Your Grace, on behalf of all the members, I would like to thank you and His Grace for such kindness to the London Society of Entomologists. And as your husband has requested, our reading room will be renamed in your honor."

What? Sara suddenly felt rather dizzy. The amount Ian had gifted for them to rename the reading room after a woman had to be quite substantial. "You are more than welcome, Mr. Graham."

"Your Grace, do you have something you wish me to read to the group or wish to read yourself?"

"No, Mr. Graham."

He turned to Mary. "How about you, Miss Plum?"

"Nothing today, sir."

He shifted his regard to Henrietta and a softness settled in his eyes. "Miss Bailey?"

"No, Mr. Graham."

It was odd that Henrietta didn't realize how Mr. Graham cared for her. His emotions all but radiated out of him when he looked at her. And it was Sara's turn to truly feel envious.

Sara returned home and quickly made her way to Ian's office. She wanted to thank him for his benevolence to the London Society of Entomologists and for asking them to name the library within it after her. She wondered if it had anything to do with what she'd told him—that the men there did not appreciate female members. Doubtful. It was probably just another way for him to make others believe he loved her. But for her, it was a prized gift.

She stepped into his office to find him standing by the window, looking out into the garden. She'd noticed since living here, he rarely walked in it. No, he was always working, amassing more wealth. Though he'd said he liked overseeing his finances, she wanted to know what really drove him.

He faced her, and she wondered how one who possessed eyes that could be so assessing could also radiate such heat within her. Perhaps it was because she'd experienced firsthand what his mouth and body could do to her.

"Thank you," she said.

"For?" He casually leaned back against the sill, allowing the sun streaming through the pane to highlight his handsome face.

"Your gift to the London Society of Entomologists." She held her breath, hoping he would say something. Anything that would show he'd not done it as just a way to sway others into believing that he loved her, but that he'd done it because he truly did care for her.

"I'm glad it pleased you."

Though not an admittance of undying love, it was a step. "I have hired a new nanny, whom I believe is the perfect match for the boys. She grew up with five brothers, so I think they will have their work cut out for them."

He stared at her for a long moment. "Where did you find her?"

"The Governess and Nanny Association. I didn't tell them who I was, at least not at first, and Mrs. Reynolds set me up with three candidates to interview. Miss Turner will start in two weeks." Sara beamed proudly.

"Well done." He grinned, then the pleased look on his face slipped away.

The quick change in his expression caused the hairs on her nape to prickle.

He walked over to his desk and lifted what looked to be an invitation. "We have been invited to a ball at Bertram Floyd's residence. I think if we are to convince Floyd that our marriage is a love match, we should take to the floor and waltz at least once."

Sara's stomach clenched. "I don't care for dancing. And I don't believe anyone would question me not doing so. They know . . ." Her voice trailed off. Everyone knew about the angst she suffered at balls when asked to dance. She could feel the flush of warmth working its way up her neck to settle on her face.

"Why do you think you laugh when asked to dance?" Ian inquired.

She peered down at the rug, then back at him. "During my first ball, I worried I'd forget the steps and trip. That I'd not only fall but drag my partner down as well. I became so nervous that I began to laugh. Somewhere along the way, my fear about falling became secondary to my fear of laughing."

Ian nodded. Not in a judgmental way, but as if he understood. "I saw you dancing with Lord Ralston once."

Sara recalled how Nina's husband had once bumped into her at a ball and noticed her dance card was blank. He'd kindly asked her to waltz. How did Ian remember that incident? Silly question. Probably everyone in attendance had watched and waited to see what would happen. If she'd had her eyes open, while dancing, she would have seen women whispering behind their fans and men staring blatantly at her—all waiting to see her make a fool of herself. But she hadn't.

"When I started to get nervous, Lord Ralston suggested that I close my eyes."

Ian's brows lifted. "And that helped?"

"It did. He told me he would carefully guide me through the steps."

"Then that is what we will do. You can close your eyes while I lead you. Perhaps you won't need to close your eyes. You've never seemed that nervous with me."

"We've never danced together."

A slight smile tipped up the left side of his mouth. "You've danced with me, Sara."

Sara knew what he was thinking—that they engaged in something so much more intimate. Surely if she could do such things with him, she could waltz. Yet she feared she might not be able to. She fought the urge to avoid his direct gaze. Instead, she tipped her chin up. "We didn't have an audience. Everyone will be staring at us, waiting for me to make a cake out of myself. They will anticipate it, and so will I, which will increase my anxiousness."

He rubbed the back of his neck. "I have to attend to some business this evening at my club." He pulled out his pocket watch. "Before I go out, why don't we meet in the ballroom in two hours? We can practice waltzing."

Practice? Her heart fluttered before it picked up speed. She didn't want to practice dancing with Ian. Was she telling herself a lie? Yes. Some part of her. The part that wished she didn't get nervous wanted to dance with him— wanted to overcome her fear. But dancing in an empty ballroom was not the same as dancing in a crowded one. But perhaps if she closed her eyes once again, she could do it.

Or she could fall flat on her face and send them both tumbling to the floor.

Chapter Twenty-Five

Before going downstairs for her dance lesson with Ian, Sara eyed the gowns she'd bought from Madame Renault's shop. Her gaze settled on the ruby red one with a low décolletage. Though the bodice was not as revealing as the shepherdess's gown she'd worn to the Farnsworths' masquerade ball, it was more revealing than any of the others Madame Renault had made. And not like any of the girlish gowns her father had insisted she wear. As soon as she'd walked into the modiste's shop, she'd been drawn to the vibrant bolt of material like a butterfly to nectar.

Madame Renault had stepped next to her and in her lilting accent had said that a gown made of such a brilliant shade would bring out the color of Sara's cheeks and lips.

Wringing her hands together, Sara had stared at the fabric, then impulsively ordered a gown made from the material. She had not expected Madame Renault to style it with off-the-shoulder sleeves and a décolleté neckline, along with extravagant beading and embroidery, but the woman had told her it was the height of Paris fashion.

Sara ran her hand down the silk, doubtful she would

ever wear such a garment in public. One could never blend into anonymity in such a bold gown.

The mantel clock in her room chimed the hour.

She was late for her dance lesson with Ian. Not that she was in a hurry. She felt like the butterflies she studied fluttered in her stomach. She closed the armoire and stepped out of her bedchamber. As she headed toward the ballroom, she repeated in her head, *I will not giggle. I will not giggle. And I will not fall.*

Drawing in a deep breath, Sara stepped through the open double doors of the massive ballroom. A sudden tightness settled in her chest. This was the last place she'd seen her father alive. How many times had she relived that evening in her head? Too many to count. She could not stop wondering if she had not gone to find solace in the library, and instead tried to intervene in the heated conversation her father had been engaged in, he still might be alive.

She pushed away the memory, along with her guilt, and walked farther into the ballroom. A movement caught her eye, and she looked left.

Ian leaned against the far wall, waiting for her. He still wore his dark gray trousers, white shirt, and charcoal damask waistcoat that he'd worn earlier, but he'd removed his coat.

Not for the first time, Sara could not stop her gaze from traveling over his masculine frame and admiring it.

"Are you ready?" He pushed off the wall and crossed the room to her. Casually he removed his cuff links, slipped them into the pocket of his trousers, and rolled up his sleeves, exposing more of him to her eyes.

"We don't have any music." As if her words conjured up a musician, a harried-looking gentleman in a simple sack suit entered the room. Even from the distance that separated them, she could see the beads of sweat prickling the fellow's brow as he fumbled with the sheet music he held.

"Mr. Mills, I'm glad you could join us," Ian said.

"Sorry I'm late, Your Grace." The gentleman rushed across the room to where a grand piano sat on a dais. His fast moving heels made a clicking noise against the polished wood flooring. The sound echoed in the massive room. He sat at the bench and arranged the music sheets on the rack.

Sara was pleased that the man's back faced them.

"Whenever you wish me to begin, Your Grace." The pianist glanced over his shoulder at them.

Ian stepped up to her, dissolving the space separating them.

She couldn't recall ever seeing Ian dancing. Probably because he would have been off meeting some rare beauty for an assignation. But surely a man of his station knew how to waltz.

As he took her right hand in his left and set his other hand on her back, she swallowed hard. A small laugh escaped her lips before she could tamp it down.

"If you are nervous, close your eyes as you did when you danced with Lord Ralston."

A bead of sweat moved down her spine like an icy finger. "If I close my eyes you won't let me fall?"

"Trust me," Ian said, his voice a soft, comforting whisper, similar to the voice he used when they were tangled in each other's arms in bed. "Begin, Mr. Mills."

The man's fingers glided across the keys as he began one of Johann Strauss's compositions.

Sara felt frozen.

* * *

His wife looked like a rabbit about to be caught by the talons of a hawk. Setting his index finger under Sara's chin, Ian brought her gaze up to his. "I promise I won't let you fall."

"I've never seen you dance. Do you know how?"

"Yes. You need to trust me. Close your eyes." Some emotion within him wanted to help her overcome her fear. Not for his benefit, but for hers.

Sara closed her eyes, and Ian began moving with her in tandem across the dance floor.

She missed a step and tugged her lower lip between her teeth. "I don't think I can do this," she said with her eyes still closed.

"Yes, you can. Relax and concentrate on the steps."

She took an audible breath and executed the next several steps with perfect precision.

With her eyes closed, Ian examined her face. He could practically see the cogwheels turning as she concentrated, while her lips were pinched so firmly together, they were growing pale. She looked to be in pain.

"Am I holding you too tight?"

"No."

"Then, darling, relax your face. We want those gathered to think you are enjoying dancing with me. Not look like you are in excruciating pain."

A stiff, clearly forced smile turned up the corners of her lips. "Better?"

"Yes. Now you only look as if I am botching this up by treading on your toes."

"That bad?" She opened her eyes.

"Close your eyes again and pretend we are in the garden with butterflies fluttering above us."

"In the garden?"

"Yes. It's your favorite place, isn't it?"

"It is one of them. Very well." She closed her eyes again.

"Do you smell the flowers?"

Sara grinned. "No. I smell your cologne, but it is just as pleasant."

"Is it?" He couldn't look away from her face.

"*Mmm.*"

"You know flattery will get you whatever you want."

"Will it get you to tell me we don't have to go to the ball and dance?"

"Well, flattery will get you *nearly* everything you want."

"That's what I thought." She laughed.

It was a lovely sound. Not high-pitched or nervous sounding in the least.

"Right now, as you laughed, you looked like you were enjoying yourself."

"I haven't fallen or dragged you down with me or laughed like a fool, so I believe I am enjoying myself."

Ian grinned. "We've reached the end of the dance floor. I'm about to bring us back up the other way. Ready?"

She wet her lips, and he thought of how whenever they were in bed, she liked to set her tongue to his skin as if she wished to know what he tasted like. Preoccupied with those memories, he misstepped.

Sara bounced into him.

He wrapped his arms around her waist and pulled her body against his so she wouldn't tumble.

Her eyes flew open. "You said you wouldn't let me fall."

He looked down at the absence of space between them—

to where her breasts were flattened against his chest. "As you see, I didn't."

"True, but you missed a step. Your mind was on something else, wasn't it? Perhaps the next business you hope to acquire."

He'd been thinking of business, all right. Their *business*. He was tempted to tell Sara the truth. That he'd been thinking of her mouth on him. Everywhere. He glanced at Mr. Mills who was still playing a waltz and didn't realize they'd stopped dancing.

"I don't think this is a good idea." She narrowed her eyes.

"Let's try it again."

"Do you promise to concentrate?"

She sounded like an irate nanny upset with her charge. "I promise," he said, unable to halt his grin.

"This isn't funny. Not at all."

"I agree. It's extremely serious." Ian forced a serious look and led Sara around the dance floor. After a while, the tightness in Sara's face lessened again. As they took the turn at the end of the ballroom floor, a slight smile lifted one side of her mouth.

The music came to a stop.

Sara opened her eyes, and the grin on her face broadened. "We did it."

"Why don't you try it with your eyes open?" Ian suggested.

She nibbled her lower lip.

"Try it. Just once." Ian thought Sara would refuse, but instead she gave a reluctant nod. "Another waltz, Mr. Mills."

The man's fingers glided across the ivories as he began another one of Strauss's tunes.

As Ian led Sara down the length of the room, her gaze seemed to be locked on the third button of his waistcoat, but she didn't falter. He could see her lips moving and softly hear her counting the beats. *One, two, three. One, two, three.* Ian couldn't stop his desire to hold her closer.

Her large eyes widened, and she glanced up at him.

"If we are to have people believing we are in love . . ."

She gave a slight nod, and he was pleased when her gaze didn't return to his buttons. Instead, they held each other's gazes. The way she looked at him made him want to protect her for eternity. He realized something was happening between them, but he feared it as much as he wanted it. "You dance well," he said, forcing himself out of his thoughts.

"Do I?" Her expression revealed she thought it false praise.

"Yes. Very. Did you have a dance instructor?"

Her body visibly tensed. "I did."

"You didn't care for him?" He knew the answer before he even asked the question.

"Not particularly. He was more like a militant general."

Had the man bullied her? Anger flared in his gut. "Was he cruel to you? Did he hurt you?"

"No. Not physically." Red singed Sara's cheeks. "But cruelty can be delved out by other means."

Ian knew exactly what she meant. The dance instructor had verbally insulted her. Belittled her. No wonder she had worried she would make a cake of herself. Ian knew what it was like to be made to feel like you aren't good enough. It was the true reason why he worked so hard. Even though his father was dead, he was always trying to prove himself beyond capable of running the duchy—of amassing a wealth his father had never attained.

"Tell me his name." Ian tipped her face back to his with a gentle touch of his hand under her chin.

"Why?" She tilted her head to the side.

"I'm curious."

Something in her eyes revealed she knew it wasn't only curiosity on his part. "I don't recall."

"I think you do."

"Sometimes it is best to let go of the past and move forward."

Wise words from a wise woman, but Ian didn't know if he was capable of such forgiveness, even for those long buried. He stepped back and flipped open his pocket watch. "I have another meeting to attend to. Should we try another lesson in a couple of days?"

She nodded. "Very well."

He watched as his little sparrow of a wife moved toward the exit and slipped out of his sight, leaving him with an almost uncontrollable desire to follow her.

After arriving home, Ian noticed that the doors to the ballroom were open and a light shown from within.

Who was in there at this late hour? At the threshold, he peered inside.

Sara danced by herself. She held her arms outward as if she danced with a partner. Ian could hear her low voice repeating, *One, two, three, one, two, three* as she practiced the steps to a waltz.

For a minute, he was reminded of the young, frightened child he was when his tutor informed him that his father wished to see him in his office. He remembered the rolling motion in his stomach, and his fear he might cast up his accounts, and receive more of a severe birching than what he presumed lay ahead.

He couldn't make Sara attend Floyd's party and dance.

Not if she suffered those same fears. He stepped into the ballroom.

As Sara turned, her gaze settled on him. She missed a step and almost fell.

He was by her side in a heartbeat with his hands on her waist, steadying her.

"You frightened me," she scolded, tipping that stubborn little chin of hers in the air.

Normally, he would have raised his brow in that arrogant way his father had done so many times to those below his station, but instead he said, "Forgive me. We don't have to attend Floyd's ball."

Her body visibly stiffened. "Are you that worried I'll embarrass you?"

"No, I'm trying to be thoughtful."

She narrowed her eyes as if she thought his statement plain old balderdash. "Really?"

"Yes, really."

"You don't think I can do it."

He released a heavy breath. "I didn't say that."

"But you think it?"

"No. I think you can do it, but if it makes you uncomfortable . . ."

Sara averted her gaze, her eyes settling on a spot to the side of the room. "For the last few years, I have relived my first Season. I've decided I want to overcome this as best I can. If I cannot, I will at least know I tried, but not trying . . ."

She looked back at him.

Ian wanted to pull Sara into his arms, as he wished someone would have done to him when he was a child and scared.

"I want to conquer this fear, and I think I can do it."

He held out his hand. "Then dance with me."

Sara placed her hand in his.

"Whether we are here or in a crush, I will never let you fall. Never."

There was such conviction in the way Ian said *never*, that Sara experienced a lessening in the tightening in her chest, and though her heart beat faster than normal, she also experienced a sense of safety as he took her fully into his arms.

Throughout the first dance, she couldn't completely release the apprehension within her, but the more she and Ian danced together, the more at ease she felt. She reminded herself that there was no one watching. No women whispering behind their fans. No men gawking, waiting for her to laugh and make a fool of herself. At Bertram Floyd's ball, all eyes would be on them.

That thought caused her heart to flutter wildly in her chest and her body to stiffen.

As if sensing it, Ian, who was humming a waltz, spoke. "Relax. You're doing quite well."

"Yes, but no one is watching us."

"When I was younger, I would become nervous quite frequently. To combat it, I would breathe slowly in through my nose, then slowly exhale."

She blinked. She couldn't imagine him being nervous, and the thought that he frequently experienced that emotion when a child tugged at her heart. "You did?"

He nodded.

"Did this breathing help?"

"Yes. If you feel your laugh coming on, center your

mind on your breathing. Distract yourself with that task. Then pretend we are the only two people in the ballroom."

Perhaps she could do that. "That would surely be better than imagining everyone naked."

Ian's eyes widened, then he laughed. "If that's what you're doing, no wonder you are giggling."

"I've never done it while at a ball. My sister suggested I do it during our wedding if I became nervous."

"Did you try it?" Humor sparkled in his eyes.

"Just once."

"Did it work?" he asked.

"It was distracting."

"Don't tell me it was the vicar."

"No! Certainly not."

"Then who?"

"I don't wish to say."

"Was it Julien?"

Ian actually sounded jealous. "Do you know you can be rather tenacious at times?"

"Yes, I've been told."

"If you must know, it was you. And I did not imagine you completely naked. You wore a loincloth."

His bark of laugher was so robust it shocked her.

"Are you laughing at me?"

"Oh no, darling. I'm not laughing at you. I'm laughing at the thought of myself wearing a loincloth."

She grinned.

"Do you realize that while we conversed you danced the whole time, looking content?"

He was right.

They stopped dancing. "Maybe you should picture me wearing a loincloth at the Floyds' ball."

Oh, the arrogant man. "It wasn't that at all."

"Hmm, really?"

"Yes, really."

They danced several more dances, and Sara noticed that Ian smiled throughout them. His expression made her feel lighter on her feet, but she still couldn't disperse her fear of what would happen at the Floyds' ball.

Chapter Twenty-Six

"Edward, will you push that clay pot with the astilbes over to that corner?" Sara asked, the following day.

"This one with the red flowers?" Edward pointed to the pot beside him.

"Yes, thank you, dear."

Over the last couple of days, the boys had been helping Sara work on the butterfly house, which was turning out quite lovely. She'd purchased a set of cushioned-wicker chaises so anyone visiting the sanctuary could observe the butterflies or simply read while enjoying the atmosphere. That was where Jacob presently reclined, staying very still since a Vanessa cardui butterfly, more commonly known as a painted lady, was perched on his head.

The orange-colored butterfly with a dark outline took flight, and Jacob grinned. "Did you see how long it stayed on me?"

Sara couldn't help her own smile. "I did."

"One stayed on me longer yesterday," Edward said.

"No, it didn't," Jacob shot back.

"I think it might be a tie." Sara looked at the watch pinned to the bodice of her brown dress. "I think you better head back to the schoolroom. I told Mr. Marks I would not keep you too long."

"Do we have to go?" Edward frowned.

Sara's heart felt light. Edward wished to stay here with her. Though she realized that might be due to whatever lesson the tutor had planned.

"Can we?" Jacob added. "You could give us another science lesson in the garden."

"Though I'd enjoy that above all else, I did promise Mr. Marks I would not keep you all afternoon."

Their shoulders slumped, but they opened the door and all three of them stepped outside and made their way into the house.

As the boys trotted up the stairs to the schoolroom, Sara made her way to Ian's office. A bubble of excitement filtered through her body over both Edward and Jacob wishing to stay with her. And for some reason, one she didn't wish to examine too thoroughly, she couldn't wait to tell Ian. She stepped into his office to find he wasn't there.

Disappointed, she made her way upstairs to her study. At the threshold she stilled.

Inside the room, Ian held the glass case that contained her malachite butterfly. As if he wished to examine it more closely, he lifted it up toward the light streaming through the windows before setting it down and opening a drawer in one of her specimen cabinets.

"Those are yellow-legged tortoiseshell butterflies." She stepped into the room.

He closed the drawer and faced her. "How many butterflies do you have?"

"I've given up counting." She lifted the case holding the Adonis Blue butterfly. "The color of this one makes me think of your eyes."

He took it from her hands, and his fingers brushed against hers.

Odd. No matter how many times their hands touched, it never lessened the current that shot through her body.

"My eyes, huh?" He grinned.

"Yes." At one time she'd thought his eyes too assessing, but now she thought them fascinating. "I was looking for you."

"Were you?" He set the butterfly case down.

"Yes. I think I have finally broken down the wall the boys have erected. If you had seen them today while we were in the garden, you would agree."

The broad smile on Sara's lips sent a wave of something through Ian. Pleasure at her pleasure. Contentment at her contentment. "That's wonderful."

She cocked her head to the side. "Did you come up here to tell me something?"

He wasn't sure how he'd ended up here. He'd been sitting at his desk and, for the umpteenth time, found himself wandering to the window to see if he could spot her in the garden. Then he'd found himself moving up the stairs, heading to her study.

"No. I happened to be walking by the room and became curious."

"The butterflies are beautiful, aren't they?" She motioned to her collection with a gentle sweep of her hand.

They were, but somehow they paled in comparison to her. And with that unsettling thought in his head, he told Sara he would see her at dinner, and quickly left the room.

* * *

Since returning from Scotland, Sara, the boys, along with himself now took all their meals in the morning room. Sara had explained that while he was gone, she'd insisted that both Edward and Jacob join her instead of them eating in the nursery, hoping the smaller, round table would be more conducive to conversation.

This evening as Ian ate dinner with them, he realized that he'd come to enjoy the chatter at the table. Edward and Jacob acted more content than they had since arriving at Dorchester Hall. They smiled more, especially at Sara. She was correct; she'd broken down the wall they had erected.

As each day passed, Ian also realized a warmth settled over him when he stepped into Dorchester Hall, one he'd never felt before. Sometimes, Sara would be playing at the piano, the lads seated beside her listening. She'd show them where to press the ivories for the next note. Other times, he'd arrived home to find her reading to them or cheerfully playing cards.

Laughter in this house was an anomaly. Surely he'd not heard it growing up.

This old structure made of brick suddenly felt like a home. It was as if a gentle summer wind blew inward, dispersing the cold chill that had permeated the interior throughout his life—banishing the ghost of the past. Hadn't some inner part of him wanted that?

Edward laughed at something, and Ian looked at Sara's smiling face. Since the episode at the pond, she'd welcomed him into her bed every night, yet he left before she woke up. He was avoiding her. Avoiding the intimacy of cuddling in the morning. What type of milksop could not open their heart up to another?

"I counted fifteen butterflies in the butterfly house this

afternoon." Jacob put a heaping spoonful of butterscotch pudding into his mouth.

"There are more than that." Edward licked what was left of his pudding off his spoon.

While contemplating his thoughts, Ian had heard their chatter in the background, but the mention of a butterfly house caught his attention. "Butterfly house?"

The boys glanced at each other before shifting their regard to Sara, both brandishing concerned expressions on their faces as if they realized they'd divulged a secret.

She cleared her throat. "The boys and I have turned the old glasshouse into a butterfly house."

The old glasshouse. Over the years, he'd thought of tearing it down, but couldn't since he had a vague memory of being knee-high in there with his mother as she'd tended to the flowers inside.

"Can we be excused?" Edward asked.

"Yes." Ian nodded.

Jacob lifted his napkin off his lap, wiped his mouth, and followed his brother from the room.

As he watched the boys, Ian could feel Sara's gaze on him.

"You're not upset about me taking over the old glasshouse, are you? The gardener said it hadn't been used in years. And Edward and Jacob have found a great deal of pleasure setting up the butterfly house with me, and they've learned quite a bit in the process."

"No. Not at all."

"Would you like to see it?"

He hadn't stepped inside the glasshouse in years, avoiding that singular memory. "I have things I must attend to."

"It will only take a few minutes," she said, a hopeful tone in her voice.

Before he could stop himself, he nodded.

* * *

As they made their way to the glasshouse, the sun started its downward descent toward the horizon. Ian examined Sara's face. As soon as they'd stepped into the garden, a smile had turned up her full lips. It was evident that she found the garden soothing.

As they strolled past several tall flowers, her fingers reached out to touch the petals. She might feel uncomfortable in a ballroom and hide away, but every time he watched her, Ian saw the sensuality of her movements. Even her steps seemed lighter as they made their way to the glasshouse. Sara was like a garden nymph. A curious creature that brought about more curiosity in him than he could recall any woman drawing forth.

They reached the pebbled pathway that led into the less manicured part of the parkland where trees took over the landscape. Sara turned to him. "Is something the matter? You look miles away."

Did he? "No, I was thinking how you fit in here."

Her brows drew together. "Here?"

"This garden."

"I love it."

"So you married me for my gardens?"

She made a solemn face, as if her secret had been found out. "True."

"Oh, how you wound me."

"It was not the only reason."

Why did his heart skip a beat? "Why else?"

"There was also your promise that my inheritance, along with my dowry, would remain in my possession."

He tamped down his disappointment.

"And . . ." She grinned.

He searched her face.

"The sentimentality of your proposal."

"It was rather beastly, wasn't it?"

"A little?" She laughed.

"And here I thought it was my charm that caused you to accept my proposal."

Her laugh deepened. "What do you think?" Sara asked, suddenly stopping.

He looked ahead to see the glasshouse with the setting sun reflecting off the structure, making it look like a beacon of light, as one might see in a fairy tale. He almost laughed at such a fanciful thought.

"Come inside." She grabbed his hand and pulled him into the building.

The atmosphere was thick with a profusion of scents. Next to the entrance were bright flowers in red and pink.

"The asters are flowering nicely, aren't they?"

Wondering if the flowers next to him were asters, he pointed at them. "These?"

"Yes." She beamed and started pointing to each species of flower and rattling off their names. "I thought men knew the language of flowers."

"Flowers have a language?"

"No, each flower when given has a meaning. Friendship, respect, admiration."

"Which one means love?"

"Red roses." She bit her lower lip. "Have you ever given them to a woman?"

He had, but never one he loved. "It seems I have made a grave faux pas."

"So some poor, disillusioned woman believed you loved her when you didn't?"

"Hopefully, she didn't know the meaning of them."

"Doubtful."

That would explain why she'd called him a lying bastard when he'd ended the relationship. He peered around. "You don't have any roses in here?"

"Though a lovely flower, they are not a butterfly's favorite."

"Just a woman's?"

"If she loves the man, I presume so."

He nodded. "Where are the butterflies?"

"It's late. They are most likely in a quiescent state. Resting." She glanced around. "Ah, there on the thistle is a Vanessa cardui, commonly known as the painted lady."

Ian spotted the orange butterfly with black markings. "Can you tell if it is male or female?"

"Many male butterflies are more colorful than the females. However, the male Vanessa cardui is quite similar to the female." She bent slightly to examine the butterfly. "But the female has a thicker body." She straightened. "This is a female."

Listening to Sara talk about butterflies enthralled him. Perhaps because he admired her intelligence. He'd also admired her derrière when she'd bent over.

"The male painted lady pursues the female. Sometimes he circles her in the air. A form of courting."

Ian realized he should have courted Sara. She deserved to be sent flowers with secret messages. Roses. Good Lord, was he admitting that he was falling in love with his wife? If he were honest with himself, he would admit he'd felt an attraction to her that day in his library when she'd tipped her chin in the air and censured him. But attraction wasn't love. Yet something was growing between them. Something that easily surpassed what he'd felt for Isabelle. Isabelle's beauty had caught his eye, but he now realized he'd never really known her.

The setting sun cut through the glass roof to pick out the gold flecks in Sara's brown hair. Without thought, he closed the distance between them. Her gaze followed him as if she knew even before he did what he intended to do.

He pulled her into his arms and kissed her as if she were a lifeline—a buoy to cling to when one is tossed overboard and into a rough sea.

She wrapped her arms around his neck and returned his kiss.

The idea of stretching out on one of the wicker chaises and making love to her with the sun descending until they were under the glow of the moon nearly overwhelmed him. He pulled back, reined in his control.

Sara's already-full lips were puffy from his demanding kiss and the way she'd responded.

She rubbed her hands over her arms.

"The night is getting cool." He took her hand in his. "Let's go inside."

Like two eager lovers who were about to experience each other's bodies for the first time, they quickly made their way to Sara's bedroom.

As soon as the door closed, Ian pressed her against it. His mouth sought hers. A firm kiss that spoke of desire; then it gentled, and his mouth coaxed hers open.

Sara pulled back. The sparkle in her lovely hazel eyes dimmed.

It felt like a punch to his gut. "Is something wrong?"

She held his gaze for a long moment. "I want to wake up beside you. I want you to stay the whole night. Will you promise me that?"

"Sara, I—"

"Promise me."

He realized how much he wanted to wake up beside her. "Yes."

Pleasure lit up her face.

Ian kissed her again.

Without hesitation she opened her mouth.

A knock on the door froze them like droplets of water on a cold metal sign. Ian rested his forehead against Sara's and inwardly cursed. Whomever it was better be dying, or they soon might be.

"What is it?"

"Your Grace, I beg your forgiveness for interrupting you, but you have a caller," Jeffers said.

Who the bloody hell would be calling on them this late? "Tell them we are not receiving callers at this time."

"Yes, well, quite understandable, sir, but it is the Dowager Duchess of Dorchester."

Isabelle. Ian's stomach lurched.

Chapter Twenty-Seven

Sara peered at Ian's face. A nerve ticked in his jaw. She'd thought his mother had died. "Your mother . . . ?"

As if her voice snapped him out of a fog, his gaze shifted to her. "Isabelle is my stepmother."

Jeffers cleared his throat, reminding them he still stood on the other side of the door awaiting a response.

"Jeffers, please show her to the yellow drawing room," Sara replied.

"Yes, madam."

Ian stepped back with a hard look on his face. "I would have preferred we sent her away."

"We could not do such a thing."

"I would have suffered no qualms doing just that."

The fine hairs on her nape lifted. Obviously, Ian did not care for his stepmother. The dowager must be an overbearing dragon of a woman if Ian didn't wish to deal with her.

Without another word, Ian opened the door and motioned for Sara to precede him.

Sara straightened her dress and stepped into the corridor.

As they made their way to the drawing room, Ian didn't

speak a single word. They stepped inside to find the dowager standing with her back to them; her gaze seemed to be directed at the painting of Dorchester Hall that hung above the mantel. The emerald-green traveling dress the woman wore caught the light from the gas lighting. Even without seeing the front, Sara knew it a costly garment with the layers of lace that trimmed the bustled back.

The dowager turned around.

Sara tried not to gape.

Ian's stepmother looked to be only a few years older than herself. Her thick and glossy auburn hair was coifed in a loose style with curling tendrils that framed her lovely, heart-shaped face.

The dowager smiled at Sara, then at Ian. "I hope you will both forgive me for calling so late, but I only arrived at Victoria Station a short time ago."

"If we had known, we would have sent a carriage to the train station," Sara said, and peered at Ian who still hadn't spoken.

"Ian, aren't you going to introduce me to your wife?" the dowager asked.

Sara watched the interaction. Though the dowager smiled, Ian's mien remained distant and cold. She would have sworn the temperature in the room dropped several degrees. She wondered what had transpired between them to cause his obvious dislike of his stepmother.

"Sara, might I introduce you to my stepmother, Isabelle McAllister, the Dowager Duchess of Dorchester."

The woman gave Sara a benevolent look and stepped up to her. "You, dear, must call me Isabelle, and I hope you will allow me to call you Sara since we are now family."

"Of course," Sara returned the woman's warm expression, hoping to defuse the almost-tangible tension in the air.

"It is quite late, Isabelle. Is your carriage outside waiting?" Ian asked.

Startled by such boldness on her husband's part, Sara's gaze jerked to Ian.

"No." Isabelle's expression looked stunned as well. "My trunk is in the entry hall, and I sent my maid belowstairs to ask Mrs. Pullman where she can sleep. I thought I would be welcome to stay here."

Ian's jaw clenched as if he were grounding his molars.

"You are," Sara replied, when it looked as if Ian would not respond.

"Thank you, dear." The woman patted Sara's hand. "I must admit I am quite exhausted."

"Yes, you must be. Might I ask where you have traveled from?"

For a moment, the woman's expression soured. "It is obvious that Ian has not mentioned me or my son. We live in Northumberland. But I was traveling on the Continent when I heard Ian had married." She turned to him. "I should scold you for not having invited me to your wedding. I would have returned for it."

"Your son did not accompany you to the Continent?" Sara asked.

"No, I thought it best to leave him with his nanny. He's not fond of traveling."

Sara desperately wanted to know how old the child was, but asking would only confirm that Ian had never mentioned them.

"Ian, I thought it about time I visited. We need to mend fences, as they say."

"You cannot be serious?" Ian narrowed his eyes.

"We need to leave the past behind us."

Sara wondered what past Isabelle referred to. What had happened to cause such a strain between Ian and his stepmother? Though seeing their age difference, it seemed rather odd for Sara to think of the woman that way.

"It's late and I'm weary from traveling. Might I use the lavender guest room? It was always a favorite of mine."

Ian didn't respond.

"I'll have a footman bring your trunk upstairs," Sara answered, breaking the quiet.

"Thank you, dear. Good night, Sara, Ian." The woman moved toward the door, each step as graceful as the next, leaving Sara alone with Ian.

"You don't care for her?"

"No, Sara, I don't care for her."

"Might I ask why?"

"I have my reasons."

Though Sara wished for more information than Ian's succinct responses, she decided it was best to let it go and approach the subject perhaps tomorrow. "How old is your brother?"

"Charles is seven." Though his answer was brief, Sara noticed the taut set of Ian's jaw ease slightly when he said the child's name.

"When was the last time you saw him?"

"Right before Edward and Jacob came to live here."

Startled, Sara blinked. The way he'd looked at Isabelle had led Sara to believe he had not seen her in years. "Isabelle and her son visited here?"

"No, Isabelle has not been in this house in years. I occasionally see him at my estate in Northumberland."

"You visit them there?"

"Not them, darling, just Charles. Isabelle spends a great

deal of time on the Continent. He is a happy child, but that cannot be credited to his mother, since she has left his care in the hands of servants. Isabelle is not the fawning motherly type. As she alluded to earlier, she enjoys traveling to Europe. I am informed when she is on one of her extended holidays and visit my young brother then."

"Does she know this?"

"I'm sure she does. Children tend to talk. And though I pay for the salaries of the staff there, I'm not naive enough to think they remain mum."

Sara had heard that Ian's father had died around seven or eight years ago. "If he is seven, then he was born close to the time your father died."

Ian nodded. "Yes, my father died eight months before Charles was born."

As they walked out of the room and up the stairs, Sara could tell Ian was deep in his own thoughts. She clasped his hand. His normally-warm fingers felt cold.

He smiled. It was the type someone gives when they feel they should, but it takes some effort, yet he gave her hand a gentle squeeze.

At her bedroom door, he brought their clasped fingers to his mouth and kissed the back of her hand. Both their actions attested to the relationship growing between them. It spoke of a deeper bond. It also signaled he was saying good night to her. That he would not be joining her in bed tonight.

He pressed a kiss to her cheek. "I have an early meeting with Julien tomorrow morning," he said as if reading her thoughts. He turned and took several steps, then pivoted back. "Your butterfly house is lovely."

It felt like a week since she'd shown it to him, when in truth it had been only a couple of hours ago—before

Isabelle showed up and seemed to turn everything upside down.

"Thank you." She forced a smile and stepped into her room.

The following morning when Sara went down to breakfast, Jeffers handed her a missive from Ian, informing her that he would be gone for the better part of the day.

She placed the note in her pocket and smiled cheerfully at the boys, hiding the worry swirling in her stomach. "Jeffers, do you know if the dowager will be joining us?"

"I doubt it, Your Grace. She doesn't usually rise this early."

The butler's words brought about the realization that the staff who had been here when Isabelle had been married to the old duke knew her habits.

While they ate breakfast, the boys chatted excitedly about the kitten.

"I heard Jeffers telling Mrs. Pullman that Cousin Ian was holding Snowball and petting it. Is that true?" Jacob made a face like he thought it rubbish.

Sara grinned and glanced at Jeffers who looked shamefaced but then smiled. "Yes, I think he likes Snowball." She looked back at Jeffers. "Did His Grace have a pet while growing up?"

The smile on the butler's face vanished. "No, madam. His Grace's father did have hunting dogs, but they were only used for that. They were not kept in the house since the old duke thought affection toward the dogs would make them less aggressive. They were not the type of dogs one could call companionable."

After what Mrs. Pullman had said about the old duke not even allowing Ian to have toys, she should have realized that would be the man's attitude. Why would he show compassion to dogs, when it appeared he hadn't shown it to his son? More and more she despised Ian's father. She suddenly wondered why Isabelle would marry such a hateful man. Only two reasons came to mind. The first was that her family commanded it. The second reason was not charitable—she'd done it for the social standing.

Near noon, Mrs. Pullman informed Sara that Isabelle had only woken up a short time ago and taken a late breakfast in her room. Though the housekeeper's voice hadn't conveyed anything, the look on her face left Sara with the impression that the woman wasn't overly fond of Isabelle.

After Edward, Jacob, and Sara ate lunch the boys returned to the schoolroom. She decided she should read a book in the yellow drawing room and wait for Isabelle, instead of going into the garden or working in her study as she normally did.

At two o'clock, Isabelle, dressed in a lavender walking dress with intricate embroidery on the bodice, finally appeared. She wore a smart-looking hat and kid gloves of the same color.

"Morning, Sara," she said, patting at the loosely styled bun at her nape.

Sara was tempted to tell her it wasn't morning but held her tongue. "Isabelle, I hope you slept well."

"Fairly well." She glanced around the room. "Ian isn't home?"

"No, he had business to tend to."

As if disappointed, the woman's lips pinched together.

"Are you going out?"

"Yes, I wish to call on a dear friend in Mayfair. Do you have a carriage I might use?"

"You can use mine."

"You are such a dear, thank you. I'll go and tell Jeffers to have it brought around."

Sara's gaze followed the woman as she stepped out of the room. Though Isabelle smiled warmly, there was something disingenuous about her.

Only a few minutes after the woman's departure, Sara stepped into her study intent on distracting herself by working on a watercolor of the Adolias butterfly. She set up her easel and was arranging her paints and brushes when Jeffers stepped into the room.

"Your Grace, Lady Ralston wishes to know if you are in."

"Yes, of course!" Sara couldn't contain her excitement. Nina's smiling face would help settle the uneasiness coursing through her.

Jeffers's lips turned up briefly. "I have shown her to the yellow drawing room."

When Sara stepped into the room, Nina's smile faded. "Sara, is something wrong?"

"No, everything is fine."

"Fiddlesticks. I've known you too long. I can tell when you are bothered by something. Is it Dorchester? Has he done something abysmal? If so, you can come and live with Elliot and me."

"No, it's not that drastic. And it's not Ian." Sara motioned for her friend to take a seat on the settee, then sat next to her. "Ian's stepmother has arrived for a visit."

Nina glanced around. "She is here?"

"Yes, but she has gone to call on a friend in Mayfair. Ian is less than pleased."

"He doesn't care for her?"

"It appears not."

"Is she a dragon, like my grandmother?"

"First, she is not old enough to be anyone's grand-mother."

"Really?"

"She is closer to Ian's age. And she has a young son. The current heir."

Nina's eyes widened.

"You didn't know this either?"

"I have a vague memory of my brother mentioning the old duke and his new wife, but I was not out in Society when it all unfolded."

Sara hadn't been either. Besides, she'd never gossiped much. Now most of the gossip she heard was from her sister, and since Louisa had only made her bow last year, she must not have heard.

"There is definite animosity between her and Ian. Something happened in their past. I just don't know what."

"I know someone who might know." Nina grinned.

"Who?"

"My grandmother."

As Nina had said, the Dowager Marchioness of Hunt-ington was a dragon. A cantankerous woman with piercing gray eyes. Sara gave an exaggerated shiver.

Nina laughed. "I know visiting her is an unsettling thought, but if anyone knows, she does."

Her dear friend was right. If there was something to learn, the elder Lady Huntington would have the information. She seemed to know nearly every scandal that had occurred, even those not known by most members of the *ton*. Yet, Sara thought she might prefer to fall into the devil's pit than visit the ill-tempered woman. "I do not think your grandmother likes me very much."

"Of course, she likes you."

Sara arched a brow and held Nina's gaze.

"Well, if it is any consolation, you should know that my grandmother isn't particularly fond of anyone. Even her grandchildren. But truthfully, her bark is worse than her bite." Nina glanced at the watch pinned to the bodice of her dress. "Her afternoon callers will have left by now."

Sara drew in a deep breath. "You wish to go now?"

"Yes, you said Isabelle went to call on a friend and isn't home. This seems the perfect time."

True. Calling on the tetchy old woman would be worth it if she could enlighten her. Sara drew in a deep breath. "Very well, let's go."

Chapter Twenty-Eight

As Nina's carriage traveled from Richmond to Mayfair, Sara tried not to twist her hands together. She hoped Nina's grandmother could shed some light on why Ian showed an almost tangible animosity toward Isabelle.

The vehicle stopped at an intersection in Kensington, and Sara looked out the window. Her gaze shifted through the crowd of pedestrians on the busy street to settle on a woman in a lavender walking gown with a matching wide-brimmed hat in the same shade as the one Isabelle had worn before leaving Dorchester Hall. The woman disappeared behind several people before becoming visible again. She stepped toward the curb and glanced up the street, giving Sara a better view of her face.

"Isabelle," Sara mumbled more to herself than to Nina who sat next to her.

"What?" Nina turned to her.

"The woman crossing the street is Isabelle, the Dowager Duchess of Dorchester. I wonder what she is doing here. She said she wished to visit a friend in Mayfair."

"Perhaps she has and is now doing some shopping."

Nina slipped into the seat across from Sara and peered out the window to get a better look. "Where is she?"

Sara pointed to Isabelle. "The woman in the lavender gown with the matching hat."

"Oh . . ."

She knew what her friend was thinking—that Isabelle was breathtaking. Almost lovely beyond words.

They watched as Isabelle opened the door to a building and stepped inside.

The carriage moved again, and as it passed the building Sara read the sign at the door. NEWTON AND NEWTON, SOLICITORS AND NOTARY PUBLIC.

"She never mentioned calling on anyone besides her friend."

"She probably just forgot," Nina said. "Sara . . .?"

"Yes."

"I wished to know how you and Dorchester are doing?" Nina's expression turned concerned.

In the bedroom they were very much compatible. Sara loved the way Ian touched her and loved touching him. In bed they seemed incendiary. Though she didn't like that he left her before morning.

However, when it came to Sara and Ian outside the bedroom, it seemed less clear. She thought of their conversation in the butterfly house. Something between them was changing. They were reaching beyond the physical to something much deeper. More emotional. She recalled Ian's expression as she'd spoken in the butterfly house. Unlike her family, he'd not dismissed her but listened intently. She cared for him. Perhaps she was even falling in love with her husband.

Sara only realized she was smiling when Nina grabbed her hand. "You love him, don't you?"

"I care for him so much more than I did when we stood before God and spoke our vows. And I believe he is coming to care for me, but my marriage is not like yours and Elliot's. You married because you both loved each other. Ian and I made a deal."

"But you now wish it to be more, don't you?"

"I believe I do." And admitting that to someone besides herself was monumental.

Nina hugged her. "I'm sure it will."

Sara pulled back. "I do have good news."

"Yes?"

"Edward and Jacob have grown closer to me."

"That is wonderful."

"It pleases me more than I can express."

A short time later, the carriage pulled up to Nina's brother's Park Lane residence where Nina's grandmother lived.

A frisson of unease worked its way through Sara's body. Apprehension about what she might find out, along with concern over dealing with Nina's crabby grandmother.

Without ringing the new electric doorbell, they stepped into the entry hall at the same time the butler did.

"Lady Nina, Your Grace." The butler inclined his head.

"Hello, Menders, is my grandmother in the blue drawing room?"

"Yes, my lady."

"How is her mood?" Nina asked.

One side of the man's mouth twitched downward. "Your brother Anthony and his wife have left their parrot here while they are in Manchester. She is not fond of the bird, and they have been arguing with each other all morning."

"She and the bird?" Sara asked. "Can one actually hold a conversation with the parrot?"

Nina chuckled. "Atticus has a very colorful vocabulary. And I'm sure being with my grandmother has added to it."

Sara twisted her hands together. "Perhaps we should come back another day, when she's in a better mood."

"Better mood?" Nina echoed. "Tomorrow she might be even grumpier. We have come this far, my dear friend. Let us not turn back." Nina linked her arm through Sara's, and they moved up the stairs.

As they neared the drawing room, they heard the matriarch. "I'm sure Cook could find a tasty parrot soup recipe."

Mouth gaping open, Sara looked at Nina.

"Remember, her bark is worse than her bite. She wouldn't really do it."

"Are you sure?"

Nina nodded, and they stepped into the room.

The thin, gray-haired woman sat in a chair. She pointed her cane at a large green parrot in a sizable birdcage. "Stop your endless prattling," the dowager snapped.

Squawk. "Love you. Love you!" The bird made kissing noises.

The elderly woman turned to Sara and Nina. "Atticus is driving me balmy with his romantic drivel that he obviously picked up while living with Anthony and Olivia. I liked the bird better when he talked like a drunken sailor."

"Grandmother," Nina said, "you should be happy Anthony has finally settled down and found a woman he loves."

Humph. "He should have married Lord Pendleton's granddaughter. Not my companion."

"Be honest. You care for Olivia a great deal."

Without responding, the woman asked, "What brings you both here?"

Nina motioned to Sara. "We wish to ask you some questions."

The elder Lady Huntington's gaze pivoted to Sara and her eyes narrowed.

Deciding she would not allow the woman to browbeat her, Sara tipped her nose in the air. She was a duchess now, and of a higher rank than the old woman.

"You're the one with the nervous laugh, aren't you?"

"Grandmother!" Nina scolded.

Sara lifted one brow in the arrogant way her husband did when displeased. "Only when asked to dance, so unless you intend to ask me, we are safe."

Briefly, the dowager looked taken aback, then her lips twitched, and she motioned to the settee. "I hope you have that bluster when dealing with your arrogant husband. He'll respect you for it. Now what do you wish to ask me?"

"We wish to inquire about Isabelle, the Dowager Duchess of Dorchester," Nina said, as both she and Sara sat.

The old woman wrinkled her nose. "Why?"

"I sensed tension between her and my husband."

"Tension? Don't tell me she's in Town."

"She arrived late yesterday at Dorchester Hall and is visiting," Sara replied.

"Your husband allowed her to stay at your residence?" The old woman's thin fingers clutched at the gold knob on her cane.

The question confirmed that something had happened. "*I* did, but he didn't seem pleased."

"I cannot imagine he would be."

Sara's heart picked up speed. "Why?"

"I hate gossip, and I will not take part in any chin-wagging. I think it best you ask your husband."

"Grandmother . . ." Nina said in a pleading voice.

The woman stared at Sara for a long minute, then released a *huff.* "Very well. It's said he desperately loved her."

Loved her? Isabelle's beautiful face flashed in Sara's mind. She recalled how she'd asked him if he'd ever been in love. He'd said he had. Had he meant Isabelle? Surely it was her he'd referred to. But she'd married his father. "She didn't return his affection?"

"I don't know. Perhaps she did. But she wanted to be a duchess more and decided not to wait. So while he was away at university, she married his father. I heard he was devastated. It caused a terrible rift between him and his father, though their relationship was said to have soured long before that."

"How could his father do that to him?" Sara asked.

The elderly woman uttered a hollow-sounding laugh. "The old Duke of Dorchester was a cruel man. He wanted a spare and his wife had only begotten him the one healthy child. Ian's mother died the first year he attended university. Everyone knew the duke was on the hunt for a young wife. One who would give him his beloved spare. I think he also wanted to hurt his son because your husband turned his back on the old duke. Even before he married Isabelle."

Sara swallowed hard. "So he'd loved her."

Nina reached out and clasped Sara's hand. "It doesn't mean he still cares for her. You said he seemed angry over her arrival. He probably despises her."

Squawk. "Love you. Love you forever," the parrot said.

Love you forever. Some loves were like that. Eternal. They held on tight, and no matter what turns life gave, they never diminished until one drew in their last dying breath. Sara stood. "I need to get home."

As Sara neared the door the dowager called out, "The wicked will do anything to achieve their goals. Don't leave that cunning woman alone with your husband. Don't trust her."

After arriving back at Dorchester Hall, Sara stood in the library and stared at the ceiling's mural, hoping the beauty of Frederick Armstrong's painting would distract her from what Nina's grandmother had said. Yet the words that Ian had *desperately loved* Isabelle still echoed in her head.

Did he still feel the same way?

The expression on Ian's face when he'd seen Isabelle hadn't reflected such an emotion. Disgust was more like it. A person jilted often must feel that way, but that didn't mean he still didn't hold a torch for her.

Sara thought of her own feelings toward her husband before she'd come to care for him. Emotions could shift over time like the wind.

"Your Grace, would you like some tea?" Jeffers asked, stepping into the room, and interrupting her unyielding thoughts.

"No. Has my husband arrived home yet?"

"No, madam."

"Is the duchess still in her room?" The woman had arrived back at Dorchester Hall only a short time before Sara.

"Yes." There was a brief crack in the butler's expression, which made Sara believe Jeffers did not care for the woman any more than Mrs. Pullman. He'd been a servant in this house a long time. He'd witnessed things. She fought the urge to ask him. Though she and Jeffers had grown closer, she doubted the reserved butler would provide her with the information she wished to know.

"Thank you, Jeffers." Sara climbed the stairs. She stepped into her bedroom and bit back a gasp when she saw Isabelle inside, standing by the bed, staring at it.

The woman turned around. "I hope you will forgive me. I know I should have asked before coming in here, but I was curious if anything had been changed."

Sara swallowed her shock. It moved down her throat like a leaden weight. Naturally this had been Isabelle's bedchamber as well. "Has it?"

"The furniture is the same. But"—she reached out and touched the edge of one of the silky blue pillows, then ran a hand over the matching floral counterpane—"this is all new."

There was an odd look on the woman's face and Sara had the impression that this room, specifically the bed, didn't hold cherished memories. And the smile on Isabelle's face looked more forced than genuine. Clearly, the woman had not loved the old duke. Her expression betrayed that. She had loved his title. Sara suddenly felt sorry for her.

"I should get ready for dinner," Isabelle said, her voice low, almost too sweet, as she stepped toward the door and out of the room.

After Isabelle left, Sara stared at the door. Nina's grandmother's words replayed in her head. *The wicked will do anything to achieve their goals. Don't leave that cunning woman alone with your husband. Don't trust her.*

Chapter Twenty-Nine

"There, Your Grace, all done." Wallace placed a pearl-tipped hairpin into Sara's hair as she got ready for dinner.

Sara viewed her reflection in the dressing table's mirror. Once again, the lady's maid had coifed Sara's hair in a loose topknot with curling tendrils framing her face.

"Thank you, Wallace. You are a magician." Sara stood.

"Do you need me for anything else, madam?"

"No, that is all. You may have the rest of the day off."

"You don't wish me to return tonight and help you get ready for bed?"

When she retired tonight, she intended to talk to Ian. "Thank you, but I shall be fine."

"Very well, madam." The lady's maid stepped out of the room.

In front of the cheval glass, Sara smoothed a hand over the skirt of her copper gown. For a minute, she'd contemplated wearing the red one she'd purchased. Was she trying to compete with Isabelle? The woman's heart-shaped face, auburn hair, and delicate features flashed in Sara's mind. She was beautiful, but Sara sensed malevolence in the woman. Perhaps she was letting her imagination run wild because of what Nina's grandmother had said.

As she headed toward the door, Sara heard a noise in Ian's room. She stilled and wet her lips. So he had arrived home in time for dinner. She'd wondered if he would. Part of her felt relieved she wouldn't have to dine alone with Isabelle, while another part of her wished she would not have to sit at the table with the woman and perhaps be compared.

Ask him about his past with Isabelle, a voice in her head whispered.

She pivoted and with measured steps moved toward the adjoining door. For a long minute, she held her hand in midair, questioning herself, fearing she might see something in his face that revealed his feelings toward Isabelle lingered. She remembered the look on his face when he'd seen Isabelle standing in the drawing room. He'd been hurt, but she needed to know how he felt. Truly felt. Yet, she was torn between learning the truth and staying oblivious to it.

You are no coward. Do not be detoured. She knocked.

The door opened and Ian stood before her. He'd already removed his neckcloth and waistcoat. His handsome face looked strained. She peered past him, hoping his valet wasn't in the room. Not seeing the manservant, she skirted past Ian and into his bedchamber.

"Where's Adams?" She moved to one of the upholstered chairs near the fireplace and braced her hands on the back of it.

"He wasn't feeling well. I told him to rest, since I don't really need his assistance dressing."

It was another action that showed Ian was not as cold-hearted as he let society believe.

"Was there something you wish to ask me?" Though the words were spoken without inflection, his countenance left no doubt in her mind he was not in the mood to be interrogated.

The questions swirling in her head and how to ask them caused her mouth to feel excessively dry. She swallowed, trying to remove the parched sensation. Her gaze dipped to his waistcoat draped over the back of the chair. She fought the urge to pick it up and draw in the scent of him that lingered on it. It had become as familiar to her as her own scent. Lately it gave her a sense of comfort. But she realized that though Ian's proximity might soothe her frayed senses, she was also a strong woman who had her own inner strength that she could rely on.

She rounded the chair and moved closer to him.

As if he knew she would not be detoured from her quest, his mask slipped slightly, and she saw concern reflected in his face. She also noticed that he looked even more tired than she'd initially thought. The small lines near the corners of his eyes appeared more pronounced.

"I need to ask you something."

"I don't love her."

Startled, she blinked. "How did you know that was what concerned me?"

"You are undoubtedly the smartest woman I have ever known. I figured you had heard the rumors about Isabelle and me."

His compliment about her intelligence made the last barrier she held between them slip. She admitted she was falling in love with Ian. "I've never been one to spend time gossiping with other women."

"Then how did you know?"

"You looked . . . well, you looked so strained when you

saw her. I realized something was not right. And when she said, 'We need to leave the past behind us,' it confirmed my suspicions that things were not satisfactory between you." She looked down at the rug, then back at him. "So when Nina stopped by today, I asked her if she knew what had transpired between you and Isabelle. But, like me, she didn't know, so we asked her grandmother."

If possible, the tightness around his mouth seemed to stiffen even more. "I can imagine what she said. Then you should understand that the look you saw on my face when I saw Isabelle was not longing, but abhorrence."

"Yes, but some emotions like love can become so ingrained within us that they can linger for a lifetime, while others fade."

Ian gave a bitter laugh. "Whatever I felt for Isabelle died the moment I found out she had married my father."

Was betrayal such a barrier that it could cause one to despise the person they once loved? Was the line between love and hate so fortified that it could not wither? No, she didn't believe so. People held a great capacity to forgive, even if they might not forget. Sara thought of her own feelings toward Ian when she first met him. She had believed she would never come to care for him, but he had touched her heart. Would Isabelle reclaim a place in his?

"Don't doubt me, Sara," Ian said as if he could read her thoughts. "What was between Isabelle and me turned to ash the moment she chose to marry my father. Especially when she knew I detested him."

Sara thought of the scars on Ian's backside. He'd said he'd fallen against a hot grate. Was that true? Had the old duke struck his son? Or allowed someone else to do it? She believed she saw the answer in the way Ian's lip curled when he'd mentioned his father. How awful to be abused by one's parent in such a brutal way. Sara recalled him mentioning he'd frequently been frightened as a child. She wanted to wrap her arms around Ian's waist and ask him if she had guessed right about his sire.

"I'll be ready shortly." Ian stepped into his dressing room.

Deciding it might be best to ask him after dinner, Sara returned to her bedchamber and waited for Ian to inform her he was ready to go down to dinner. While waiting for him to dress, she paced and turned over their conversation in her mind. Isabelle and his father had wounded Ian. The latter perhaps not only emotionally, but physically. Was that why he'd initially only offered his body so freely to her, yet had been hesitant to open himself up to a deeper relationship?

Yes, two of the people he'd trusted had scarred him. And now one of those individuals was trying to insinuate herself into their home and lives. Sara was tempted to ask Isabelle to leave. But the thought that Ian had a younger brother that he only saw occasionally stopped her. They were family. Perhaps Isabelle was right that the past could be put aside, and Ian could become part of his brother's life, but Sara didn't like the idea that life might include Isabelle being around.

Ian knocked on the connecting door.

She stopped her anxious pacing. "Yes, come in."

Ian stepped into her room. As usual, he looked virile and handsome in his evening attire, yet the stiffness in his jaw revealed a man who was not at all pleased.

"Ready?"

"Yes." She forced a smile, attempting to lighten the mood, but Ian seemed too deep in his own thoughts to notice.

They stepped into the morning room to find Isabelle,

dressed in a white gown, standing by the French doors that were open, allowing the evening's cooler air to circulate around the room. The hair near her face was pulled into a topknot, while the strands in the back were left to trail down her back. A breeze drifted through the doors and lifted the loose strands of her auburn hair, while the moon highlighted the varying shades of red. She looked like a painting. Delicate. Ethereal. An almost whimsical figure.

Isabelle turned around and faced them. Once again, her beauty struck Sara. She was as breathtaking as one of Sara's butterflies. The woman's gaze shifted over Sara with lightning speed before slowly taking in Ian.

There was tension between Ian and Isabelle, but it was obvious the woman thought him handsome. Sara realized what a striking couple they would have made.

"I was surprised when Jeffers told me we were to be eating in here instead of the dining room." Though Isabelle smiled, Sara was given the impression that Isabelle took it as a snub of some sort.

"We have taken to eating our meals in here, and the boys seem to like the less formal nature of the morning room," Sara said.

"Boys?" Isabelle cocked her head to the side.

Sara looked at Ian. Was it possible she did not know about Edward and Jacob?

"Edward and Jacob," Ian said as they took their seats at the table.

"I know about the children. I just wasn't aware they joined you for dinner."

"They do," Sara said. "But today they ate earlier and will not be joining us."

Unaware of this, Ian's regard shifted to her. He seemed to

comprehend why. She hadn't wanted the boys to experience the tension Sara had known would permeate the room.

As the first course was served, Sara peered at Isabelle. "I hope you had an enjoyable visit with your friend."

"I did."

Several footmen stepped into the room and began serving under Jeffers's watchful eye.

"You went to Mayfair?" Sara asked, wondering if the woman would mention she'd also gone to Kensington.

"Yes." Isabelle spooned soup into her mouth.

"It's been a while since you were in London. There are so many new shops. Did you go shopping afterward?" Sara hoped she wasn't coming across as if trying to interrogate the woman, which was exactly what she was attempting to do.

"No, I only visited a friend."

Sara forced another smile at the lying woman. What secret was Isabelle hiding?

"Thank you for the use of your carriage."

"You're quite welcome. It was a gift from Ian."

Isabelle's hand tightened on her spoon, causing her knuckles to whiten ever so slightly.

Ian set his utensil down and glared at Isabelle.

As if she felt his gaze on her like a probing stick, she glanced up.

"How long has it been since you have seen your son?" His already-hard jaw tightened.

Red singed Isabelle's cheeks. "I don't think that is any concern of yours."

"Perhaps not, but a child needs his mother."

"If I recall correctly, your mother was absent most of your life."

Isabelle's sharp words confirmed what Mrs. Pullman

had said—that Ian's mother had not lived here for most of Ian's childhood.

The steely look he shot at Isabelle appeared capable of withering one quite soundly, but the woman seemed unaffected.

"You should return home," Ian said. "Spend some time with Charles before you go gallivanting again."

This time her smiling façade cracked. She narrowed her eyes. "Ian, you seem determined to make me feel quite unwelcome." She glanced at Sara. "I have come here to try to heal the tattered bond between Ian and myself. We are family, after all. Sara, won't you intervene? Can't you make your husband see that we cannot go on this way?"

Sara wasn't sure what to say. She didn't want the woman here either, but her son. . . Maybe if they could get closer to her, her son could stay at Dorchester Hall while Isabelle was on the Continent. Yet, knowing Isabelle had lied to her made Sara leery. She didn't trust the woman.

Before Sara could respond, Isabelle stood and lifted her napkin to her eyes and sniffled. "I've lost my appetite," she said and stormed out of the room.

"Crocodile tears," Ian mumbled.

Sara turned to Jeffers. Before she could ask the man to give her and Ian a few minutes alone, the butler exited the room.

Sara reached for Ian's hand. "I think it's about time we talked."

Lips pinched tight, he nodded.

She waited.

"I cannot believe there was a time I loved her."

Sara could imagine it. A young man could be swayed by such beauty. She presumed like her sister, Louisa, the woman had garnered a great deal of attention. That hordes of men had wished to court her.

"She is beautiful."

"Perhaps. But she is quite ugly inside." He took a deep breath. "I thought she loved me. I believed that with every fiber of my being, but she was only after the title of duchess. Before I went away to university, I asked if she would marry me. She said yes, but she married my father instead. Obviously too impatient to wait for the title. She married him just like that." He snapped his fingers.

Nina's grandmother had told her most of that, but in a less emotional way. But there were other things Sara wished to know. "Your scars—how did you get them?"

He closed his eyes for a moment as if blocking out a memory from his past or attempting to drown it. "My father."

The idea that a parent could be so cruel made her want to retch. Sara could feel the tears pooling behind her eyes. She blinked, intent on trying to absorb them, since she knew how difficult this was for Ian to talk about. Her appetite gone, she pushed her bowl of soup away, trying to rein in her own hatred for a man she'd never met.

"Why?" Her voice was barely audible to her own ears, but the expression on Ian's face conveyed he heard the question.

He looked at her with those intensely blue eyes of his. "I have spent most of my life trying to figure it out. He said that hitting me would build character. He also expected perfection, and no one is perfect, so he was never satisfied."

Suddenly all the pieces of the puzzle were tumbling into place. The reason Ian worked so hard. Why he guarded his heart. Sara curled her fingers so tight, her nails bit into her palms.

"The last time he came after me it had been with a

horsewhip. I ripped it from his hand and raised it to strike him. I wanted to draw blood. My own father's blood. It was then, I knew if I continued to be part of his life, I might turn into him, and I didn't want that, so I walked away and built my own life. I told him I never wanted to see him again. That I would make a new life for myself. That I was going into business with Julien after university. That didn't settle well with him. He knew I would one day come into the title. That he could not stop that. So I believe he set out to hurt me. And he figured out how to go about doing that. He asked Isabelle to marry him."

Sara wanted to hug him, but hesitated, fearful he would see it as pity. But it was more than that.

The hell with it. She stood and settled on his lap.

He closed his eyes and bent his head, so their foreheads touched. She listened to the sounds of his breathing—low and steady. Soothing to her own frayed nerves. For a long moment they just sat there.

She needed to admit to him her own emotions. "I believe I've fallen in love with you."

She waited to see what he would say. His arms tightened about her waist, almost painfully crushing her body to his, but he said nothing.

"It's fine if you don't say it, Ian. I feel it in your touch." She glanced up to see his eyes still closed and saw the movement of his throat as he swallowed. Then he nodded, confirming he did love her, but she would give him time to say the words because she knew in time he would.

"Let me show you how I feel. Not with words but with actions." He took her hand and led her to his bedroom.

Chapter Thirty

Opening her eyes, Sara stretched like a contented cat, lying in its favorite sun-drenched spot. Though she lay alone in Ian's bed, earlier this morning she'd awoken with him beside her. Well, actually, he'd woken her up with kisses over every inch of her body before he'd made love to her with the same gentleness he'd shown her last night. Sated, she'd drifted back to sleep. She remembered him kissing her cheek and telling her he needed to leave to attend several meetings. She wished he didn't work so hard, but she feared he did so because of the demons that shadowed him, causing him to feel he had to prove himself worthy. Hopefully, he would come to grips with them in time.

Naked, she slipped out of Ian's bed and stepped into his bathing room to take a shower bath.

An hour later, still feeling as if the world had been set back on its axis, she made her way downstairs. Yet something kept niggling at her brain. Why Isabelle had lied about going to Kensington. Had she gone anywhere else? Determined to find out, she stepped outside and crossed the courtyard to the carriage house. Jasper could tell her where he'd taken the dowager yesterday.

Inside, the scent of horses and manure permeated the air.

A groomsman mucking out the stalls stopped working and stuttered a greeting.

"Could you direct me to where Jasper is?" she asked.

"I'm here, Your Grace." Her coachman stepped out of a stall.

"Jasper, where did you take the dowager yesterday?" Sara inquired in a low voice, so as not to be overheard.

"Mayfair."

"And afterward?"

"I didn't take her anywhere after, madam."

Sara rubbed at her temple. She was positive she'd seen Isabelle in Kensington.

"Once we reached Grosvenor Square," Jasper continued, "she asked me to let her disembark. I told her I could convey her to whichever address she wished to visit, but she said she wanted to walk the square first."

"Then you picked her up at which residence?"

"No, madam. She sent me on my way."

"You mean you did not drive her back to Dorchester Hall?"

"No. I presume she hired a cab."

"Interesting," Sara mumble.

The coachman nodded. "I thought it rather odd."

"Thank you, Jasper."

Confused even more by her coachman's revelation, Sara stepped back inside Dorchester Hall. As she walked past the library, she was startled to see Isabelle sitting at the desk in the room, penning something on a sheet of paper.

Just like when she'd found the woman standing in Sara's

bedchamber, the sight of Isabelle surprised her. The woman never rose early. She usually slept past noon.

Isabelle glanced up. Her eyes widened, and she quickly folded the paper. Obviously, whatever she'd been writing she didn't wish Sara to see.

"Morning." Sara stepped fully into the room and up to the desk.

"I'm writing to my friend in Mayfair," Isabelle said in way of explanation. "Might my lady's maid have the benefit of your vehicle to deliver it?"

"She doesn't need to go. I can have a footman convey it."

The nearly imperceivable stiffening of Isabelle's body revealed she didn't want anyone to know who the missive was for. More and more, Sara didn't trust the woman.

Isabelle flashed one of her ingratiating smiles and waved a hand in the air. She shoved the note into the pocket of her blue dress. "I suppose I should go to Mayfair and pay a call on my friend instead of sending her a note. Do you mind if I use your carriage?"

Where was she going? An uneasiness gripped Sara's stomach. Ian was right. Isabelle had not come here to make amends so the family could grow closer. She was up to something and most likely something nefarious. She wished she could have seen whatever Isabelle had written. "Of course. When would you need it?"

The woman peered at the clock on the desk. "One o'clock."

"Oh! How perfect. I'm going to meet Lady Ralston this afternoon and do a bit of shopping. We might as well ride together." It was a lie, and Sara hoped she was as skilled an actress as the deceptive young dowager. Isabelle was up to something, and Sara intended to find out what the woman was about.

This time Isabelle's agitation was not so easily masked. The woman's lips flattened out as her faux smile dissolved like a sugar cube dropped into a cup of steaming tea.

Your move, Isabelle. Sara waited for the woman's response.

"Yes. How lovely. We can ride together." Isabelle's overly sweet smile resurfaced, yet the tension in her body remained, revealing she was not as pleased as she wished Sara to believe.

A few hours later as they traveled to Mayfair—to Grosvenor Square—the woman talked lightheartedly about the weather, the season, and fashion, yet Sara noticed the way her companion's foot occasionally tapped against the floor. It was the only sign that revealed Isabelle wasn't as calm as the facade she portrayed.

"What door address should I give my coachman?" Sara asked.

"I've decided to do a bit of shopping before paying my call," Isabelle said as they neared Mayfair. "Will you convey me to Madame Renault's shop? I have heard she is the best modiste in London."

There it was. The subterfuge. What Sara had been waiting for. Confirmation that whomever Isabelle was paying a call to was someone she didn't wish either Sara or Ian to know about. She forced a smile, acting as if she didn't suspect a thing—playing the game as well as Isabelle. She had a feeling the woman thought Sara rather dull-witted, since she appeared to be the type of person who believed their intellect far surpassed others.

That *belief* might cause her to make a mistake.

Sara slid open the front glass panel. "Jasper, will you convey Her Grace to Madame Renault's shop?"

"Yes, madam."

When the carriage pulled in front of the modiste's shop, a brilliant smile lit up Isabelle's pretty face.

"I shall be visiting Lady Ralston for a couple of hours," Sara said. "Would you like my carriage to pick you up at your friend's residence?"

"No." Isabelle's response was too fast. Too sharp. "I mean you need not bother. I'm not sure how long I will be. I'll take a hansom to convey me back to Richmond." Offering another clearly forced smile, Isabelle stepped from the carriage and entered the modiste's shop.

Before the coachman climbed back onto the box, Sara motioned to him. "Jasper, will you pull ahead and park the carriage so it is not noticeable to anyone leaving Madame Renault's shop?"

A thin line momentarily formed between the man's brows. "Of course, madam." He pulled from the curb and into the traffic, then parked the vehicle in front of another carriage farther up the street.

Sara stepped out of the vehicle, and keeping herself out of sight, she waited for Isabelle. She had a strong suspicion the woman wouldn't be in there long.

"Madam," Jasper's raspy voice said.

Startled, Sara clasped the bodice of her dress and spun around.

The coachman stood next to her on the pavement. His face flushed. "I beg your forgiveness, madam. I didn't mean to frighten you. I only wish to know if there is something you would like me to do?"

She knew the man could be trusted. Besides, Wallace had told her that most of the servants didn't care a great deal for Isabelle. The staff who'd been employed when the old duke was alive remembered her with little fondness. It appeared the leopard had shown her spots on more than one occasion.

"I think the dowager is up to no good."

"Ay, that's what I've heard whispered, Your Grace. Bad rubbish and all that. If you forgive me for saying so."

"I agree. When she comes out of the shop, which I expect any minute, I want us to discreetly follow her."

A cunning grin broadened the coachman's lips. "I can do that." Jasper's eyes widened. "Look, madam."

She turned.

Isabelle stepped out of the modiste's shop and looked both ways as if making sure Sara was not still about, then she moved to the curb and waved down a hansom cab.

Sara jumped back into her carriage and ducked below the windows, while Jasper jumped up onto the perch and lowered his hat, shielding his face.

After the cab drove by, the coachman slid open the door behind his perch, "I'm following, madam, but I don't want to be directly behind them. Best to give her a wide berth, so she doesn't spot us." He looked as serious as an agent for the Crown, then grinned before closing the sliding window.

After a couple of vehicles passed them, Jasper called to the horses. "Move on, my fine fellows."

The carriage smoothly pulled into the fray of traffic.

Sara peered out the front window. Luckily, the hansom possessed no rear window, which made the chance of Isabelle spotting them less likely. Moving north, they drove past Barkers of Kensington in Kensington High Street, confirming in Sara's mind where they were going—the solicitor's office she'd seen Isabelle stepping into the last time the woman had lied. Why was visiting a solicitor such a secret?

A few minutes later, they neared the office. Sara cracked open the front window. "Jasper, pull the vehicle to the curb. I believe I know where she is going. I don't wish her to see us driving by and realize we followed her."

"Yes, madam." The coachman called to the horses, pulled in front of an apothecary's shop, then climbed down from his seat. He moved to the door and opened it. "Do you wish me to follow the vehicle on foot?"

"No. If my hunch is correct, the hansom will be stopping just about . . . there," she said as the vehicle pulled to the curb in front of the solicitor's office.

"What do we do now, madam?"

"I suppose we wait and see where she goes afterward."

After a half hour, Isabelle stepped out of the office with a gentleman with ginger hair. Even from this distance, Sara could see Isabelle looked agitated. She poked her finger several times into the man's chest. His face reddened, and then Isabelle climbed back into the waiting hansom.

Sara scrambled back inside her carriage.

Jasper returned to the box and urged the horses into the traffic.

After several turns, Sara realized that Isabelle was returning to Dorchester Hall.

She'd never visited Mayfair. When Ian arrived home, she would tell him what she'd witnessed. Perhaps he could deduce what Isabelle was about.

"Jasper," Sara said, "before returning home, take the carriage through Richmond Park. I don't wish us to arrive home on the woman's heels. And don't tell anyone what we did. The dowager cannot find out."

"Madam, my lips are sealed."

* * *

An hour later, Sara stepped inside Dorchester Hall.

"Your Grace, I hope you had a pleasant outing." Jeffers said, offering a warm smile.

She clasped the butler's hand.

His eyes widened. "Is something the matter, madam?"

"Truthfully, I'm not sure. Where is Her Grace?"

The man's nose twitched slightly as if forced to smell rotten eggs and wished to cover his sour expression. "She is in her room."

Sara was tempted to march to the guest room and confront the woman about her secrecy. Tell her she'd seen her in Kensington and find out what lie she produced. See if she mentioned the solicitor's office and the redheaded man Sara had seen her speaking with. No, she would tell Ian about the woman's subterfuge and see what he thought about it.

"Jeffers, as soon as His Grace returns, tell him I wish to speak with him."

After checking in on Edward and Jacob, Sara went to her study. Hoping to distract herself, she pulled out a book on butterflies common to Europe.

Isabelle stepped into the room. "One of the servants told me I might find you in here." The woman's shrewd eyes glanced around before she stepped up to the display shelves. Her gaze settled on a wood-and-glass case with preserved butterflies. "Do you kill them?"

There was something unsettling in the tone of the woman's voice as if she would think more highly of Sara if she did.

"No. I bought most of them. And the ones I've gathered . . . Well, their lifespan is not long."

Isabelle nodded and turned to the easel with the water-color of the Adolias butterfly Sara had begun painting. The woman studied it for a moment and turned to Sara. "I came to inform you that I've been invited to dine with my friend in Mayfair, so I won't be here for dinner. I won't need your carriage. I asked the hansom cab I rented today to return to Dorchester Hall to convey me. Though I will be leaving soon since I want to go shopping beforehand."

"How lovely," Sara said, her mind spinning. She was tempted to ask Isabelle her friend's name. No, she didn't wish her to grow suspicious. Sara suddenly wondered if the redheaded man was the woman's lover—a man whose station was not equal to Isabelle's. Sara saw nothing wrong with that, but a woman like Isabelle, well, she would be more conscious of social standing. Could that be what was going on?

Isabelle drew in an audible breath and let it out as if somewhat frustrated. "For my son's sake, Ian and I have to forget the past. Move on. I want us to be a family."

The woman's words rang false. She didn't even seem to spend time with her own son. "Yes, that would be for the best."

"You are so sensible. I have a feeling we are to be great friends." Isabelle clasped Sara's hand. The woman's fingers were cold, almost bloodless.

Sara fought the urge to pull her hand out of the woman's grasp. Instead, she forced a smile. "That would be lovely."

Isabelle released Sara's hand, smiled broadly, and exited the room, leaving Sara feeling as if Isabelle had just com-pleted a performance as worthy as any actress who tread the stage.

* * *

Sara sat in an upholstered chair in the library petting Snowball as Edward and Jacob sat on the rug, playing a game of Old Maid.

Jacob glanced up from his cards. "What is an old maid?"

Before she could respond, Edward rolled his eyes at his brother. "Her picture is right on the card, silly. She's an ugly old woman."

Sara frowned. "Old maid means an older woman who hasn't married."

"Because she's ugly, no one wanted to marry her, right?" Edward asked.

"No. Not at all. She might be beautiful, and some women *choose* not to marry."

"Why?" Jacob tipped his head to the side.

"There are several reasons. Independence. Education. At one time, I did not wish to marry. I wanted to study my butterflies."

"But you're married now, and you still study them," Edward said.

How did she explain to the boys that a woman didn't always have that choice? That a husband might not accept a woman's desire to further her scientific endeavors. "I was fortunate to marry your cousin Ian." Saying the words out loud made her realize how true they were. "He doesn't mind me furthering my studies. I hope you both will be like him and want a wife who has her own interests."

Jacob smiled. "I will. I want a wife like you. One who lets me search for butterflies."

She couldn't halt her smile. "What about you, Edward?"

He nodded. "I think they should change the picture on these cards to someone pretty like you."

Her heart fluttered. "You know I love you both dearly, don't you?"

"Yeah, we know," they said in tandem.

Sara gazed at the doorway. Isabelle had left a half hour ago for her dinner party. Sara had almost followed her but decided to wait for Ian so she could tell him about Isabelle's lies. All day, she'd been trying to convince herself that Isabelle's deception meant nothing. That there might be a simple explanation for the woman's lies, but in her gut, Sara didn't believe so.

She glanced down at Snowball, purring in her lap, and wondered what was taking Ian so long? Last night in bed, Ian said he would arrive home before dinner. Where was he?

Jeffers stepped into the room. "A messenger brought a missive from His Grace."

Sara set the kitten down and rushed across the room to take the note from the butler.

My darling Sara,
My meetings are taking longer than I believed they
would. And I still need to stop at my solicitor's
office afterward. If I'm not home in time for dinner,
please start without me.

Always yours,
Ian

She released an impatient breath.

"Is there anything you need, madam?" the butler asked.

"No, Jeffers."

The man turned to leave.

"Jeffers?"

He pivoted back. "Yes?"

"Who is His Grace's solicitor?"

"Mr. Miles Newton of Newton and Newton in Kensington."

Sara's heart skipped a beat. "Are you sure?"

"Yes. The solicitor has called here several times to conduct business with His Grace."

The uncomfortable feeling in Sara's stomach ratcheted up. "Is he a ginger-haired gentleman?"

"Yes."

Sara remembered the letter Isabelle had penned in the morning. Since she'd gone into Town, she'd not needed to have it delivered. Sara recalled the blue day dress Isabelle had worn and how she'd hastily shoved the note into her pocket.

Isabelle had changed before leaving. Was the note still in there?

"I need to do something," Sara said to the boys. She darted up the stairs and stepped into the bedchamber Isabelle used. The room was filled with the cloying smell of the woman's perfume. She marched to the armoire and flung it open. Upon seeing the gown, she searched the pocket.

Empty.

Was she going mad? Spinning a cloak-and-dagger situation in her head when there wasn't one? No. Her intuition insisted that Isabelle was up to no good. She moved to the small writing desk and opened the drawer. Not seeing the missive, she closed it.

This was foolish. Isabelle was too smart. She would have destroyed it. Sara peered at the unlit fireplace. Her gaze shifted to a box of matches on the mantel. She darted toward the hearth and crouched. Small bits of burnt paper were visible.

Whatever Isabelle had written, she'd burned. Sara was about to stand when she spotted a piece of paper that was not completely charred. She snatched it up. The only words that remained legible were *kill* and below it *tonight*.

Sara blinked at the piece of paper, then dropped it as if it remained hot and singed her fingers.

Then she was out the door and down the stairs as if the hounds of hell were on her heels.

The butler stood at the base of the stairs staring at her. "Madam, what is wrong?"

"I don't have time to explain. Have Jasper bring my carriage around."

"You're going out?"

"Yes. If Isabelle returns before me, don't let her out of your sight. Use whatever means you must take. Now, please hurry. And send someone to get my husband's bow and arrows. I might need them."

Chapter Thirty-One

As Ian leaped down from his carriage, he glanced at the sign that read NEWTON AND NEWTON, SOLICITORS AND NOTARY PUBLIC. Late yesterday evening, the solicitor had sent word that Ian's new will was completed and ready to be signed this evening. He surveyed the building. Except for a light shining from Mile's office window, the building remained dark as did most of the buildings on the street this late in the day.

"I shouldn't be long, Fletcher," Ian said to his coachman. He stepped inside the building to find Newton's secretary was not at his desk. In fact, the office was so quiet, one could most likely hear a mouse if it crept by. He entered the solicitor's office.

A desk lamp illuminated Isabelle, sitting at the man's desk.

"What the deuce are you doing here? Where's Newton?" he demanded.

The sound of the door closing behind him caused Ian to spin around.

"Here, Your Grace." Newton took a single step out from

the shadowed edge of the room, allowing more lamplight to spill onto his body.

Ian's gaze dropped to the revolver in the solicitor's hand.

"Take a seat, Your Grace." Newton waved the gun.

"Yes, Ian, please sit." Isabelle motioned to the chair facing the desk.

"I prefer to stand, while you both tell me what the bloody hell is going on." Though he demanded an answer, the gun in the solicitor's grip left no doubt as to what their intentions were.

Isabelle's gaze shifted to Newton.

The man stretched out his arm and pointed the weapon at Ian's chest. "You need to sit."

"Yes," Isabelle said. "This might take some time. There is so much I wish to tell you."

Ian sat, while his mind tried to figure out how he could disarm Newton. Keeping Isabelle talking might help him settle on a plan. "What is it, Isabelle? Get on with whatever you wish to say."

She smiled. The expression looked smug more than anything else. "Have you ever wondered why the old duke hated you?"

Too many times to count, Ian thought, but he said nothing.

"As he was dying and on laudanum to dull the pain, he rambled. He didn't believe you were his son. He thought your mother had been unfaithful."

Ian tried not to react, but his body tensed. If true, it would explain a lot. Too much.

"He believed Frederick Armstrong was your father."

The painter? "That's ridiculous."

"Think of it, Ian. He worked on the library mural throughout the year before you were conceived."

"That's your proof?" He gave a humorless laugh.

"No. My proof is that your father killed him. Ran him over with a carriage while he crossed the street."

Ian suddenly felt as if someone struck him with a blow to the head, causing a sense of vertigo.

"Amazing how when one believes they are about to meet their maker what they will ask forgiveness for," Isabelle continued. "In the old man's case it was not so much forgiveness, but an explanation that the painter deserved to die for cuckolding him. Even when close to gasping his last breath, he rationalized all the vile things he'd done throughout his life."

For all he knew, Isabelle was lying. But Ian wouldn't put such a heinous act past the old duke. As far as what his mother did, he didn't know. The only people who could tell the truth, and whether Isabelle told it, were dead.

"My son is the rightful heir," Isabelle said, interrupting his thoughts.

"Even if my mother did have an affair, it doesn't mean I'm not the old duke's son."

Looking distracted, as if she hadn't heard his words, Isabelle tapped her index finger to her lips. "You shouldn't have asked Miles to change your will. And you most certainly shouldn't have married. I want Charles to be the next duke."

Ian's gut spasmed. If Newton and Isabelle were set on killing him, what would they do to Sara if she were with child—a child who if male would supplant young Charles as the future duke.

"Sara," he said, his voice low and raspy.

As if frustrated, Isabelle drummed her fingers on the desk. "Yes, your poor little wife. So sweet. So naive. She will be devastated when she learns you were set upon by thieves and fatally wounded. I'll have to be the shoulder she leans on. I'll have to comfort her. While keeping my eye on her belly. If it swells with your babe, she might have an accident. Or perhaps I'll wait and see if she bears a boy. Then I will have to deal with the child instead."

Bile moved up Ian's throat. "You're mad."

"No. I'm determined that Charles be the next Duke of Dorchester, and I control everything. Thankfully, Miles sent word to me that you'd married and had asked him to change your will. You haven't changed it. Have you, Miles, darling?"

"No. Only one part. Julien Caruthers, Lord Dartmore, is no longer the executor of your estate. I am."

If Ian wasn't killed tonight, he was going to beat Miles Newton to a pulp. "I'll never sign such a will."

"You don't have to. Miles has become exceedingly skilled at forging your signature."

Isabelle stood. "I must be on my way." She spoke as calmly as if they'd just shared a pleasant conversation over a cup of tea and were both about to go on their merry way. "I need to be at Dorchester Hall when your poor wife hears the news of your unfortunate demise."

"My coachman is outside. He'll hear the gunshot."

"True, but by the time he makes it into the alley, you will be dead. Miles will testify that two thugs entered the back door, robbed both of you, and when you tried to stop them by following them into the alley behind the building, they shot you and ran off. While waiting for your coach-man to find a policeman, Miles will get rid of the gun."

Ian glared at Newton who had remained quiet through-out Isabelle's diatribe. "You want this? You want blood on your hands?"

He shook his head. "No, not especially, but money has a way of persuading one to do things they thought themselves not capable of doing. Isabelle has promised me that I will be wealthier than I ever imagined."

Isabelle walked over to Newton and drew the back of her gloved hand down the man's cheek. "So much money, Miles. It will be ours for the taking. All of it. Now, you know what you must do, don't you?"

"Yes." The solicitor nodded like a marionette whose strings were being pulled.

Isabelle patted the man on the head as if he were her lapdog, then she walked out the back door in Miles's office that led to the alley.

After she left the office, Ian noticed the gun in Newton's hand shake. The normally nervous solicitor looked like a rabbit that wanted to flee a horde of hounds. It appeared Isabelle was the man's backbone.

Ian stood and took a small step toward him. "You don't have to do this, Newton."

"Your Grace, don't take another step." The man waved the gun.

He was a good fifteen feet from the man. By the time he tackled him, Newton could lodge a bullet in his chest. Could he overpower him even if shot? He realized that would depend on where the bullet struck him. But he needed to try something. He could not allow Isabelle and Newton to hurt Sara. But first he would try to convince the man that Isabelle was using him.

"Newton, do you really believe Isabelle intends to share the wealth?"

The man's jaw tightened. "She does. You heard her.

Besides, you're robbing her son of his just place in this world."

"Am I?"

"Yes."

"Have you ever seen Isabelle's son?"

The man shook his head. "No, but what does that have to do with anything?"

"Charles looks nothing like the old duke. It wouldn't surprise me if Isabelle took a lover while married to my father. She's a woman who will do almost anything to get what she wants. Did you know she once professed her eternal love to me? You know what happened. She married my father. So what do her words really mean?"

"Shut up."

"I'm sure she told my father she loved him. You know she didn't, don't you? He was a means to an end, as you are. As I would have been. If anyone finds out you killed me, do you think she will admit to having planned this? No. You will be the one they hang. Not her. I can see her denying everything. Perhaps that is her plan."

"I don't believe a word you're saying."

"Yes, you do. I see it in your eyes. Give me your weapon and put an end to this madness."

"No." Newton cocked the gun.

As Sara's carriage rumbled through the London streets toward the offices of Newton and Newton, her heart thundered in her chest, feeling capable of leaping from it. The word *kill* on the sooty paper kept flashing before her eyes. Something horrible was about to happen. She felt it in her bones—deep within them as if ice replaced the marrow.

The vehicle turned and twisted through the dim roadways until the clopping of the horses' hooves slowed and the carriage pulled up to the solicitor's brick building.

Ian's carriage was parked in front with the coachman sitting on the box.

That was a good sign, wasn't it?

Sara snatched up Ian's bow and the arrow-filled quiver and leaped from the vehicle, while she surveyed the building. All the windows were dark except one on the ground floor.

Jasper jumped down from the box and moved to her side. "I'll not let you go in there alone, Your Grace." His gaze dipped to the weapon she held. "Do you know how to use that, madam?"

"Not very well. Do you?"

"No, but I know how to use my fists." He lifted them in the air.

Seeing them, Fletcher, Ian's coachman, climbed down from his perch. He looked at the weapon Sara carried, and his brows pinched together. "Your Grace?"

"How long has my husband been in there?"

"About half an hour."

"Has anyone besides him come out?"

"No one that I saw, madam."

"Fletcher, stay here, and if anyone comes out, stop them."

"Yes, madam."

Together, she and Jasper moved to the front door. Not sure whether it would be locked, Sara held her breath and turned the handle. The door opened on quiet hinges. She let out a relieved puff of breath, and they stepped inside.

The room contained a desk, then there were two closed doors, along with a stairway to the first floor.

Sara moved to the door on the left where a light shown

from under it and pressed her ear to the surface. The quiet from within the lit room unsettled her. Her hand wrapped around the bow grew sweaty.

Jasper reached for the handle and waited for her signal.

She placed the arrow into the bow as Ian had shown her and pulled it back. She could not seem to stop her arms from shaking. She took a calming breath, the way Ian had suggested, then nodded.

Like the front door, this one swung inward on quiet hinges. A lit lamp illuminated the sizable desk it was perched on, but no one was in the office. She lowered the weapon and slumped against the wall, feeling a dichotomy of emotions. Relief. Fear. Confusion.

Where are you, Ian? She turned and made her way to the other door.

Jasper opened it.

The office had the smell of a place that had been closed up for a while. White dustcloths were draped over the furnishings.

"Should we go upstairs, madam?" Jasper whispered.

"Yes." Ian had to be here somewhere.

They made their way up the steps. Just like downstairs, there were two doors, but instead of the stairway, directly in front of the steps, there was a window at the end of the corridor that looked over the back of the building. The curtain fluttered, and Sara realized the lower pane was partially raised.

A voice alerted Sara that someone was outside. She moved to the window and moonlight highlighted two men in the alley. Pressing her fingers to the glass, she leaned closer.

The man facing the building was Ian, the other, with his

back to them, looked to be the redheaded man she'd seen Isabelle conversing with.

Ian. Thank God he's alive.

The man was talking. "Now, Your Grace, toss over your gold watch. If this is to look like a robbery, I'll need that, along with your signet ring."

Robbery? It was then that Sara saw a moonbeam reflect off a gun in the man's hand.

Jasper must have seen it as well since he uttered a low oath before he spun around and darted out the room, his feet heavy on the treads as he made his way down them.

Fearing the coachman might not make it in time, or could end up shot himself, Sara quietly raised the lower sash all the way up. Thankfully, it made little sound. With hands that shook, she removed an arrow from the quill and placed it in the bow.

Heart thundering in her chest, she once again took a slow breath in and out to calm herself and took aim.

Chapter Thirty-Two

Ian stared at Newton in the alley behind the solicitor's office and listened as the man told him to remove his gold pocket watch and signet ring so when the police arrived it would look like a robbery.

"I'll tell them how I tried to stop you from following the thieves, but you didn't heed my warnings."

Slowly Ian removed the watch from his fob pocket and unclasped it. When he tossed it to Newton, and the man switched his attention to the timepiece to catch it, he intended to lunge for the solicitor.

Even if Newton moved fast enough to get a shot off, hopefully it would only incapacitate Ian, not kill him, because he intended to rip the man apart. Limb by limb. No one would hurt his wife. He loved Sara. And if it was the last thing he did, he needed to return home and tell her that. Say it out loud—even if it meant doing so with a bloody bullet lodged in him.

Ian was about to toss the watch to Newton and carry out his plan when a movement from a second-story window caught his attention. The silhouette of a woman. For a second, he thought it was Sara. No, that couldn't be, but as she leaned farther out the window, allowing moonlight to reach her, he realized it *was* her.

Good Lord. What is she doing here?

She lifted something in her arms. He blinked, thinking he might have become delirious because it looked like his bow. Before he could absorb that thought, he saw an arrow flying through the moonlit ally, heading right for Newton.

It struck the bastard in the shoulder. The man dropped the gun and let out a scream. Stumbling sideways, he tried to grasp at the protruding arrow to pull it out.

Ian lunged.

Newton's eyes grew wide. He bent to pick up his fallen gun.

"No, you don't, you bloody sod." Ian planted a facer on him. Once, twice, and again until the man slumped to the ground like a rag doll, out cold.

The back door of the solicitor's office flew open.

Ian grabbed the gun and aimed. He uttered a blasphemy and lowered the weapon when he realized it was Sara's coachman.

The man rushed forward and observed Newton with an arrow lodged in his shoulder, along with his battered face. "Gorblimey. She hit the blackguard." Jasper's gaze shifted to Ian's bloodied knuckles. "Well done, Your Grace. Well done."

Sara ran out the door Jasper had exited and flung herself into Ian's arms and started pressing kisses to every inch of his face.

He grabbed her shoulders. "Sara, what are you doing here?"

"Saving you."

"I've seen the way you aim an arrow. I'm damn lucky I'm not the one lying on the ground."

Humph. "Men and their male pride. Admit it. I saved you."

He wrapped her tightly in his arms. "Yes, my little Amazon warrior, you saved me." He turned to the coachman. "Jasper, see if you can find a policeman. We need this bastard locked up."

"Yes, Your Grace. Right away." The coachman trotted off.

"Where is Isabelle?" Sara asked.

"She hadn't returned to Dorchester Hall before you left?"

"No. This was her doing. She wanted you dead."

"I know."

"Why?"

"Greed. She wanted Charles to be the next duke. Now, my sweet-little-bow-carrying wife, tell me how you knew to come here."

While they waited for Jasper to return, Sara told Ian what she'd seen.

After the police arrived and carted Newton off in cuffs, Sara and Ian headed back to Richmond in Ian's carriage. Following them in their own vehicles were several policemen, along with detectives from Scotland Yard.

Ian pulled Sara onto his lap and held her tight against his chest. "While Newton pointed that gun at me, one thing kept drifting through my mind."

"What?"

He cupped the side of her face. "That I might not get to tell you that I love you."

Sara pressed a soft kiss to his lips, then snuggled closer to him.

"Do you have anything you wish to tell me?" She'd said she believed she'd fallen in love with him. He desperately wanted to hear her say it.

"I love your garden."

"Anything else."

"I love Jacob and Edward."

"Minx, is that it?"

She pulled back and gazed at him. "I love butterflies."

He released a frustrated breath.

She combed her fingers through his hair. "And I love you. Dearly. With all my heart."

He pulled her tight, closed his eyes, and promised himself that not a day would go by where he wouldn't tell Sara how he felt—how he loved her.

A short time later, they walked into Dorchester Hall to find Jeffers grinning broadly.

Confused by the man's jovial expression, Ian peered at Sara whose expression looked as baffled as his.

"Oh, thank goodness you are both safe."

"Is that why you look in such a jolly mood?" Ian asked.

It was then they heard Isabelle yelling. "You'll pay for this, Jeffers. Let me loose! I'll see you tossed in jail."

Smiling broader, the butler opened the double doors to the receiving room off the entry.

Inside, Isabelle sat on the settee with her wrists and feet bound with what looked like Ian's four-in-hand neckcloths.

Seeing both Ian and Sara, the woman paled. "That idiot Newton. I should have known he'd botch things up. I hope he's dead."

Ian turned to Jeffers. "You should have gagged her as well."

"We should have."

"We?" Sara echoed.

"Yes." Jeffers motioned to Edward and Jacob who stepped into the entry hall, wearing matching devilish expressions.

"Those boys are beasts. When I get loose, I will summon a constable."

"No, Isabelle. You will be spending a long time in jail."

"No one will believe it. I'll tell them I had nothing to do with Newton's plan."

"Good thing she wasn't gagged," Sara said. "She's admitted to knowing why you aren't dead. How would she have known about the plan if she wasn't privy to it?"

Isabelle's smile disappeared when two of the detectives stepped behind Sara and Ian in the doorway.

Ian turned to them. "You heard what she admitted to?"

"We did, Your Grace."

"Then take her away."

Kicking and screaming, they dragged Isabelle from the room and out of Dorchester Hall.

"I feel like a black cloud has been lifted." Sara clasped Ian's hand.

After the detectives questioned them, Ian entwined his fingers with Sara's and led her upstairs, intending with *both words and actions* to show his wife how much he loved her.

Chapter Thirty-Three

The following week, Sara laughed as she and Ian played pirates in the garden with Edward, Jacob, and Ian's younger brother, Charles. Ian had told her what Isabelle had said about his parentage, along with Isabelle's belief that Ian was not really the old duke's son but Frederick Armstrong's. But as she looked at his younger brother, she realized that Charles looked nothing like the old duke's painting that hung in the family's portrait gallery, while Ian had the man's square jaw and blue eyes. Eyes that Sara now thought were not cold and distant but loving and kind.

Since Ian's near brush with death, he'd changed even more. It was as if that stubborn brick wall had completely crumbled. He spent every evening home and lounged late in the mornings in bed with her. Well, sometimes they didn't just lounge. And every day he told her he loved her. Several times. Yesterday, she'd found him standing outside her study staring at her. "Do you wish to go for a walk in the garden?" he'd asked.

Once there, he'd asked her about every butterfly they'd seen. She'd delighted in telling him about them and

318 Renee Ann Miller

basked in his rapt attention, while for seven days in a row, a bouquet of red roses had been delivered, signed *Forever and always, Ian.*

"Come here, you scallywags, and walk the plank," Ian said, chasing the boys and drawing Sara from her thoughts.

Charles laughed and darted away with Edward and Jacob to hide. The child had settled in better than they'd thought. He'd been lonely in Northumberland. He hadn't asked about his mother. Both she and Ian presumed the child thought her off gallivanting on the Continent when in truth, she was in prison awaiting trial, as was Miles Newton. Both Sara and Ian knew the child needed to be told the truth, but they wished to give him a few weeks to adjust first.

Ian turned back to her. "I've scared them off. Now we can kiss."

She giggled, then swallowed her laugh as Ian pressed his lips to hers.

"You two kissing again?" Edward grumbled.

They stepped apart to see the child peering around an evergreen tree, looking thoroughly disgusted by what he'd witnessed.

Ian walked over to him and ruffled his hair. "One day it won't disgust you."

The child wrinkled his nose as if he thought that impossible.

"Let us go find those scallywags, matey." Ian set his hand on the child's shoulder.

"Ian?" Sara called out.

He faced her. "Yes?"

"Don't forget tonight we have the Floyds' ball."

He returned to her side. "You still wish to attend?"

She knew what he was thinking. That normally they

would garner a great deal of attention, but more so after Isabelle's foiled plot. She nodded.

"Are you sure? We don't have to go."

"No. I want to."

"Truly?"

"Yes."

"There. All done, madam," Wallace said, beaming as she placed the ruby-encrusted comb in Sara's hair that the woman had styled in a loose chignon. "You look like a princess."

Sara stood from the chair in front of her dressing table and walked over to the cheval glass. Butterflies fluttered in her stomach. She shook her hands to stop the tingling in her fingers and stared at her reflection. She'd already changed twice. First she'd worn a simple ball gown of brown taffeta. Then she'd impulsively asked Wallace to help her put on the red gown she'd purchased from Madam Renault's shop. Though she thought it the most beautiful thing she had ever worn, she would stand out like a full moon on a dark night.

She looked at Wallace. "I think I'll put the brown one back on."

"If you wish, madam, but you look lovely."

Sara stared at her reflection again. She fancied the red color, and the vibrant shade did make her cheeks look rosy, as Madame Renault insisted it would.

You can do this, a voice in her head said. *You want to wear it.*

True. And she did feel like a princess, or at least like a duchess, and though it was a bold choice, she was the

Duchess of Dorchester, a woman who could set fashion trends if she wished. She swallowed. "Very well."

A knock on the connecting door drew her attention to it. She took a deep breath, knowing it was Ian. Knowing he was about to see her.

"If there is nothing else, madam, I'll leave," the lady's maid said with a sparkle in her eyes.

"Thank you, Wallace."

The woman exited the bedchamber.

Sara drew in another deep breath and faced the door. "Yes, come in."

Ian stepped into the room. His eyes met hers, then slowly drifted from her face to the hem of her gown before returning to her face. "Good Lord, you are the most beautiful woman."

She blurred behind unshed tears.

He was by her side, wrapping her in his arms. "Don't cry, love."

"They are happy tears. For the first time in my life, I am nervous to attend a ball, but also relishing the thought of dancing with you."

He stepped back and held out his hand. "Then let's show the *ton* that we truly are happily married."

In the carriage, Sara tried not to imagine the worst thing that could happen—that she might become nervous and laugh.

The carriage pulled in front of Mr. and Mrs. Floyd's residence.

Ian clasped her gloved hand. "Are you ready, my duchess?"

She squared her shoulders. "Yes."

As they walked into Bertram Floyd's ballroom, all heads turned when they were announced.

Though her stomach felt queasy, Sara tipped her chin up. "Everyone is looking at us."

"Of course, they are. The men are envious that I have the most beautiful woman on my arm. The women are envious that you are wearing such a glorious gown. Tomorrow every woman in attendance will be rushing to their modiste to order red gowns, following your lead."

"Ha! I think the women are envious that I have snagged one of the last Infamous Lords."

Ian shook his head. His wife still didn't comprehend that she was as beautiful as her butterflies. Before he could say so, Louisa and Ned approached them.

Louisa's eyes said it all. They reflected the confidence Sara had achieved. She was a duchess in every sense of the word. Powerful. Influential. Radiant.

Ian waited to see if Louisa would try to cut Sara down, but without hesitation, his wife arched her brow in that way he did, and he nearly burst out laughing because suddenly Louisa looked as nervous as a debutante about to make her bow before the queen.

"You look lovely, Sara," her sister said.

"Thank you. As do you."

"It's the oysters. They help the complexion." Ian grinned.

Louisa wrinkled her nose. "I'm not fond of oysters, but . . ." She turned to her brother. "We must order some."

Ian gave Sara a sly wink. His wife's lips twitched, but he knew she would scold him for telling such a lie when they arrived home.

Louisa glanced down at her pink gown as if realizing

Sara's vibrant red one outshone hers, and a pout settled on the girl's face before she started talking to Sara about who was in attendance.

While Louisa and Sara chatted, her brother leaned forward and spoke in a low voice. "The way you are looking at my sister, everyone will believe you do love her, Dorchester."

Ian's jaw tensed. He held the earl's gaze. "Make no mistake, Hampton, I love her with every fiber of my being, and if you ever do anything to hurt her, by God, you will answer to me."

Hampton paled. "I would never . . ."

"Good. I'm glad we understand each other."

Just then Bertram Floyd and his wife, Clarissa, approached and Ned and Louisa moved away.

"Your Graces, welcome. I am so glad you could attend."

Floyd looked at Sara, then Ian. "Dorchester, if you would like to go into my study, we can discuss the sale of Floyd Ironworks."

As the man spoke, the violinist drew his bow against the strings of his instrument, announcing the first dance was about to begin.

"Floyd, the orchestra is about to play and the only thing on my mind this evening is dancing with my lovely wife. We can discuss business another day."

The man's face flushed red. "Yes. Of course."

The orchestra began a waltz, and Ian led Sara to the dance floor.

"How could you walk away? He was finally ready to sell his company."

"Sara, I have everything I want. If Floyd sells it to Julien and me, that will be nice. Something I can pass down to the boys and any children we bring into our lives, but it isn't the most important thing in my life. You and the boys are. In fact, I don't know if I want it. I was thinking I'd like to spend more time with my family. Perhaps we could go to Cornwall to watch the migration of butterflies."

"Ian, if you make me cry, right here in front of everyone, I will never forgive you."

"I love you, Sara." The words that had felt so hard to once say came easy to him now when he looked at his wife.

She smiled. "I love you, Ian."

He knew that and cherished it.

As they danced, neither realized how everyone watched them. No, they only had eyes for each other.

Epilogue

Two weeks later . . .

The cliffs in Cornwall were a sight to see. Ian placed a hand over his eyes, shading them from the sun as he viewed the ocean beyond. The scent of the salty water carried on the breeze. Lowering his hand, he entwined his fingers with Sara's. She had taught him that love was not something only poets wrote about, but an emotion that could latch on to one's mind and heart and be eternal. He brought her hand to his mouth and kissed her fingers, one by one.

Sara snuggled closer to him.

The sound of children laughing drew their attention. They turned to see Edward, Jacob, and Charles running. Each child held a butterfly net, but instead of trying to catch the colorful insects, they were chasing one another. Georgiana Turner, their new nanny, was also trying to snag the children in her net. The boys had grown quite fond of her in such a short time. Perhaps because she possessed the patience of a saint and as much devilment as the lads.

Their laughter was a wonderful sound.

They still hadn't told Charles about his mother, and he

still never asked about her. Though he had asked if he could live with them. They had assured him they had no intention of sending him back to Northumberland.

"I see them," Jacob shouted, pointing at the sky.

Ian and Sara looked. And there they were, a swarm of butterflies, crossing from the Continent.

Sara squealed with delight.

Seeing her smiling face made Ian happier than he'd ever been. He stepped behind her and pulled her back against his chest. "After we leave here, what would you think about us going on an extended holiday?"

She turned around in his arms. "You're serious, aren't you?"

"Yes."

"What about Magnus Shipping? What about your other businesses?"

"I've realized that they can run fine without me."

She beamed. "Where would we go?"

"France. Italy. I've told Julien I won't be returning for at least a month."

"You've had this planned all along?"

He nodded.

She got up on her toes and kissed him.

All three boys grumbled over having to witness such a scene.

Ian laughed. It felt good to laugh, and it felt even better to do it with Sara in his arms.

Visit us online at
KensingtonBooks.com
to read more from your favorite authors,
see books by series, view reading group guides, and more.

BOOK CLUB
BETWEEN THE CHAPTERS

Visit us online for sneak peeks, exclusive giveaways,
special discounts, author content, and engaging
discussions with your fellow readers.

Betweenthechapters.net